Society in India:
Ambedkar's Vision
Essays from Christian Perspective

Society in India:
Ambedkar's Vision

Essays from Christian Perspective

Monodeep Daniel

(Ph.D Amsterdam)

Delhi Brotherhood Society
2019

Society in India: Ambedkar's Vision-*Essays from Christian Perspective* — Jointly published by the Rev. Dr. Ashish Amos of the Indian Society for Promoting Christian Knowledge (ISPCK), Post Box 1585, 1654, Madarsa Road, Kashmere Gate, Delhi-110006 and Delhi Brotherhood Society (DBS), Brotherhood House, 7 Court Lane, Delhi-110054.

ISBN: 978-81-938241-5-3

Laser typeset at **ISPCK,** Post Box 1585, 1654, Madarsa Road, Kashmere Gate, Delhi-110006.

Tel: 23866323, Fax: 91-11-23865490

e-mail: ashish@ispck.org.in • ella@ispck.org.in

website: www.ispck.org.in

Dedicated to

Rev. Dr. (habil.) James Massey
a foremost Dalit Theologian
and a faithful son of the Indian Church

Contents

SECTION THREE
Manusmriti • Caste • Violence

SECTION FOUR
Constitution • Development • Democracy

Acknowledgements

I want to express my gratitude to Revd Fr. Solomon George, Director of Delhi Brotherhood Society for fecilitating the printing of this book and Revd Dinesh Singh of the Center for Dalit Studies, New Delhi for editing and giving his valuable suggestion for the arrangement of chapters. I also acknowledge the support of Ms. Ella Sonawane, Asst. General Secretary (Publishing & Mission) for publishing this work from the ISPCK, New Delhi. The project could not have been accomplished without the support of ICCO Kerk in Actie, The Netherlands. I thank them for their partnership with the DBS.

The Author

Preface

I'm very happy to see that the author has published these papers on Dr Ambedkar which he had presented on different occasions now in the form of a book. It is clear that these studies focus on Dr Ambedkar's vision of society. This means that in the line of his vision we must endeavour to build a society that would be pluralistic, equal and free. However, to attain this is not possible without power. But where does power come from? True power comes from political participation without which people remain unorganized with weak identity i.e. they remain nameless and faceless. The guiding light for political engagement comes from Dr Bhimrao Ramji Ambedkar (14 April 1891–6 December 1956).

Dr Ambedkar was clear that the monopoly and domination of the so called upper castes propelled by brahminical culture needed to be checked. At a later point when he had expressed his concern to protect the Indian culture it was not to uphold the domination of Brahmins but should be understood as his concern to protect cultural diversity. It must be accepted that culturally diverse society which is dominated by one section cannot be called pluralistic. In Dr Ambedkar's line of thinking the emergence of a genuinely pluralistic and egalitarian Indian culture would occur when the society embraces justice by annihilating caste system. It is this phenomenon of emergence that has to be propelled and protected.

If, therefore, society after Ambedkar is to be just then it needs to be pluralistic, equal and free. Let us discuss of these below.

Firstly society must be pluralistic, which means that the Indian citizens would take the right to profess, practice and propagate diverse forms of religions, cultures, languages, scripts and cuisine to a logical conclusion of strengthening our pluralistic culture. If all cultures were to be treated equally then the caste system which aims at social stratification will have to be annihilated. There is a false idea that national integration can only be achieved by preserving the pervading culture and practice of caste system. This is far from truth. The fact of the matter is what Dr Ambedkar had underscored. He held that national integration has to be achieved not by imposition of one culture but by cultivating a firm "will" of diverse Indian people to be united as a nation.

Secondly society must be equal which entails diverse people, even if they cannot become uniformly equal, they must at least be treated as equal. In other words their dignity must be respected and every one must equally have access to opportunities. A great gift of Ambedkars's democracy to India is that at least on the day of voting every citizen irrespective of gender, colour, creed and language, becomes equal in terms of one vote and one value. This sense, attitude and practice of social equality should be given a stronger push to enable the Indian society to emerge as one consisting of free and equal people.

Thirdly society must be free, which means that every individual and each community irrespective of their cultural or linguistic affiliations must freely enjoy their human and civil rights as provided in the Indian Constitution. They must be free to travel anywhere in Indian and express their opinions and concerns. For this reason, the journalists, media and press should be protected.

We must further affirm that politics is the game of acquiring power. However, to gain power for the sake of power should not be the aim of political activism; rather the aim should be to attain and manage it. It means that by acquiring power the person should become a catalyst for the emergence of a just Indian society. But what does power gained through political process entail? Power entails control over the national assets and human resources. The aim of justice should be to have these assets and resources redeployed for the emancipation of the Dalit and Adivasi. This should be done so that the gulf between those who "have" and the rest who "have not" vanishes.

Rev'd Fr. Solomon George
Director
Delhi Brotherhood Society

Introduction

It is now sixty years since Dr B.R. Ambedkar died but the question is this: what did the Indian society achieve in his line of thinking? In other words, did our national society restructure itself on egalitarianism? It is no secret that the foundation of Indian culture is caste system giving expression to inequality and segregation in various ways. Therefore, after Ambedkar what has been done to diminish inequality or overthrow the idea of caste? These are hard questions to assess our own failings and achievements in the area of social transformation. If anything in this line has ever been achieved, the credit must go to the Indian Constitution which was drafted under the chairmanship of Dr Ambedkar. At least on the voting day our Constitution makes all citizens legally equal each with one vote and one value.

But still the query and quest for social equality is left unattended. Instead of attending to the evil of social inequality the attention is diverted to the issue of national integration namely, how can we keep the Indian republic united? The answer comes loudest from the dominant section which refuses to accept the fast growth of cultural pluralism. Their answer is reductionist i.e. reduce India to a singular culture of brahmanic flavour which is the caste system. This alarms the rest of the Indian citizens.

The fact of the matter is that national integration cannot be achieved apart from justice, which involves equality in every aspect of life. Both have to be taken up with equal urgency. National integration is a matter of peace and social equality is a matter of justice. Peace can only be achieved by justice. Discontent in forms of social and political unrest will raise its ugly face as long as people feel socially and politically excluded from the mainstream.

This book consists of papers which I had delivered in different forums. I have struggled to show the challenges which must be addressed and hurdles that must be overcome for the social restructuring of India as an egalitarian society. The studies are in line with Dr Ambedkar's thinking.

These essays have been divided into four sections by the editor, Rev. Dinesh Singh. Essays in each section have similar connecting ideas to help the reader see this connection I have written a brief foreword for each section.

The first chapter is on "Society" which envisages a pluralistic society of equal and free people. I had presented under the title *Towards a Rainbow Community* at a national seminar at Dharma Jyoti Vidyapeeth Faridabad, on 11th September 2013.

The second chapter titled "Religion" is on Dr Ambedkar's Response to Religions in India. His chief point is that religion has a power to sanctify places, people, elements and also ideas. Therefore it is important to assess religion whether it was sanctifying that which was good or that which was bad. Indian religions, particularly, Hinduism had sanctified the caste system and other religions in India had imitated its practice. The challenge is to dismantle this system.

The third chapter is on "Education". Tracing the start of western education in India both by the missionaries and the Wood's Dispatch 1854. It draws out Dr. Ambedkar's point that education in order to be a serious effort, should be taken up as a programme of political parties in their agenda.

The fourth chapter on "Identity" was presented as a paper titled as, *Identity and Diversity: Citizenship, Vocation and Common Good* at the International Triennial Conference at Madras Christian College in Chennai on 5th January 2017. The essay is an extension of the theme on education and its role in creating fearless individuals who would endeavour to create a society of free, equal, secure and happy people.

The fifth chapter deals with "Leadership". I had presented this as a paper titled *Models of Leadership in the Indian Church*. I have highlighted four leadership models, namely, ministerial, magisterial, managerial and transformational models. For all these I have drawn examples form historical figures of Asoka, Akbar, Pandita Ramabai and Dr Ambedkar respectively.

The sixth chapter deals with "Christians". This was a paper I had presented under the title *Influence of the Bible on Dr B.R. Ambedkar* at conference in Delhi at a Christian Academic Conference in January 2016. I had underscored egalitarianism as the attraction that the biblical tradition had for Dr Ambedkar.

The seventh chapter is on "Manusmriti" which I had presented as a paper in Sakus College, Dimapur under the title *Dr. Ambedkar's Response to Manusmriti*. It is a study on Dr. Ambedkar's exposition of the codes of Manu highlighting the point that the provisions of this ancient law was not based on justice but on caste system. This is evident in the form of penalties and awards; and the construction of laws and the perception of conflict with in it.

The eighth chapter is on "Caste System" which I wrote in September 2015 where I have explored what Dr Ambedkar had discovered about the caste, namely, the way they over centuries had operated, originated and evolved. Annihilation of Caste will only be possible if we understand these aspects properly.

The ninth chapter is on "violence" where I have explored the structured order of violence springing from the caste system. Originally the paper was titled as *Structured Violence: A Fierce Approach to Dominate* which I wrote on 24 November 2009.

The tenth chapter is on "Indian Constitution" originally under the title *God's Kingdom and the Indian Constitution*. Here I explored the biblical influence on it which came via Dr Ambedkar. To do this I have underscored the three features of the Indian Constitution, namely, justice, equality and fraternity and its seven merits which are political democracy, parliamentary system, protection of private property, fundamental rights, facile procedure of amendments, principle of federalism, and power of the centre.

The eleventh chapter deals with "Development". It highlights the development of society and individual. Social development should seek individual's happiness.

The twelfth chapter is on "Democracy" which sums up the vision of Dr. Ambedkar for a just society. The chapter is a short study tracing the history of democracy through the ages starting from the Greek civilisation in the antiquity till the rise of the modern Indian republic.

SOCIETY · RELIGION · EDUCATION

The first section is a set of three essays on Society, Religion and Education. Dr Ambedkar's concern for justice and enlightenment interconnects these three subjects. It must be accepted that to make society equal, religion must sacralise egalitarianism but to enlighten people, society must promote education. Granted that these essays highlight Dr Ambedkar's ideas on these issues, nonetheless we study these from a Christian point of view.

The first essay on "Society" is based on the Christian commitment on social and cultural inclusion and pluralism. Both society and culture are aspects of justice. Let us take cue from the bible. In contrast to the narrative of the tower of Babel (Gen 11) when God scattered the people to speak different languages all over the face of the earth, on Pentecost God fused diverse people together into one community of Christ (Acts 2).

The aim of this social engineering was not to impose cultural uniformity but to celebrate diversity so that the community would be culturally and intellectually enriched. This feature of the Christian community *ekklesia* offers a social design for the world, namely, inclusive and multi-cultural society, where discrimination based on caste, race, colour, or language would have no place. This is opposite to what the caste system stands for, namely, to forge society on graded inequality, fixity of occupation and fixation of people by birth.

The second essay on "Religion" underscores Dr Ambedkar's point that religion has the authority to sanctify i.e., to make sacred. In other words, it not only sacralises objects, persons and places; but also ideas, worldviews and social designs. By declaring them sacred religion lends validity. Social designs are also sacralized. Dr Ambedkar described the sacred design for social order as the *ideal-scheme-of-divine-governance* which could be either hierarchical or egalitarian. However, in his view egalitarianism was an important feature of a just social design. This scheme was diametrically opposite to the caste system. This also resonates with the leading principle of equality in the Law of Moses and the gospels. According to the gospels, the Kingdom of God involves fairness, generosity, graciousness, gratitude, compassion and unconditional love. These are not valued in a caste based society.

The third essay on "Education" highlights Dr Ambedkar's point that traditionally education was the speciality of the dominant castes. It was not open to all people; certainly not to the Untouchables. However, in a just society it will be available for all without discrimination. It is pointed out in the essay that the missionaries and the British government broke the monopoly of dominant castes on education and opened up western education to all through the system of government and missionary schools.

Learning was tied up with Christian tradition which was rooted in its liturgy and evangelism. The aim of this was to make God's people to read God's Word to all people. For this people were to be educated; the Bible to be translated in their languages and educational resources, like grammar books, text books and dictionaries to be made available. The concern to make Bible a book for all people became a basis for ushering modernity. Moreover, education from Christian point of view was to help people find traces of Christ, who is the living Word of God, in their context.

Chapter 1

Society

The pluralistic feature of human society is an accepted fact. The question however is this, how can this plurality be harmonious? I will deal with this question in four sections below. In the first section we will have a bird's eye-view of the nature of our Indian society, in the second section we will bring to fore some approaches to social pluralism; in the third we will take instances of pluralism in the bible and finally the vision of a harmonious society.

NATURE OF INDIAN SOCIETY

Figuratively rainbow points to harmony of social diversity but not social plurality. Acceptance of plurality does not mean that all is well with the community. This has been the reality of the Indian society where varied social groups have existed together. At their best they have been disinterested in the other or at their worst they have been in conflict with each other. The reason for this has been the caste system or *vernavyavastha* which was propounded in the Rig Veda (c. 1200 BCE), reinforced in the Bhagavad Gita (c. 300 BCE-300 CE) and crystallized in Manusmriti (c. 100 CE).

The Caste System

Caste system is uniquely Indian. It is its *dharma*. Over the centuries it evolved defeating all who challenged it till it became the backbone of Indian culture and civilization. It is the source of discrimination of people and degradation of human personality. There are three reasons why this system, as Dr. Ambedkar (1891-1956) had identified, obstructs harmony. These reasons are its features of graded inequality, fixity of occupation and fixation of people.[1] We will discuss these in the three sections below.

Graded Inequality

People are born in their communities i.e. *jatis*. Now each *jati* has been placed in a *verna* i.e. caste. The castes are placed in descending order of purity. So at the top level are the *Brahmin*-priests, the second are the *kshatriya*-warriors, on the third are the *vaishya*-traders and on the last level are the *shudra*-servants. All the rest who are not housed in this graded social order of caste are treated below human dignity and segeregated as untouchables. Here we introduce the term "Dalit" which connotes the broken and feeble condition of these people.

This graded system reinforces inequality. Clearly the *jatis* who are placed on the lowest level and those who are casted out are adversely affected by various socio-economic disadvantages. So perennial poverty and persistent lethargy has made Dalits depended. Largely, the Dalit infants for the first five years do not have adequate nourishment which ends in their permanent intellectual retardation. This ensures that they would never be able to compete in the mainstream. Added to this is the discrimination which is the practical outcome of untouchability and revulsion which the clean castes have towards Dalits who they regard as polluted and dirty. The most visible form of discrimination is segregated residential areas of Dalits at the outskirts of every Indian village. These are called variously as *thatti* (laughter), *cheri*, *maharwada* in different regions. These areas are marked by poverty, unhygienic conditions and backwardness.

It must be admitted that there can be no social harmony between the segregated groups of clean and unclean people. They do not compose a rainbow of diverse colours; instead they are as distinct as chalk and cheese.

Fixity of Occupation

According to the caste system the occupation of each community is fixed in the society. So the jobs that are deemed to be unclean, like doing the hide work or removing the night soil, are done only by the Dalits; whereas teaching of scripture and the rituals are performed by the Brahmins. It must at once be said that prior to *Manusmriti* this was not so. For instance, the Bhagavad Gita directed that individuals should take up their occupation according to their innate abilities yet the injunctions of *Manusmriti* prevailed over the principle of Gita.

So the occupation of each *jati* is fixed according to the caste and is non-transferable. The dilemma of this arrangement is this that on the one hand this arrangement ensures jobs to people but on the other it offers no secure alternative to the surplus personnel. So a large number of Dalits either remain unemployed or underemployed. Dr. Ambedkar was quick to notice that the facade of the division of labour in the community was actually the division of labourers. This deprived the workers to form solidarity or trade unions to protect them against exploitation. Far from harmony caste system was the tyranny of the owners-of-the-means-of-production before whom the Dalits were silenced.

Fixation of People

As discussed above, the people in their *jatis* and *vernas* i.e. castes, have fixed place in the hierarchical arrangement of the society. People are fixed at different levels with no stairs joining one level to the next. One way to change this was by marrying into another caste, but by doing this the lowest caste was thrown out of the caste system altogether. In this way, the people were left with no option but to adhere to the Manu's law of marriage. Far from the ideal of the pluralistic and hospitable community, this arrangement ensured that each individual was fixed within his/her caste.

There were also restrictions on inter-dining among the communities. Let us take the example of Mahatma Gandhi. In 1921-22 he elaborated his thoughts on the caste system in *Navajivan*, a Guajarati journal. Dr. Ambedkar translated this article and published in his book "What Congress and Gandhi have done to the Untouchables". This is what Gandhi wrote,

> (1) I believe that if Hindu Society has been able to stand it is because it is founded on the caste system ... (5) I believe that interdining or intermarriage are not necessary for promoting national unity. That dining together creates friendship is contrary to the experience. If this was true there would have been no war in Europe ... Taking food is as dirty an act as answering the call of nature. The only difference is that after answering call of nature we get peace while after eating food we get discomfort. Just as we perform the act of answering the call of nature in seclusion so also the act of taking food must also be done in seclusion.[2]

His critique of Gandhi's most extraordinary reasoning to restrict interdining was that it was "really an argument of a mad man."[3] In other words Gandhi's reasoning was flawed altogether arising out of his deeply dyed casteist psyche. Dr. Ambedkar's critique of Gandhi's position was this, that "the Hindu Society has been able to stand while others have died out or disappeared is hardly a matter for congratulation". It has survived not because of caste but because the foreign conquerors did not find it necessary to exterminate them. Hindus survived not by beating the invaders but by abject surrender to them.

Clean and Unclean

The second feature of the Indian society is the practice of untouchability. As discussed above the descending order of caste is accompanied with a descending levels of purity. The line of reasoning here is that the clean castes should protect themselves against the contact of the unclean or polluted castes. Somewhat the idea is that such physical contacts will render the clean castes unclean. The anxiety of this kind was so intense that it ignited Mangal Pandey to kickstart the 1857-uprisings against the East India Company Officers in India.

The reason was that Dalits came to be regarded not only as the most unclean beings but also were the most hated beings. Not created from the body of the *purusha*, they have never been regarded as full human beings. Following the model of the social isolation of the priestly castes for cultic observances, the other castes too insulated themselves from the lower castes and the untouchables i.e. Dalits. And so the society instead of evolving into the harmonious community increasingly became a community of broken people.

Honour and Shame

The third feature of the Indian society is the feeling of honour and shame. This is particularly visible in the area of socializing. Special care is taken in dining and contracting marriages. Food and fellowship has to be strictly within the limit of the one's own caste, similarly marriage also has to be within one's own caste. The only respite is the *gotra* which are sub-castes within the larger orbit of a caste. So the marriage across the *gotra* was a way of keeping the genetic pool viable.

The violation of the strict norms of dining and marriages became a matter of deep shame for a family, conversely adherence to these rules was deemed to be a matter of honour. This is deeply ingrained in the mind of people even in our times. Any association with Dalits in these matters brings shame to a person. At the same time marriage within the *gotra* was also a matter of dishonour. So the cases of *khap panchyats* where severe penalties are inflicted by the elders on the young people who deviate from these age-old norms end in honour killings and lynching. Dr. Ambedkar and other reformers were quick to understand this apartheid. To overcome this problem they advocated inter-dining and inter-marriages.

SOME APPROACHES TO SOCIAL PLURALISM

Clearly what emerges out of this is that there exists no community in the Indian society which is not ordered on the design of the caste system. The society may look cohesive but it is broken. Each community lives independently with no interest in the other. As a result of this arrangement the Dalit communities suffer social isolation. It must also be pointed out that all religious communities in India—Muslims, Christians and Sikhs—have adopted and absorbed casteist practices. In this regard, Nehru made an interesting observation in his book *The Discovery of India*,

> Rebels against caste have drawn many followers, and yet in course of time their group itself has become a caste. Jainism, a rebel against the parent religion, and in many ways utterly different from it, was yet tolerant to caste and adapted itself to it; and so it survives and continues in India, almost as an offshoot of Hinduism. Buddhism, not adopting itself to caste, and more independent in its thought and outlook, ultimately passes away from India, though it influences India and Hinduism profoundly. Christianity comes here eighteen hundred years ago and settles down and gradually develops its own castes. The Moslem social structure in India, in spite of its vigorous denunciation of all such barriers within the community, is also partly affected.[4]

In other words religions, even of foreign origin, that adopted the caste system survived in India; conversely those like Buddhism which originated in India but did not adopt caste system, could not survive.

Now in the modern democratic republic and in an increased pace of industrialization of India the challenge for those who benefit from this social arrangement is to maintain the status-quo. The feeling of discontent of the disadvantaged communities needed to suppressed both across the lines of caste and religion. I feel that three important approaches were developed for this. The aim was to maintain social order by retaining the social system. These in my view are toleration, function and dialogue. Let us discuss these:

Tolerant relationship

Toleration has been promoted as a social virtue where all, despite their differences, are allowed to live in peace. At its best it is like a relationship of pets with their owners who tolerate them. The determination of the members of the dominant castes to tolerate instances where their precautionary lines to protect their purity are flouted is appreciable. But this flouting has its limits. A well known way to promote toleration has been by inter-dining. However, toleration does not mean that dignity is extended to Dalits rather it is a way of co-existence.

Functional relationship

Functional relationship involves cooperation between different communities that perform diverse tasks in the society. It is often referred to as the *jajmani* system as propounded by William H Wiser (1890-1960), an American Presbyterian missionary and an anthropologist who worked in Uttar Pradesh. *Jajman* resembled a Yardman in English i.e. the one who was compensated for the services he rendered.[4] However, unlike the yardman in the western society who was paid for his work, in the *Jajmani* system the servile castes *neechi zat* was in a fixed relationship with the dominant castes *oochi zat*. This relational fixity was despite the fact that the servile castes were compensated for their work, for instance merely with grain, by the dominant caste.

Admittedly, the term *jajman* was used primarily for the so called upper castes, whereas the people of the servile castes were referred to as *kam-karne-wala*.[5] Wiser observed that that the relationship between the high caste *jajmans* and the low caste *kam-karne-wala* is clear, but this arrangement does not describe the relationship between low caste *jajmans* and the high caste *kam-karne-wala*.[6] It is very interesting to note that towards the end of the twentieth century religious rituals, albeit in specific territories, were offered for the latter by some Brahmans.[7] This was done in view of the fact that not only the existence of the servile castes was a necessity but also that they could afford to pay the officiating priest. Yet this did not mean that dignity was extended to the servile castes or that they were treated with equality. Wiser observed that

> The higher caste although they cannot move up the scale of occupation, can move down ... But those who are the lowest have nothing left to which to descend and they cannot ascend. They are shut up to nothing but the dregs of occupational tasks. Even a greater weakness is the attitude of the higher caste to the low. ... Manu's (Law) ... reveal that the Sudra has the relationship of a slave to the Brahmans. This relationship holds particularly for the lowest Hindu groups, such as the leather workers and sweepers.[8]

All it meant was that in functional relationships plurality was forged as an arrangement of utility and convenience without producing social harmony based on justice. It must be admitted that at its best the *jajmani* arrangement is the recognition of economic interdependence of one caste on the other for food and labour, rather than social justice.

Dialogical relationship

This idea was developed from within the Christian world. The first to seriously consider the subject of dialogue was Stanley Jedidiah Samartha (1920–2001). He contributed to this area as the first director of the *Dialogue with People of Living Faiths and Ideologies* a sub-unit of the World Council of Churches His famous quote is,

> Dialogue is a spirit, a mood, an attitude towards neighbours of other faiths. In a multi-religious country like India where the destinies of different religious communities are intertwined and where people of different religious persuasions and ideological convictions face the same human problems in the life of the nation we need to remove suspicion, and build up confidence and trust between people. Thus, in a community where people of different faiths live and work together, dialogue can become an expression of Christian neighbourliness and part of the Christian ministry in a pluralist world.[9]

Clearly Samartha's concern was to bring change in people's thinking rather than a change in the social system. Through dialogue people who learn from one another would appreciate one another and so peace would prevail. However, mere mutual understanding may lead to the appreciation of plurality but it will not produce a harmonious community we are looking for.

Transformational relationship

In the three approaches above the idea to maintain social order supersedes the concern for justice. I contend that no social harmony can be achieved without justice. I will be taking my cue chiefly from Dr. B.R. Ambedkar's line of reasoning and his view of what justice entails. In a transformational relationship the aim is towards social transformation i.e. towards creating a just society. The rainbow of social harmony will appear only when the cloud of justice gathers. In other words harmony in society will result when the society is established on justice. But before we do that let us provide ourselves with some biblical foundations for harmony.

BIBLICAL INSTANCES: PLURALISM OR HARMONY

From Babel to Jerusalem

The biblical narratives show that besides ethnic conflicts, there were linguistic conflicts also. This is true in our times too. A way to overcome these conflicts is to learn the language of the dominant groups. However, the first instance of reckoning multiple languages is in the story of Babel in Genesis. This primitive human society was cohesive but up to no good. Their endeavour to build a tower was not what God intended them to do. So God confused them with languages. The consequence was dramatic. The community disintegrated into linguistic groups and each group moved away from the centre of activity (Genesis 11.1-9). In this linguistic plurality there was no intermingling because each group started to live its own cycle of life. Diametrically opposite to this story was the event of Pentecost in the Acts 2. Here people of different linguistic groups were brought into one community by the Holy Spirit. This community in Jerusalem was heterogeneous yet cohesive and the agenda of its life-and-work was set by God. They were not to raise a tower up from earth but to build the city of God. In other words they would bring God's blessings down to all the families of the earth reversing the earlier curse (Genesis 12.1-3).

So the character of the Christian community right from the start was the combination of harmony and heterogeneity. The cause for harmony was equal share in the Holy Spirit. This brought the ideal of social equality to fore. All who were baptized and had the Spirit in equal share. No one was superior.

From Olive Tree to a Grafted Tree

In Romans 11 we read St. Paul's illustration to describe the relationship of the gentiles (unclean) and the Jewish (clean) communities. Figuratively the wild olive branches (unclean gentiles) were grafted on to the cultivated olive (clean Jewish) tree. The miracle which never happened in nature but occurs as a social phenomena was this that the nature of the wild olive branches got transformed. To reiterate the wild olive branches become equal beneficiaries of the nourishment of the root of the cultivated olive tree. Thus the distinction of the clean from the unclean classes is ended by equality of advantage of the spiritual heritage. All classes and ethnicities become one in the body of Christ. Attention should be drawn to the fact that harmony in society can be possible only in equal treatment of all communities of people.

From Structural Body to Organic Body

The third instance of harmony in St. Paul's letter is in the metaphor of the organic body in 1-Corinthians 12. Here he was arguing that the differentiation of functions in the community does not mean social inequality. Functions and offices entrusted to different people do not make them superior or inferior. Just as all the members of a body are equally honoured, and all feel the joy and the pain, so do all the different members of the body of Christ. The list of functionaries "first the apostles, second the prophets, third teachers, then miracles, then gifts of healing ...." (Rom. 12.28) are not indicative of the order of status but it indicates the chronological sequence. Initially the

Lord Jesus appointed the apostles, and then emerged the prophets for example Agabus (Acts 21.10) and subsequently others. In this metaphor all members of the body are equally honoured. The social tasks are not monopolized by any class; instead the variety exists like the colours of a rainbow on the single arc.

Looking back we learn from the three sections above that harmony is the result of equal treatment of people and equal access to resources. Harmony will not result from imposing monoculturalism but equality among people diversified by occupation, languages, religions, ideologies, education and finances.

TOWARDS A HARMONIOUS COMMUNITY

Dr. Ambedkar had pointed out that justice is another name for liberty, equality, and fraternity. He had also traced the Christian root of this slogan highlighting that it was not original to the French revolutionists per se. In this he underscored a very important point to prove his thesis of religion and society. According to him the primary occupation of religion was not God; instead religion propounded the *ideal scheme of divine governance for society*.

The problem, however, before him was that each religion propounded its own scheme. So each religion needed to be assessed whether its ideal scheme was good or bad. If the ideal scheme advocated *justice* and promoted *human rights* as foundation for establishing society, then the scheme was good. It is beyond our scope here to explore Dr Ambedkar's theory of religion and society in detail but we accept that liberty, equality and fraternity are foundational aspects for a multi-cultural community, where heterogeneity and harmony will join together, and where people will be just and generous in their dealings.

I have shown that various models put forward for turning pluralism into a system of harmony had not succeeded. The reason I reckon is that harmony in a heterogeneous society cannot be achieved unless a society is founded on justice. In the following section we will discuss three aspects of justice namely, equality, association and liberty.

Equal but not Hierarchical

Social equality is the hallmark of justice. Equality does not mean uniformity as such. As discussed above, equality means justice. It means that all communities will have accessibility to civil liberties, dignity, opportunities and protection of their human rights. But as Dalits have been historically disadvantaged, therefore, in the race for achievements they cannot be treated on par with the privileged communities. Justice will take practical shape only when Dalits are compensated with preferential treatment. This has been extended famously as the policy of reservation and quota. Yet we know how the 1950 Presidential Order curtailed the benefits of reservations to those Dalits who chose to embrace Christianity or Islam. Subsequently, the Sikhs and the Buddhists in 1956 and 1990 were included but the rest are still excluded. Having said that discrimination creates injustice, we must also affirm that inequality equally creates injustice.

We know that castes are not distinct communities; rather they are unequal communities. It must be accepted that justice and harmony will be possible only if the caste system is dismantled. This entails a radical social transformation. For the ambedkarites the way forward is conversion of Indians to an egalitarian religion.

In Dr Ambedkar's line of thinking facilitating conversion of masses to an egalitarian religion is a positive service one can offer to this country. For himself Dr Ambedkar chose *Navayana* or Neo-Buddhism, a religion which he himself had established on the principles of his theory of religion and society. In his view all religions in India were unfit for Dalits to embrace because all had shaped themselves up in line with the caste system. Over and against this the *Navayana* aims to create a community of equal and free people.

Association but not Isolation

We know that the Indian society which has been established on the design of the caste system not only discriminates and treats people unequally; it isolates communities especially the Dalit communities. The curious nature of the caste system is such that hatred is served by the hands of the co-religionists. The routinely reported cases of fratricide in the newspapers demonstrate the extreme nature of the alienation of people. A multi-ethnic society does not mean that it is necessarily a casteless society. The point is to understand that a harmonious society cannot be established without social equality. Therefore, in the Indian social context justice involves annihilation of caste.

In other words the diverse communities of the society and its people, like various colours of a rainbow, have to merge into a single ray of associated life. The associations have to be more human than the client-patron relationship of the *jajmani* system. We took cue from the biblical metaphors of the *body* and the *grafted olive tree* in an earlier discussion to understand what such associations entail.

Liberty but not Anarchy

We have already discussed that obsession of the caste system has been to maintain social order without taking social justice into consideration. This is a system which establishes apartheid and slavery, not harmony and justice which we are looking for. Our vision of harmony is pluralistic and inclusive community. In other words, we are looking forward to a society where people will be emancipated from untouchability and segregation. Anarchy is not what we desire but a society liberated from the caste system. To protect ourselves from anarchy, we must ensure that society is firmly re-established on democracy. In other words, worldview of democracy should replace the religion of caste.

A harmonious community can only be possible when the associated life of the people is established on justice i.e. social equality. In other words, where all people are included in the community, all are treated with equality and all communities within the society are treated with fairness. Where no one is isolated and where all enjoy equal opportunities and civil liberties of a democratic society. Now we know that the democratic State desires to establish a harmonious community on the basic principle of justice, but it has failed to accomplish this desire. What the State cannot do, religion can because religion commands the loyalty of the people in a way that the State cannot. If this is so then the Church must take a lead in the direction of establishing a just society. In this respect there has to be a double pronged approach i.e. on the one hand interreligious dialogue and on the other the politicization of Dalit Christians.

Firstly, by dialogue I do not mean sitting together for a cozy conversation; instead the leaders of the diverse religions and ideologies must deeply search for a *shared-moral-standard* and agree to it. It will be possible only if they engage with the best aspects of every religious tradition. Justice is one such aspect. If justice is to be the criterion, then the shared-moral-standard should accept fostering egalitarianism, freedom and kinship within every community and among all the communities in the society. Here the Sermon of the Mount should provide the prompt "do unto others what you want others to do to you" (Matt 7.12).

Secondly, the politicization of Dalits is in answer to the question, can Dalit-Christians have power? If the answer is in the affirmative, then the step to acquire it is to politicize the community. It means several things. Firstly it means that politicization has to do with organising and empowering the people to come out on the streets to demand their rights in the society. Secondly, it means mobilizing people in an organized way to demand for their civil liberties and human rights, thirdly, to field candidates for the legislative assemblies and the parliament, and fourthly, to enhance the education of the Dalits because knowledge is power.

IN THE ABOVE DISCUSSION AMBEDKAR'S VIEW THAT SOCIETY SHOULD BE JUST, INCLUSIVE AND PLURAL HAS BEEN UNDERSCORED. This resonates with the Christian ideal of community *ecclesia* where God welcomes diverse people into the body of Christ without discrimination on linguistic or ethnic grounds.

Endnotes

[1] B.R. Ambedkar, '*Hindu Social Order*' (1946) Writings and Speeches, Vol.3. pp. 106-113.

[2] B.R. Ambedkar, '*What Congress and Gandhi have done to the Untouchables*' (1945), Writings and Speeches Vol-9, Education Department. Govt. of Maharashtra. Mumbai: 1990. pp. 275-76.

[3] Ambedkar. *Idem.*, pp. 287-88.

[4] William Henricks Wiser, *The Hindu Jajmani System: A socio-economic system interrelating members of a Hindu village community in services.* Lucknow Publishing House. Lucknow. 1936.

[5] *Ibid.*, p. 6.

[6] *Ibid.*, p. 181.

[7] This was shared in a personal conversation with my employees from Garhwali region.

[8] *Op cit.* Wiser, p. 164.

[9] S. Wesley Ariarajah, *A World Council of Churches Perspective on the Future of Hindu-Christian Dialogue* in Harold Coward (Ed.), Hindu-Christian Dialogue - Perspectives and Encounters, Motilal Banarsidass Publishers, Lucknow, 1993. pp. 251-52.

Chapter 2

Religion

D r Ambedkar was disturbed by the behaviour of his coreligionists towards the Untouchables. This being his own experience, he reflected on this social problem of untouchability and segregation i.e. revulsion and rejection of the Dalits as inferior and unfit for human association by the 'clean' castes. He held that social change was possible by changing people's behaviour, and that people's behaviour would change if they changed their thinking. He drew a line under religion to emphasize that it was wholly responsible for shaping people's thinking. Therefore, religions needed to be assessed. In doing so he was also searching for a possible home into which he would lead his people.

For this assessment he developed a theory of religion and society. He defined religion as propounding the *ideal-scheme-of-divine-governance* i.e. a design sacralized for social order.[1] Accordingly, the first purpose of religion was to offer a design to organize the society and the second was to sacralize whatever was vital for cohesion of society. Therefore, a religion needed to be scrutinized if it offered a just social design. Justice for Dr Ambedkar was synonymous with liberty, equality and fraternity.[2] Unlike the French, Dr Ambedkar gave priority to equality in this slogan and underscored its religious roots.

Having thus reduced the relevance of religion to social utility he started his assessment of each religion. His aim was to explore two things; one, the roots of social inequality and two, the central concern of society. Tracing the evolution of religion and society he brought out two norms for assessing the contemporary religions, namely, *utility* and *justice*. He pointed out that in the three phases of society's evolution—primal, antique and modern—religion had distinct concerns.[3] These were to protect life, society and individual. The former two he valued for *utility* and the latter one for *justice*. Religion's *utility* for preserving life and society was important for the survival of the human species but the protection of individual's interest was important to make him/her a free and equal being. This was justice.

These then were the norms that Dr Ambedkar would employ for assessing the *ideal-scheme-of-divine-governance* of religions. Admittedly, there was no obvious role for deity in his theory of religion. This in his view was rational. Nevertheless, religions when found faltering needed to be reformed on this rational principle namely of *justice* and *utility*, so that their ideal scheme for society's governance would be just and useful for the people i.e. one that would promote egalitarianism, freedom and kinship. Once a religion was reformed the reordering of society would be easier. This was his basic principle for social change. All the rest which was esoteric and metaphysical was superfluous for him.

Dr Ambedkar's line of reasoning is both interesting and problematic. The problem is the dilemma between *utility* and *justice*. There would be situations where the collective advantage for society—*utility*—would not be in the interest of an individual's justice and vice versa.[4] Dr Ambedkar did not really see this drawback in his argument. He also had no explanation for resistance of the adherents to reform their religious worldviews to their own advantage even by the force of law. One example is the Hindu Code Bill which failed in the Indian parliament in 1951. His way to transcend this dilemma was to intellectually articulate his ideas hoping that those who read his books would be persuaded by his arguments to reform religion and society.

Now let us return to our discussion on assessment of religions. The method to assess religion was to cull out its sacred design for social order by scrutinizing its rituals, not its doctrines. What did the ritual actually intended to do? He pointed out that the rituals indicated what kind of scheme was being sanctified for the social order? It could be unjust or just i.e. hierarchical or egalitarian.[5] Justice meant two things for Dr Ambedkar. Firstly, it meant that social order should ensure that all people to enjoy freedom, equality and intermingling. Secondly, it meant that unequal people should not be treated equally under the law. Therefore, Dalits who were disadvantaged needed to be compensated. This meant that the individuals were protected. This is in line with Dr Ambedkar's reasoning that what was good for the individual was also good for the society. In this way the dilemma of justice versus utility was transcended. In Dr Ambedkar's thinking if the laws of a religious tradition contradicted this principle of *justice* and *utility* they had to be changed. In his view nothing was eternally fixed in a religious tradition except to protect life, society and individual.

At this point we must draw attention to three things highlighted by Dr. Ambedkar about religion; firstly that the conflict of norms create dilemma; secondly, religious tradition is a strong basis of social inequality; and thirdly, that it is difficult to reorder society through the agency of religion alone. Keeping this predicament in mind let us proceed to see one more aspect of Dr Ambedkar's analysis of religion. Dr Ambedkar divided the religious traditions into two regimes: the *religion of rules* and the *religion of principles*.[6] He pointed out that under rules, people acted without thinking whereas with principles as their guide people had to think about why and how they were to act. Therefore, their actions had to be responsible acts. We can now concisely state Dr Ambedkar's line of thinking.

Society is a given fact where human beings are born and where they live till they die. The social nature of human beings and their interdependence to meet their needs make society an unavoidable fact. But inevitably, over a span of time, it becomes socially and economically unequal giving rise to classes and castes based on economy, occupation, gender, language, ethnicity and colour. Here some people gain dominance and others are subjugated. This injustice of inequality cause two things: the subjugation of the powerless as well as the lawlessness of the powerful. We may also note that the majority makes law so they are the masters of the law and can make them to suit their own advantages which may perpetuate inequality oppression, rejection, exploitation and exclusion.

Religion, which originally in the primal phase started as ritualized actions of socially useful roles for human beings, also changes tracks to support and sanctify unjust social order of its day. Therefore, religion needs to be assessed and reformed. This in turn will help to change the thinking of the people and facilitate to establish social righteousness. Here the importance of religion should not be underestimated for two reasons: first, that it has the power to let loose or to rein in the behaviour of the majority. This may adversely or favourably affect the minorities of a society; and second, that it gives a blueprint for structuring society, which Dr Ambedkar called as the *ideal-scheme-of-divine-governance*. This is a difficult but crucial point in Dr Ambedkar's thinking on religion, because the two things – inspiration, as well as, the practical extension of its ideals in law – have to be held together. For the State, the issue of religious plurality in the society adds to this problem of differentiation by giving rise to multiple collectivities in one society i.e. communitarianism. Understandably if a society were to be established on Dr Ambedkar's ideals, it would not tolerate alternative religions which may differ in their ideals.

A religion's blue print for the social order should be assessed on the standard of reason and human rights for the reason that the law does not affect the human heart and conscience. In other words it is the human heart, not the law, which compels us to share our goods with the poor. Having assessed various religions, Dr Ambedkar found that it was very difficult to reform them. Here a way out was to establish a single religious system based on entirely his ideals. In order to undertake the exercise of assessing a religion, Dr Ambedkar unveiled the foundational roots of religion's advancement over several millennia. These, as we have discussed earlier, were three, namely, conserving life, preserving society and protecting individual. He reduced these to *utility* and *justice* that constituted the basis of religion to govern society.

A religion that sanctified *utility* and *justice*, instead of regarding the supernatural, as normative was *rational*. It would resist propagating superstitions. A religion, therefore, that sacralized what was *useful, just* and *rational*, offered a righteous blueprint for a social order and for regulating behaviour of the people. It does this by making morality, instead of the law, sacred. Hence, a religion that would stand this test should be established in a society. Here Dr Ambedkar misses the big point of religious pluralism in society. Understandably so because as a statesman with an agenda for the emancipation of Dalits, he saw difficulties in uniting and organizing them on democratic principles of freedom and equality.

A society established on religion's intention to make people free, happy and equal would constitute a just society. This aspect of *utility* of religion was tantamount social justice. The former involved equal treatment of all people under the law and the latter involved solidarity, reciprocal responsibility and mutual care among people in a society. From this aspect of justice and righteousness Dr Ambedkar had figured out that the slogan of the French Revolutionists—liberty, equality and fraternity—in the end had religious roots.

According to this line of thinking it is essential that a State be established to make laws for the society and execute them or to punish those who break them. Therefore, it is the responsibility of the State to ensure that the people not only live peaceably in society, but also that the interests of individuals are protected. In this way the State comes mid-way of seeing society as closed home, on the one hand and on the other, the individuals as free beings. Here we should highlight Dr Ambedkar's insight that the rules of society are authorized by religion. However, all societies become unjust and differentiate into unequal factions and so do the religions especially when they sanctify unjust norms and worldviews. Therefore there arises a need to assess and reassess our religion. When this assessment succeeds to re-establish a righteous religion, then the above cycle would repeat itself.[7]

Dr Ambedkar believed that religion had the authority to sacralize, e.g. it had earlier sacralized the dharma, the *dhamma* and the gospel. This demonstrated the fact that by doing this it makes a philosophy or an ideology or a theology sacred. Once sacralised, the social order, the moral order and the worldview propounded by that philosophy or ideology or theology gains legitimacy and authority. Having reached this point, a religion propounds what it has accepted as sacred in an indisputable fashion. The drawback is that it can advocate a system of social inequality as a sacred order; here the caste system was a case in point. To counter this, every religion, in Dr Ambedkar's view, needed to be tested on the anvil of justice. But as we have already pointed out that this method was too simple to analyze the complexity of religion. Let us now study Dr Ambedkar's assessment of various religions in India with my comments below.

Primal Religions: It was obsessively ritualistic either to sterilize or to insulate or to ward off the unseen or the seen powers that threatened life. These were Religions-of-Rules, albeit, in a primitive way. Dr Ambedkar saw limited traces of untouchability in the tribal practices. It was observed around a person deemed to be contaminated till the rituals were performed to receive him/her back into their society. In as much as the Primal Religions were useful to study the nature of the primitive society, these were incapable to help the people move into modernity.

The Hindus: The Hindus had the drawback of the caste system which created social stratification. This was propounded the *dharma* which had made it to be a Religion-of-Rules. According to the rule of dharma, the society had to be ordered into four castes. Starting with the Brahmin-priest, the castes were placed in a descending order of purity i.e. the *kshatiya*-warrior, the *vaishya*-trader, the *shudra*-servant and the rest were casted out from the caste system as untouchables who were unclean. The caste system was sanctified as the *dharma*. Consequently people suffered the consequences of inequality. It caused isolation, discrimination and oppression. The people who experienced brokenness in excessive ways were Dalits.

The Muslims: Despite their religious ideal of egalitarianism they did not treat their Dalit coreligionists with equality and friendship. For example as he found in Bengal their community was vertically divided as *ashraf, ajlaf* and *arzal.* These sections corresponded to the caste system allowing limited intermixing among them. The Islamic tradition, under the injunction of *Sharia* or the religious law, on the one hand, and the caste system on the other, was a Religion-of-Rules. Consequently people suffered social stagnation.

The Christians: Free from the tradition of religious legalism Christianity was a Religion-of-Principles. However, despite its ideals of equality, freedom and fellowship the Indian Christians needed respite from the brutality of casteist practices within their community. Moreover it was politically weak and numerically insignificant in India.

The Sikhs: Although Sikhism was a Religion-of-Principles the Sikhs were affected by the caste system. For instance the status of the Ramdasi communities, who were faithful Sikhs but were classified as Scheduled Caste, was a glaring example of unequal social distinctions among them.

The Jews: They were an interesting and an ancient community in India. Despite being a Religion-of-Rules it had adapted itself to the modern society. In the Indian context it was divided up into caste-like unequal community of *gora* (white) and *kala* (black) Jews respectively. Although Dr Ambedkar was interested in the Jewish scripture to establish some aspects of his theory of religion, it was not a religion to which he had ever contemplated to convert. In fact after assessing various Indian religions he found none of them were suitable for Dalits.

The Buddhists: Buddhism was the religion he turned to. We know that there are various types of Buddhists in the world. Dr Ambedkar found these forms were irrelevant for Dalits. As if instinctively driven, as his life drew to an end due to persistent ill-health, he decided to convert to what he had created after his own ideals. He rewrote the scriptures following the gospels both in its ethics and in narrating Buddha's life by removing all those stories which he considered as irrational e.g. the narrative of Gautama's three encounters: with an old man, a sick man and a dead man. This was a diminished form of the traditional Buddhist religion. He had called it the *Navyana* or the neo-Buddhism where the *dhamma* of justice was sanctified as a norm for a righteous society. In this way he founded the Religion-of-Principles.[8]

The two formulations with which Dr Ambedkar had reduced religion into a social operation were these: one was to define religion as an *ideal-scheme-of-divine-governance*, and the other was to concentrate on two norms—*utility* and *justice*—as the scale to assess the whole universe of religions. We can call these as Dr Ambedkar's apparatus which was reductionist in approach. As a result of this, his theory ended up in contradictions and his decisions were inconsistent with what he had stood for. This diminutive approach of Dr Ambedkar looks lucid but it hindered him to appreciate the complex makeup of religion. This complexity failed to fit into his norms of *utility, justice* or *reason*. He, therefore, eliminated much of religion that fell beyond the scope of his norms e.g. transcendence. But such reduced ideas do not constitute a proper religion. Yet he was so convinced of the social utility of religion that he disregarded both, its diversity of scope, as well as, its plurality in a society. Now if his reductionist apparatus of assessing religions were to destroy its diversified nature, and thereby the religion itself, then it would bring an end to the society too. In the absence of society the operation of religion, by his definition, would become irrelevant. In other words, the *ideal-scheme-of-divine-governance* of a religion has no operational scope if society vanished and its population broke up into minute unrelated floating units.

Be that as it may, Dr Ambedkar inaugurated *Navabaudh*, new Buddhist community on 14th October 1956 in Nagpur of which he became the first member, and 365,000 followed him on the spot by converting to neo-Buddhism. In this way he succeeded to establish his new religion in the new community on the lines of his reductionist apparatus. This community was not intended to be differentiated into diverse schools of thought and types of practice. Ideally this may not look disjointed but it needs little evidence to realize that in such a homogeneous community those who differ would be marginalized.

By adopting neo-Buddhism Dr Ambedkar found a way out of his predicament of being a nationalist yet abandoning his cultural religion. He did what he had publicly announced i.e. renounce Hinduism, yet he could be nationalistic by not adopting a foreign religion. Having reached this decision to adopt neo-Buddhism, Dr Ambedkar abandoned his search for an egalitarian religion. But this was inconsistent with his vision i.e. to establish a just society with the help of an egalitarian religion. This inconsistency was the result of his reductionism.

Let us try to understand why he fell in this trap of reductionism. The reason is that his question—what is a good religion?—was wrong. I think the exercise to prove the worth of a religion fails to convince others to abandon their religion in order to embrace the better one. What he should have asked was this—how we can agree on a shared-moral-standard for all people in a multi-religious society. This question is also important for the State because it is responsible for maintaining social integration of the nation. To achieve this in a pluralistic society, people of all religions or ideologies need to agree on a common standard of morality. The State, however, can neither guarantee social consent, nor social cohesion nor a shared-moral-standard. Nonetheless once the consensus of shared morality is reached, religions can guarantee adherence to this standard because they have people's loyalty. But Dr Ambedkar did not seek this; instead he wished to establish a just society through a religion that propounded egalitarianism.

In my view the possibility of a shared-moral-standard can best be achieved by inter-religious dialogue. Dialogue is a conference of religions and ideologies where all dissimilar voices—diverse and contradictory—are heard. This demands humility to learn and hold others in a deep respect for their convictions, to be sensitive to the feelings and a desire to engage with the best-of-traditions of others, confidence in one's own faith tradition and politeness in expressing differences. It is possible for all to share a moral standard and from there to develop a value-system acceptable to each religious or ideological group. Such a moral standard can function as a civil morality i.e. as the heart and conscience of the society.[9]

We see in the Indian context that different communities and castes co-exist with mutual disinterest. Even if the laws have made life easier for the Dalits, it has not created for them a social intercourse with the other communities. Here there is a need for reconciliation between those who have been wronged with those who have wronged others. But these initiatives of active-reconciliation should not be confused with making compromises. It will be this mutual acceptance that will restore the *selfhood* of those who have been wronged. *Selfhood* is a positive emotional state of a person. It is evident at the level of personal confidence as well as in the self esteem of a person. This will also be visible in one's mental and physical wellbeing which in turn assures a person to flourish in life. The point is that justice does not automatically create social integration. Action for reconciliation must be undertaken to make the different communities of a society to meet together. Here the emphasis should be to appreciate and celebrate the common humanity of all people in spite of their region-cultural differences. Here a shared-moral-standard of a society can be of help so that justice can be accompanied with reconciliation. It will help the healing of the interior wounds which is an important aspect of restoring a broken person's *selfhood*.

ALTHOUGH MANY HAD SUFFERED THE EXCESSES OF THE CASTE SYSTEM, FEW IN INDIA HAD RESPONDED TO IT IN THE WAY DR AMBEDKAR DID. Few had reached the level of thinking that he had reached in his times. We learn from him that our faith in what our religions teach us should help us to establish society of equal and free people, in other words a just society. If our religion fails to teach this to us then we must search for an alternative. His aim was to use every bit of religion to promote righteousness and good quality of life. The importance of this is obvious in our times when the revival of Indian identity is not based on righteousness but on culture. The culture's proximity to religion has sacralized it to such an extent that its practices and norms are accepted unquestioningly. In these times Dr Ambedkar's message comes out clearly in favour of righteousness not culture.

Ironically, the one who, along with Mahatma Gandhi had founded the modern democratic republic of India was accorded no State ceremonies at his last rites in Mumbai. Although the *Ashokchakra* i.e., the blue wheel at the centre of the Indian national flag was added at his insistence, his body was not wrapped in it. Neither was he honoured with the twenty-one gun salute nor the sounding of the Last Post at his funeral. Yet millions of people have come to honour him every year since 1956 at *Chaityabhoomi* in Mumbai. This shows that Dalits will remember him and will continue to draw inspiration from him for a long time to come.

Endnotes

[1] B.R. Ambedkar, 'Philosophy of Hinduism' (1941), *Writings and Speeches* Vol. 3, Mumbai, 1987, p. 6.

[2] Ambedkar. *Idem.,* Vol. 3, p. 25.

[3] Monodeep Daniel, *Religions in India: The Vision of Dr. Ambedkar* (2016) ISPCK New Delhi. p. 30.

[4] *Ibid.,* pp. 32-36.

[5] *Ibid.,* p. 45.

[6] *Ibid.,* p. 49.

[7] *Ibid.,* pp. 265-66.

[8] *Ibid.,* p. 267.

[9] *Ibid.,* p. 275.

Chapter 3

Education

R ight at the start it must be stated that the phrase "Education for all" neatly sums up Dr Ambedkar's view of educating India. Unmasking the pretence of *Chaturvarnya* he wrote, "Education everyone must have. Means of defence everyone must have. These are paramount requirements for every one for self-preservation."[1] This was in view of the fact that education and bearing arms is neither possible nor permitted for all in a caste structured society. He dealt with this in his monograph *Annihilation of Caste* (1936) where he attacked the casteist mentality of Arya Samajist.[2] It was in this light that he wrote on education with a deep social insight. This is what he wrote,

> Assuming that *Chaturvarnya* is practicable, I contend that it is the most vicious system. That the Brahmins should cultivate knowledge ... and that the Shudra should serve sounds as though it was a system of division of labour. ... The defenders of Chaturvarnya say ... Why need the Shudra bother to take to education, when there is the Brahmin to whom he can go when the occasion for reading or writing arises? ... The theory of Chaturvarnya, understood in this sense, may be said to look upon the Shudra as the ward and the three Varnas as the guardians. ... (But) what is to happen if the Brahmins ... fail to pursue knowledge ...? What is to happen to the Shudra if the three classes refuse to support him on fair terms or combine to keep him down? Who is to safeguard the interests of the Shudra ... when the person, who is trying to take advantage of his ignorance, is the Brahmin? ... How can the fact that his neighbour is educated and armed help a man who is uneducated and disarmed? The

whole theory of absurd ... The *Chaturvarnya* ... makes no provision to safeguard the interests of the ward from the misdeeds of the guardian.[3]

The above excerpt exposes the fact that what the promoters of Caste System or *Chaturvarnya* argue is basic to what the Caste System stands for, namely, that education for Dalits is unnecessary. This was not merely in literature but has been put into practice for millennia. On account of the *Chaturvarnya* Dalits could receive no education. Dr Ambedkar observed that

> They could not think out or know the way to their salvation. They were condemned to be lowly and not knowing the way of escape and not having the means of escape, they became reconciled to eternal servitude, which they accepted as their inescapable fate.[4]

It is clear from the above excerpt that education was (and is) the key to escape bondage both externally and interiorly to liberty in life and thought. He had articulated this in his Introduction to *Federation versus Freedom* a speech which he delivered and published in 1939 on the founder's day of Gokhale Institute founded by Late Rao Bahadur RR Kale,

> First, knowledge is power as nothing else is, and secondly, not all those who wish and care for knowledge have the leisure and the patience to dig for it. As one who believes in the necessity of knowledge and appreciates the difficulties in its acquisition I am glad to be associated in this way with him and with the Institute he has founded.[5]

However, Dr Ambedkar was not the first one to realize the significance of education. It is very interesting to note that I-Tsing the famous Chinese visitor in the seventh century gave an account of education of this time. He visited when India was in its Buddhist era and education was popularized by the monks who were from different sections of society and they taught to all people. In their opinion knowledge, education and enlightenment were connected. Therefore, for a society to be enlightened its entire population were to be educated. No doubt universities in Taxila and Nalanda even attracted students from other countries to study both religious and secular subjects.

This was in contrast to the earlier non-Buddhist system where the *Gurukula* System of schooling kept the light of learning shining but only among the few. The *Shudra* and the Untouchables were kept out of the system. Instructions were mostly in Sanskrit and the subjects were irrelevant to needs of daily life. The *Gurus* were not trained specifically for teaching as a profession rather they were versed in *Dharmashastras* and later in *Puranas*.

Later during the Muslim era education was imparted in the *Maktabs* or Madarsas which were attached to the mosques. The Moulvis were not only teachers but were noted for their pious lives and knowledge of *Koran*. Delhi became a centre for learning and literary activities. Although orphans were provided with state funds since the time of Akbar and later Aurangzeb continued to provide sustenance through lands and pensions to Islamic scholars and stipends to poor Muslim students, the Untouchables stood no chance to enter the Madarsas.

Situation changed with the arrival of Christian missionaries particularly from 1813 onwards. Starting from Goa, Tranquebar and Serampore they opened their schools in every part of the country for all sections of people including the Untouchables. The missionaries assessed the standard of civilization by the measure of justice. Therefore, all that was unjust had to be eliminated for which education was important.

In 1854 Wood's Dispatch was a turning point in the Indian Education. It contained some important recommendations. *Firstly* that an Education Department should be setup in each Province and its highest official should be named as Director of Public Instruction; *secondly* that universities should be set up in Kolkata, Chennai and Mumbai. These Universities should have Chancellors, Vice Chancellor and Fellows; *thirdly* that emphasis should be to spread public education; *fourthly* that the system of grant in aid of education should be set up and; *Fifthly* that special institutions for training teachers should be set up and *sixthly* that Importance should be given to the education of women.

Revolution in education was brought by Christians by their missionary enterprise; and by legislative measures schooling was made both professional and open to all sections of society. It was in this British dominated environment that Dr Ambedkar was articulating his vision for education for all i.e. without discrimination, inclusive and universal. In 1919 his observation to the Southborough Committee about Bombay (Mumbai) Municipal schools was this,

> This most cosmopolitan city … with a greater freedom than any other Corporation in India has two different set of schools … one for the children of touchables and the other for those of the untouchables. This in itself is a point worthy of note. But there is something yet more noteworthy, following the division of the schools it has divided its teaching staff into untouchables and touchables. As the untouchable teachers are short of demand, some of the untouchable schools are manned by teachers from the touchable class. The heart-killing fun of it is that if there is a higher grade open in untouchable schools service, as there is bound to be because of a few untouchable trained teachers, a touchable teacher can be thrust into the grade. But if a higher grade is open in the touchable school service, no untouchable teacher can be thrust into that grade. He must wait till a vacancy occurs in the untouchable service!!! Such is the ethics of the Hindu social life.[6]

It is clear from the above excerpt that despite Wood's Dispatch in 1854 and Indian Education Commission (famously known as the Hunter Commission) in 1881/82 which established institutions for the training of teachers; the teaching profession was stained with discrimination and exclusion. This was true both for the students and the teachers.

What Dr Ambedkar had reflected on education had surged from his innermost being which was deeply marked due to his childhood experiences. Education in those days was not open to children of the Scheduled Caste families. They normally followed the trade of their families, for example, treatment of hide and shoe-making. Exception was made for Bhim perhaps because the boy was bright and a teacher protected him by giving him his name "Ambedkar" after which the boy never used his family name "Sakpal" which identified him as untouchable. We must remember how he was made to squat separately in the class on a piece of gunny cloth.[7]

Bhim knew that without being a competent scholar he could go no further to educate himself. Therefore, he had no option but to excel in studies at Elphinstone College, Mumbai, and thereby to gain scholarship from Sayajirao Gaekwad, the Maharaja of Baroda. He did his advanced studies at the Columbia University USA from 1913-16. Later in 1920 he did Barrister-at-Law from Grey's Inn for which he was sponsored by Chhatrapati Shahu, the Maharaja of Kolhapur.

Meanwhile his doctoral thesis, on which he was simultaneously working, was submitted albeit after he had returned to India that was published in 1923 by P.S. King & Son Ltd. London, under the title *The Problem of the Rupee: Its Origin and Its Solution.* He was awarded a doctorate from the Columbia University in USA. After returning to India he changed his track. Instead of working on economics he started to work on two fronts. The first was to practice law to earn a living and the second was his engagement with politics. His aim was to become the national representative of the Untouchables. For this he took initiatives of setting up *Bahiskrit Hitkarini Sabha* which was a welfare association for those affected by untouchability in 1924; he started a newspaper *Bahiskrit Bharat* in 1927 to bring the grievances of Dalits to public views.[8]

We may now ask ourselves, what could have Dr Ambedkar learned from his experience of educating himself? He learnt that western education could set the Untouchables free both from external socio-economic bondages and internal grip of unjust worldview of mind. To achieve this objective education was to be made possible and permissible for all Indian people in an inclusive and non-discriminatory atmosphere. For this reason the Untouchables were not only to be admitted in the schools but also the management of schools should have untouchable representatives. For similar reason the 'two-tumbler' model i.e. separate schools for touchables and untouchables should be discarded. Thus staying together, studying together and playing together would explode the myth of caste superiority.

In Dr Ambedkar's view if education was key to a non-violent revolution for social reform then it had to be taken up as an initiative of a political party. With this in view he collaborated with his colleagues to form a political party called the Independent Labour Party in 1936. It aimed to attend to the problems and grievances of the landless, poor tenants, agriculturists and workers. Education was listed as an important aspect for social reform which reflects his vision for education. In matters of education he wrote in the Party's constitution that:

Firstly, The Party will give effect to the scheme of free and compulsory primary education.

Secondly, The Party will undertake a scheme of adult education so as to make all people literate.

Thirdly, The Party will lay special emphasis on technical education.

Fourthly, The Party will endeavour to provide facilities for higher education in India and abroad by means of State aid to deserving persons from communities which are educationally backward.

Fifthy, The Party will undertake legislation to reorganize the university education in the Presidency by establishing regional universities and to make them teaching universities. The Party believes that this is the only remedy by which the course of examination which has blasted the intelligence and effort of the student population can be removed.[9]

In my view educating the Untouchables in Dr Ambedkar's reasoning was not merely to create a class of educated servants for civil services or to manage institutions of dominating castes; rather it was also to prepare them to engage with politics.

THE POWER OF EDUCATION FOR POLITICAL ACTION IN DR AMBEDKAR'S VIEW WAS THE MOST EFFECTIVE WAY TO SHAPE DALIT STRUGGLE FOR THEIR FULL EMANCIPATION. Political action was the most effective way to make people's voice lucid against the tyranny of caste and give shape to their resistance. To organize people politically would involve raising people's consciousness against the nature of their oppression and thereby build their intellectual capacity to undertake their struggle for liberation. If the initiative for such political activity was to be by Dalits then education was to be the key for people to articulate their concerns. As a convinced democrat Dr Ambedkar viewed politics as a human activity which required the art of negotiating with possibilities. Only educated and intelligent leaders could do this in order to take best advantage for their people.[10]

Endnotes

[1] B.R. Ambedkar, "Annihilation of Caste" (1936) in *Writings and Speeches* Vol-1 p. 62.

[2] His objection was their attempt to make the Hindu social structure look attractive by substituting the term *Charutvarna* for Caste System. In this way the social division would look more like social class rather than castes. Granted that the objective to use this term was to highlight that in their idea of social design where the value of individual was not by birth but by worth *guna* but their insistence to label people as Brahmin, Kshatriya, Vaishya and Shudra betrayed their intentions. Dr Ambedkar pointed out that "to allow this *Chaturvarna*, based on worth to be designated by such stinking labels of Brahmin, Kshatriya, Vaishya, Shudra, indicative of social divisions based on birth, is a snare." *Idem.*, pp. 58-9.

[3] *Idem.*, Vol-1 p. 61-2.

[4] *Idem.*, Vol-1 p. 63.

[5] *Idem.*, Vol-1 p. 283.

[6] *Idem.*, Vol-1. p. 262.

[7] Monodeep Daniel, *Religions in India: The Vision of Dr Ambedkar* (2016) ISPCK New Delhi. p. 3.

[8] Daniel. *Ibid.*, p. 5.

[9] Ambedkar. *Idem.*, Vol-17. Part-2. p. 419.

[10] Daniel. *Ibid.*, p. 276.

IDENTITY · LEADERSHIP · CHRISTIANS

The set of three essays in the second section are on Identity, Leadership and Christians. The underlying thread of these essays is the role of rationality. The reason that the importance of education is underscored in these three essays is to show that religion could be assessed on the anvil of reason. It is important to do so because identity in the Indian context is rooted in religious affiliation. Moreover caste identities emerge from religious worldview.

The first essay on "Identity" extends to include discussion on education, citizenship and common good. In Christian view specific identities are to be accepted as a matter of fact; for instance Jesus of Nazareth or Simon of Cyrene or Paul citizen-of-Rome. However, these identities which make a person stand apart from the rest could be either helpful or unhelpful. Here it must be underscored that in our context caste-based identity is demeaning for Dalits. Such an identity must be discarded for a dignified one. In a similar situation Saint Paul, two millennia ago, pointed to a new identity in Christ to erase Jewish and gentile identities which was creating pure versus polluted sections in the neonate Christian community.

In principle, therefore, identities are not permanently fixed. People should adopt a new identity by converting to another religion which offers them dignity. Therefore, religions, in order to be retained or discarded, must be rationally assessed whether or not they are beneficial for people.

The second essay on "Leadership" underscores the Christian view of it i.e. a leader as God's servant who leads in order to transform. The essay underscores the responsibility of a leader to transform society to be more just, ushering freedom, egalitarianism and fellowship. It anticipates a casteless society brought about by convinced, committed and courageous leaders. Accordingly Dr Ambedkar, who emulated Moses and Messiah, is offered as the model. A striking similarity in noticeable in the attempt of the apostles of Christ who in their times established a new community which was inclusive of diverse languages and ethnicities, and whose members were all equal who lived a responsible rather than legalistic life. At least this was the ideal they pursued.

The third essay is on "Christians". The aim is to show Dr Ambedkar's perception of Christians. In his assessment the religion of Christians was beneficial for the Untouchables; yet it had some serious defects both in its social concerns and theological doctrines. Although religion of Christians fell short of his standard of rationality, yet Christ in some way like Buddha was a compelling figure for him. If Buddha was his ideal then Christ was his inspiration. This is obvious in what he wrote during the short span of life after his conversion to Buddhism. He still drew models and examples from the Christian world.

Chapter 4

Identity

In the Indian context personal identity comes primarily with caste i.e. *verna* and *jati*. Everything else follows after that. This is unique but also oppressive. Caste identities involve exclusion or subjugation of those who are not in their particular orbit. This needs to be changed. Therefore the question is this, what can replace caste as the source of identity? To answer this most difficult question in the Indian context I propose that we turn to western education. The aim to cultivate educated personalities is to bring about both personal and social transformation. For this reason I propose the term 'transformative education'.

Personal transformation entails a change in what one values. Some values which contradict Christian values are obvious. These are caste system, consumerism and market society. In a casteist society it is the honour of a caste to trample the dignity of the one below. Similarly in consumerist society it is power of money to procure and consume from the market. The pursuit of wealth, therefore, makes people exploitative and callous to the weak and marginalized sections; needless to say that the western society has now emerged as a *market society*. Against all this the aim of education should be to wean a person away from self-centred life seeking honour and power. This change of thinking is the key for cultural transformation i.e. to create a culture of compassion and justice. As manyawar Kanshiram-ji, a pioneering dalit political activist, had said,

> We don't want social justice, we want social transformation. Social justice depends on the person in power. Suppose at one time, some good leader comes to power and people get social justice and are happy but when bad leader comes to power it turns into injustice again. Instead we want whole social transformation.

A way forward to transform society is to promote transformative education which should derive models and inspiration from *monastery* rather than *market*. The former is focused on cooperation for building community but the latter on competition. Excessive spirit of competition isolates individuals from their communities that seeks job, comfort and success and material things for its own sake with no objective to share it with others.

In this connection it must be stressed that "to teach" has no intrinsic value unless it aims at the higher goal "to educate". To be educated means to develop capability of becoming the master-narrator and thereby make the gospel the master-narrative of the society. I contend that it is the gospel that through education transforms the society. Without it education only serves the purpose for reinforcing caste-system which increases inequality in society by practices of discrimination, segregation and untouchability.

At the same time human beings do educate themselves all the time from their birth to death so that if not in life then in death their favourite story might become the master-narrative. There are various reasons for this: one is that their human nature of curiosity compels them to seek and understand; two that it is in their nature to be sensitive to what is moral and just; and three that their instinct to survive inclines them to dominate over others. This process continues beyond the formal systems of education. One way in which people are educated in this manner is culture. Here knowledge is retained and transmitted continuously from one generation to the other. At this point of our discussion we must come to terms with the Indian culture.

Cultures are fluid. They are born, they flourish and then they cease. Although they change and vanish with time, they leave something of enduring consequence which is retained over a longer span of time. One enduring feature in the flux of Indian culture has been the caste-system. Under this system, education was permitted only for the so called upper castes—particularly the priestly castes who were engaged in liturgical activities. Others in the socially privileged category were the philosophers and those keeping accounts. We all know that on the basis of religious injunction the society has been organized into four castes in a descending order of purity. Accordingly, all *jatis* have been accommodated in these four castes, namely, *brahmin, kshatriya, vaishya* and *shudra*. With the passage of time some *jatis* became casteist, others followed caste-like practices and others uncaste-like manners. Priestly castes took the privilege to legitimize social practices and others sought legitimacy from them, especially, the princely families. Consequently, such *jatis* became rigid observers of the caste system.

The remaining population which could not be accommodated in any of the four castes or those who flouted the caste norms, either by disregarding the regulation of diet or marriage, were relegated outside the caste system as untouchables. However, Dr Ambedkar, who gave India its Constitution, described four features of caste system. These were: graded inequality, fixity of occupation and fixation of people. The resultant social inequality perpetuated by caste system is gross injustice which can only be abolished by social change and by changing the thinking of the people. This exercise to change the thinking of people is education which leads to social transformation.

The point of this discussion is to draw attention to the practice of education in the Indian society since antiquity. The fact is that except for the privileged castes, education was not permitted for the populace. The practice to educate the privileged castes resulted in the reinforcement of their domination over the rest. Clearly the aim of education was to ensure domination of the privileged castes with none to challenge. Hence it is understandable why the masses in this subcontinent have remained unlettered till now.

This has seriously affected the identities of individuals and communities in the socially diverse canvas of India. In other words, how others regard and treat an individual and a community in the larger arena of society is critical for creating identity. Always it is the dominant social group that set the standard for creating an identity for others. In a socially and culturally diverse society identities reflect position of power or condition of powerlessness. It must be admitted that the dominant social groups take control of education because education is the key to unblock power. Therefore, they determine who are to be educated and how they are to be educated.

Having said this we now turn our attention with regard to education today. Let us begin with the premise that the aim of education is to cultivate human personality for social tranformation by changing the thinking of the people. Here Paulo Freira's insight about education as critical pedagogy is most useful. According to him cultivating personalities through education is useless unless they became a part of initiating social change. In the Indian context this has to be done by liberating education. The question is, how can we liberate individuals and communities to decide how are they to educate themselves? And, in what are they to educate themselves? In other words the minorities, tribal, Dalits and women must decide the method and priorities in the field of education.

How could this be done? According to him we have to help those under education to develop critical thinking. In other words they must raise questions of "why" "what" and "how" pertaining to social realities so that they challenge and critique the master-narrative of the dominant castes and offer an alternative narrative which is suitable for their emancipation from the grip of caste.

Identity and Diversity

In the Indian context identity is deeply linked with education. So we have to understand how identities are created. It is very interesting to note that identities in India are created not by education; instead they are formed within the discourse of caste from which none can escape. The conception of caste which creates a field for people to think, feel and act is transmitted through repetition of the practice of untouchability and touchability; in other words the repeated exercise of social exclusion and inclusion particularly in matters of social intermingling i.e. dining, marriage and business.

Like the master-signifiers, which Jacques Lacan propounded as the identity bearing words in the world of symbols, the caste discourse in our context propounds master narratives that mark identities.[1] One such master-narrative is the story of cosmic sacrifice enumerated in the Rig Veda. We hear about the division of society into four castes or *varnas* for the first time in the Rig Veda, which is the foremost *sruti* scripture. It tells us of the origin of castes from the body of God or *purusha* denoting the source from whom all things are born. This is what it says,

> The *brahman* was his mouth; of both his arms was the *rajanya* made. His thighs became the *vaisya*; from his feet the *sudra* was produced.[2]

The above text legitimises caste system as a sacred order. James Massey, a foremost Dalit theologian in north India, wrote,

> The description of the traits and the profession that is assigned to each of the caste or *varna* follows this. Thus a brahman was the priest with white complexion; a Kshatriya was the warrior with red complexion; a vaisya was a trader with yellow complexion; and a sudra was a serving caste with dark complexion. Having described this much about the four castes the Rig Veda does not go any further. How these four castes will function, conduct themselves in the society and carry on their duties are to be found in the *Smriti* Literature. Together these codes constitute the *Dharma* of an individual or of his caste.[3]

In this connection those people who did not belong to the four castes were named as *maleccehas* or *chandalas*. Manusmriti, which is a major *dharmashastra*, describes them as those who came through mixed marriages. Among the scores of injuctions against them one will suffice as an example,

> The dwellings of *chandalas* should be outside the village; they should be deprived of dishes; their property consists of dogs and asses. Their clothes the garments of the dead, and their ornaments of iron, and their food should be in broken dishes and they must constantly wander about.[4]

The repetition of such identity-bearing stories over a long period of time makes it appear to be true imparting security and well-being. In this way it makes the master-narrative the signifier. Persis and Saguna explain the working of this idea in verbatim,

> There are two operations here on the part of the signifier: (i) it confers identity on the subject by saying: 'You are this' or 'You are that', (ii) it induces behaviour in conformity with itself: 'You will be loved and recognized if you are like/do this or that.' In short, the signifiers of discourse have immense power over the subject; they make the subject that which they enunciate.[5]

But what causes such subservience of the subjects to the master-narrators or master-signifiers? The answer lies in the human desire for the other. Now if desire is always the desire-of-the-Other then every individual seeks recognition and approval from the Other. For this reason the subservient people also seek recognition and approval from the Other i.e. from the dominant castes who they acknowledge as superior. They think, feel and behave in ways that would be approved by the dominant castes. This imposed element of inferior identity affects the way they respond to education particularly resisting change in the way of thinking.

Having said this we know that there is diversity of identities in the Indian society. Even if there was to be one religion and one language in India, it would fail to produce uniformity. The reason is that identity in the Indian context is not created by religion or language but by caste. Caste which is constituted by diverse *jatis* will continue to create diverse identities. In such diversity the importance of identity of individuals and communities is crucial. That the castes impose inequalities in identities in a descending order of purity is unacceptable. As pointed out above caste identities are not only based on graded inequality but it propagates feeling of disgust for Dalits which heightens untouchability.

As a counter to the master-narrative of caste, post modernity may offer some respite by its emphasis on deconstruction and of equal validity of all narratives. Unfortunately progressive thinking like these has failed to appeal the Indian intelligentsia where the ideology of Hindutva has made the casteists master-narrative stronger, which is soundly based on exclusion of the adherents of Abrahamic religions from the communities of Indic religions.

Therefore, challenge for the Christian educators is this, how to make people change their way of thinking in a two-edged way i.e. on the one hand to respect diverse identities equally and on the other to be inclusive. In other words how do we celebrate diversity of identities yet welcome everyone everywhere. Where do we draw the line of social distinction and when do we erase it for inclusion? This takes us to the next section of our paper namely, citizenship.

Cultivating Citizens

First of all what is the meaning of citizenship? A citizen is a person who belongs to the free order of the Indian society. S/he enjoys rights and shares duties as enumerated in the Constitution of India. But this does not come automatically. The sense of rights and duties has to be cultivated. This cultivation comes with education. But the question is this that in the diversity of thinking what approach to education should we take? To answer this query help comes from Dr B.R. Ambedkar (1881-1956) who was a great thinker, a reformer and pioneer of Indians into modernity. In his line of thinking education was not merely literacy and training for livelihood, but it was to learn the associated way of living in a democratic society. I describe this as democratic social morality. In short it means two things: firstly, to be citizens of democratic India involves social equality, inclusion and dignity; secondly, it involves striving to create a democratic society where all citizens are equal and free. These two things mean "to be" and "to strive". Indeed we strive to be free because we were born free. Similarly we strive for kinship and community because we were born social. There are no lines of social exclusion. Clearly to be equal and to be social annihilates caste which enforces social inequality and isolation. It must be highlighted that these two erase dignity and freedom. To reiterate, citizenship is all about democratic social morality which has to be inculcated through education.

The best example in the gospel which involves all these ideas is the parable of the Good Samaritan. It is a parable which brings to fore the practical aspects of democratic morality where caste-class divide, Indic, Tribal and Abrahamic distinction are erased by human touch of care and compassion, responsibility and duty. It is also a parable for good citizenship where every individual citizen goes beyond his/ her limits of duty to attend to the "real" needs of others. In a good city citizens care for others. In the parable of the good Samaritan the individual identities of the Samaritan and the stranger are subsumed in a greater identity which constitute our citizenship.

Citizenship is an identity which includes within itself all diverse identities. Citizenship offers an alternative narrative of India which is secular and inclusive. It is the story that begins with the people of Indus civilization, it tells us of the coming of various groups of people, invasion of powerful empires, progress and fusion of ideas, blending and dissemination of religions, evolution and change of culture, rise and fall of empires. In this story the people of India from all backgrounds have a role and a contribution.

For clarity let us see these cultural streams blended in the mosaic of rich multi-cultural heritage of India, these are the *adivasi* (tribal), the *aryan* (Indic), the *dalit* and the *abrahamic* (Judeo-Christian and Isalmic). The fact of the matter is that we intentionally use words like 'blend' or 'mosaic' or the phrase 'multi-cultural heritage' to conceal the horrendous nature of conflict between diverse cultural streams each of which exist like a separate nationality. The basic cause of conflict lies not so much in the existence of these multiple streams but the challenge that the *abrahmic* and *adivasi* worldviews pose for the *aryan*. Sadly within the Indic culture the counter argumentative streams of *charvaka* and *sramana* have been snuffed out leaving only the casteist discourse to dominate as the master-narrative. Having thus eradicated this inner threat the danger is from the outside, namely from the *adivasi*, and the *abrahamic*.

The desire of the casteist stream in the Indic culture, to dominate and control the national and natural assets leads them to develop certain strategies. One is to exclude the non-Indic and *dalit* from the main stream. The strategy of exclusion is to make them powerless by depriving them of the education and nutrition. This certainly is not a good approach to citizenship of a nation that wants a place in the present global world as an upholder of the human rights.

Having said this let us turn to another impediment of citizenship. This is the rise of materialism. It takes fifteen long years to educate and prepare a child in Indian schools to serve the larger society as a productive citizen. Their capability is assessed by what they are paid for their service. Through years as student they were mentored and monitored mainly by tutors and parents. What they inculcated in them is evident from what they had appreciated as their own success. A teacher feels successful when they meet their former students who have developed the capability to buy and consume things from the market. They should be able to afford gizmos and gadgets, holiday packages, fully furnished flats or villas, cars, labelled goods and clothes and the list goes on.

Obviously only those who have had the advantage of belonging to economically privileged families would be able to afford all this. The teachers, deliberately or unwittingly, had mentored their students to believe that their advantage was due to their own deserving abilities; on the other hand, those who suffered disadvantages were regarded to be their own worst enemies. Those who have the capability to procure goods in order to consume are the ones who also dominate in the sphere of education, technology, culture, business, health, nutrition and governance.

The above is the value-system of a market-society and a consumerist outlook of life. It is clearly self-centred with no concern of the progress of society in other words attending to the *felt* rather than the *real* needs. This is the result of the master-narrative of materialism. This attitude is favourable for the economically strong individuals who belong to the socially dominant castes; but it becomes detrimental for those who are persevering to progress and are striving to be free. It creates a society of dominant and subservient classes. Social classes have no sense of community. The situation becomes complex in a society designed on caste system where the privileged castes have also become the dominant classes. This is bound to be so due to the historical advantages of education culture and funds which the privileged castes had access to. The rational of this advantage is explained through the stories which we can call as the master-narratives.

Let us look at it in another way. There are two master-narratives in India, the first is the Mahabharata and the second is Hindutva. These are master-narratives because they are the signifiers. They signify what each community is and who the individual is. The Mahabharata in the narration of ethical dilemmas brings out the significance of duty in the midst of crisis. The imperative of duty lies in the caste one is born. Hence caste signifies an individual by locating his position and work in society. In its wider application it signifies whether a person is included in the four tier caste-system or is excluded as an outcaste.

On the other hand Hindutva signifies Hinduness of people as patriotic or otherwise, on the basis whether they have embraced an Indic or Non-Indic religion. Therefore, this system of value and the outlook of life must be countered by an alternative value system.

This alternative is provided by the gospel of Jesus Christ. It is a narrative of the Son-of-God who became a human being and he explored and experienced what it was to be a man-of-sorrow by being refuted, rejected and killed. God, in his incarnated Son experiences the world of creatures in an authentic way. Metaphorically it is like exploring and experiencing by becoming blind how they negotiate through darkness. This was God's discovery i.e. what it was to be a refuted and rejected. In the Indian context Dalits are discarded as polluting people. But God does not discard or reject anyone; rather all human beings and whole creation is being saved and transformed to perfection. The way God brought this transformation was by *giving* himself to us as a weak and vulnerable human beings thereby in his body on the cross exposed what evil does. Accordingly, from Acts 20:35 we can derive the biblical philosophy for the weak in a nutshell,

It is more blessed to give than to receive.

Now *giving* can only possible by being just (Luke 16.19-31), becoming compassionate (Luke 10.29-37), becoming non-violent (Luke 9.52-56) and becoming wise (Matt 25.1-13). These qualities make us good human beings.[6]

Three more values come out in the gospels which are particularly important for oppressed people, firstly, the value of knowledge and its practice i.e. orthopraxis (Matt 7.24-27); secondly, the value of organization (John 15.1-5) and thirdly the value of struggle (Matt 10.16-31).[7] Added to this is our obligation to be a community of equals by being united (Gal 3.28), to enjoy fellowship by intermingling (Eph 2.14-19) and to be free (Gal 5.1).

Discerning Vocation

Another query for the educational institution is this, what is the purpose of educating our generation? The large opinion is as simple as to affirm that it is to build career. In other words it is all about making money from professional services. To meet this need there is a clear expectation from institutions imparting education. They must produce capable men and women of aptitude to be trained as professionals to deliver specific services. The result of this assumption is that the educational institutes operate on factory model. Accordingly they admit children as raw material. They work on them for more than a decade. After this processing those who get moulded for the utility of the consumerist society are awarded but the rest are eliminated through the examination system as waste material. From among these best suited students the companies can select according to their choice those who would render services and for which they would be paid well. In other words the institutions of education are focused to enable the students to improve their skills for the prospect of career.

The attraction to lucrative career is the human selfish instinct which takes over their social instinct. With surplus of material goods, individuals cater to their *felt* needs instead of *real* needs. In view of the fact that *real* needs are social and require collective effort, it demands that individuals should sacrifice their *felt* needs. For example conservation of environment is a *real* need therefore individuals must give up their *felt* need for automobiles. The factory model approach to education is most appealing to a consumerist society but has pushed our planet to the brink of ecological disaster. Yet it fails to find an alternative to the idea that economic and technological growths are irreversible. It is a known fact that billions in China and India aspire to achieve the American life-style standards giving little heed to the impending threat of extinction of human life from the earth. At the same time the poor oppressed with load of loans have no time to worried about the melting ice caps and receding glaciers of the Himalayas.

But the factory approach to education does not view education in the light of these concerns; rather due to this factory-like approach to produce serviceable product, (in the education sector it is the human resource), we have had no impetus to raise our universities to be counted among the world class institutions. In contrast to this, the Christian vision for education has to be larger than merely building career; instead it is to do with discerning vocation. Vocation involves excelling in the field which a person discerns as a call to undertake. Call is one's internal compulsion inspired by divine sources which is beyond the human rational grasp. The aim is to obey this call despite the economic and social losses one would suffer as a result.

In this line of thinking we affirm that educating-to-discern-vocation not only involves cultivating capacities with which a person is naturally endowed but also to enable them to acquire such expertise for which the person may not have the aptitude. Such considerations in education have to be for higher goals which are beyond merely career-building.

In all this prayer also has a place. The aim of prayer is to help the person to discover the internal sources of living waters springing from transcendental source. It is in the directive presence of the transcendent that individuals discern their immanent purpose. Despite the intention to develop one's naturally endowed capacities and to acquire capabilities, the aim of education should be to enable individuals not only to discover the call but also to prepare themselves to obey it. If this is the case then education becomes a spiritual exercise. In other words it develops a person to accomplish what this call demands. Finally it is in obedience to this discernment that a person leads a purpose-filled life. The key to discern the call is to share life, faith and joy with the weak and the vulnerable.

Having considered the unsatisfactory functioning of the factory-model of education let us explore another model.

Serving the Common Good

A better illustration for educating our people is of planting a sapling. The idea is to respect each individual treating him/her like a sapling possessing full potential to flourish into a tree. For this, the sapling has to be provided the right kind of atmosphere and soil with proper nourishment of water, manure, sunlight and air.

Similarly every student is like a sapling full of potential for flourishing provided they are given the right kind of social and intellectual atmosphere. One of the ingredients for human life to flourish is moral education which is fundamental to educate person's mind for making choices and develop values in life. Moral life of a person begins with the way s/he thinks. Now thinking is all about view and value for what is common i.e. shared space of time and commodities.

From the ecological metaphor of variety of flourishing trees we can envisage a shared space in which the trees have to grow and spread. This is the ground, the space, the resources and the environment which is common and where they exist with all other forms of life. The insight of this metaphor is that if all share the common resource then the view of majority is not to be exercised at the expense and interest of the minorities. It is only when the majority restrains its ambitions in a democracy that the minority are included and individual citizens feel that they also belong to the larger community of citizens. These ideas are not new. Rousseau expressed it in the belief that government should be based on the 'general will' or common good, rather than upon the private or selfish will of citizens. Education should, therefore, prepare the young generation to understand that common good is not only being eco-friendly but also involves political participation which is possible in democracy where the feeling amongst individuals that they belong to the larger community of citizens is strengthened. This collective feeling and belonging reinforces social equality which is an essential aspect of social justice.

In seeking common good over and against private good education must help students to develop critical thinking and power of analysis. In this line of thinking the power to distinguish the *real* interest from the *felt* interest must also be emphasised. The *felt* interests can be selfish ending in conflict, but the real interests may require collective effort. For instance the need and interest to conserve environment is a *real* interest which demands collective efforts.

IN THE INDIAN CONTEXT EDUCATION MUST AIM TO BRING SOCIAL TRANSFORMATION. This means that teachers and students together should create a society where people understand that interdependence does not erase their identity, but that they can be independent and still hold the identity of their community for themselves. This leads us to view democracy as social instead of majority mob. The aim is to generate faith in the goodness of humanity and to hold that human beings are not entirely selfish but as those who seek companionship. They are bound to one another by existence of common humanity and common good.

Furthermore education in India must strike new grounds in three more aspects. Firstly it must bring more advancement; secondly it must bring more justice and thirdly it must make us more eco-sensitive. As far as advancement is concerned we can explain it by another word progress. It must be said that progress primarily is to do with our thinking. It entails inculcation of courage in our people to leave old things behind, foremost being the caste-system and move ahead in forging social associations where all people can intermingle, interdine and intermarry. Similarly justice entails guarding each another's dignity. Power and energy in a person are released when his/her dignity is preserved. For this there is a great scope for restructuring our bureaucracy, augmenting judiciary, innovating new ways of dealing with community and family conflicts, and social and personal security. The aim is to make every individual secure, equal, healthy and free to practice, profess and propagate his/her ideas. Lastly, eco-sensitivity means that not only we realize our bonds with all other forms of life on this planet but also do our best to preserve environment with all its diversity, food-chain, vegetation and wildlife.

Endnotes

[1] Ginwalla, Persis and Ramanathan, Sugune. "Dalit Women as Receivers and Modifiers of Discourse" in *The Emerging Dalit Identity* (1996). Ed. Walter Fernandes. Indian Social Institute, New Delhi. p. 42-3.

[2] Rig Veda 10:90:12.

[3] James Massey, "Dalits and Dharma" in One Volume *Dalit Bible Commentary* (2015) CDS. New Delhi. p. 56.

[4] Manusmriti 10.51, 52.

[5] *Ibid.*, Ginwalla, Persis p. 44.

[6] These are the parables: Luke 16.19-31 is a parable of rich-man and Lazarus; Luke 10.29-37 is the parable of the Good Samaritan; Luke 9.52-56 is Jesus' refusal to destroy the Samaritan towns; Matt 25.1-13 is the parable of the five wise and five foolish virgins.

[7] These are the metaphors: Matt 7.24-27 to hear and to act is like constructing a house on a rock with quality to endure; John 15.1-5 to be organized to be ordered like branches attached to vine; and Matt 10.16-31 to struggle non-violently is to be like sheep among wolves and to be wise as serpents and harmless as doves.

Chapter 5

Leadership

Prophesy is future oriented but it does explain truthfully the present time too. In other words it involves both foretelling and forth-telling. At any rate, whether futuristic or contemporary, its message is thoroughly social. With this in view we will divide our study in four sections. In the first section we will look at our social order where the culture operates, in the second we will look at the ecclesial order in which spirituality operates, in the third we will propose what the ecclesial leadership of CNI should aim at and in the fourth we will evaluate how much we have strayed or stayed within the ideal range of the biblical vision.

The question "what should the church leaders prophecy in the midst of injustices", makes it necessarily for us to examine our social and ecclesial context. The understanding of this will clarify what to tell forth and what to foretell.

INDIAN SOCIAL ORDER

Without further delay it must be stated that social order can either be exclusive or inclusive. Whatever the merit of the two orders the fact is this that every national society is exclusive to the extent that it comprises of a mass of people who *will* to be together as a nation by excluding all the rest. This is natural to human society. Hence

Dr Ambedkar had affirmed that we are Indians first and Indian last. The problem, however, arises when within a national society there is exclusion of some who legitimately belong to it. Such exclusions could either be deliberate or accidental. Unfortunately a large section has been excluded from the Indian national society. The basis is firstly the caste system and secondly rightist ideology. For clarity we will study each of them below.

Different religions in India purport different social designs. These designs of social order are declared as sacred by respective religions. Remarkably there are only two designs to organize society—the hierarchical and the egalitarian. The Indian social order is hierarchical due to the grip of *brahmanical* worldview which promotes caste system as the social order. The classification of innumerable *jatis* into four tier *verna* or castes—Brahmin, Kshatriya, Vaishya and Shudra—is deeply ingrained in the minds of people. However, not all *jatis* were placed within these four caste categories. Many who worked with animal hides, removing carcass and night soil and sweeping lanes were segregated as Untouchables.

In the present scenario the Untouchable *jatis* are excluded from the national society. The dominant caste groups recoil with a feeling of revulsion for the Untouchables. This feeling of disgust arises from the fact that the Untouchables have to undertake tasks connected with organic matter, whether it is removing the night soil or dead animals or skinning the dead animals for hide or cleaning the streets or clearing the garbage. Although the majority of the Untouchables worship the same deities and celebrate the same festivals as the dominant castes their cycle is distinct from the dominant castes.

The problem of exclusion does not end here. The various groups in India have developed their own forms of caste system. Many who do not belong to any of the four castes imitate caste-like-practices; while those who have uncaste-like-manners have to bear the brunt. The aim to emulate caste-like-practices is to draw close to the dominant caste in order to gain credibility from them, and eventually to be absorbed into a caste. This is obvious in their patronising the ochre-robed ascetics and inviting the *Brahmin*-priests to perform sacred ceremonies for them.

The practices of such groups to shun consumption of beef, incur the expense of pilgrimage, worship the images of *brahmanic* deities, practice the rigour of fast and extravagance of festivals is aimed to gain legitimacy and acceptance from the dominant castes. It only aggravates the exclusion of the Untouchables. With this the contours of caste, namely, graded inequality, fixity of people and fixation of occupation thereby gets reinforced. This is first kind of exclusion of people from the large mass of national society.

The second kind of exclusion is based on acute cultural split-up on the fault line of religions. I contend that the idea of segregating religions of the *Indic* origin and the *Indigenous* from the *Abrahamic* by downplaying syncretistic religious movement of *Sufi, Sai, Kabir* and other forms of mysticism is at the root of the problem of exclusion. This idea of exclusion was drawn and articulated primarily by Vir Damodar Sarvarkar who after his tenure in the jail wrote and published his book *Hindutva* in 1923. However, it is beyond the scope of this paper to discuss on Sarvarkar's theme.

The above discussion brings out the fundamental unjust condition of Indian society, namely social inequality and exclusion. The result of this injustice on a large section of people shows itself in various forms of poverty, segregation, illiteracy, ignorance, subjugation, torture, unemployment, violation of fundamental and human rights.

In the urban sprawl of metro cities we see people and children on streets, abandoned old people, and people resorting to begging, homeless people of various sorts and so on. All this and much more is the result of a social order based on the culture and practice of untouchability and segregation resulting from the caste system. This is so because the Untouchables along with a very large section of people are regarded as unessential for the national society.

The alternative to the unequal social order of caste was the social order which was propounded by the *Abrahamic* religious traditions namely Judaism, Islam and Christianity. This was social equality and kinship. Dr Ambedkar had pointed out the values of Justice was thoroughly grounded in the Judaeo-Christian tradition. If justice was expanded as liberty, equality and fraternity then it is not difficult to see that each of these aspects had a biblical basis. It must be admitted that the French revolutionists who had used these words as their slogan did this from within the cultural realm of Christianity.

However, it is well attested that Indian adherents of *Abrahamic* religions falling in line with the caste system have adapted themselves to unequal social order by developing their own version of caste system. The Syrian Church in Kerala is a case in point here which largely manifests itself as a privileged by insulated community.

ECCLESIAL SOCIAL ORDER

The Christian ideal of society is where people are equal, free and can intermingle. It is diametrically opposite to a society organized on caste system. Moreover, we also believe that what is good for the Christian-community *ekklesia* is also good for the whole human society. For our purpose the study of one faith-community i.e. the Church of North India will suffice. In its Faith-and-Order[1] social equality is not affirmed exclusively for its own community of believers; rather the conviction is that all people outside the believing community should also enjoy the benefits of social equality.

In other words justice is not the sole monopoly of the Christian community *ekklesia*. So the question is this how should the ecclesial leadership conduct itself in the unjust climate of the caste based social inequality? Can we get some guidance from the CNI Constitution on this? I affirm that we can. If our leadership aims to create and sustain the faith-community *ekklesia* of free and equal people then they must have a clear understanding of the FO of the CNI Constitution. For this purpose I have reduced the FO of the CNI into four categories, namely, *astha, vyavastha, sangathan* and *sangat*. To help us sum up the social order that the FO propounds for its adherents let us examine each of these below.

FEATURES OF C.N.I. ECCLEISAL ORDER

Astha, which means faith of a person which should be firmly fixed on God, the one who is revealed in the Bible, and who has disclosed himself in the Lord Jesus Christ. Secondly God has created human beings in his own image. In this sense all are equal in dignity and splendour. Thirdly, God has created human being not to live in isolation but in communion.

Vyavastha or the social order is therefore based on our *astha* that all human beings created in God's image *imago dei* are equal and need to live in communion. Therefore the society should facilitate communion of free and equal people. In other words the Christian vision of society is egalitarianism, freedom and fellowship. The example of this is set out in the faith and practice of the Christian community *ekklesia*. In our case it is the CNI.

Sangathan is the organized aspect of the Christian community. In other words the community is not *ochlos* or a crowd; rather it is *laos* or God's people. People *laos* have no power unless they are organized in the form of pastorates, dioceses and synod under the care of presbyters, bishops and a moderator. In this form of organization *sangathan*, the Community *ekklesia* becomes God's gift to the world. Without the structure of an organization *sangathan* the people *laos* will disperse and vanish into oblivion.

Sangat in Punjabi language denotes fellowship or communion. By fellowship Christians mean the intermingling of the God's People *laos* by inter-dining and intermarrying across cultural, racial, linguistic, territorial and national frontiers. Hence, the name 'Church of North India' indicates a fellowship which includes all cultural and linguistic diversities.

MODELS OF ECCLEISAL LEADERSHIP

The system of Caste assimilated in the warp and woof of society gives rise for all forms of injustices. In whatever way the caste system may be justified by those who benefit from it —occupational, racial, colour, family, religious or lineage—the fact remains that it promotes discrimination of Dalits by the practices of inequality untouchability and segregation. The Indian Church is adversely affected by it. However, the encouraging thing is that this system has not been left unquestioned in the Indian history. Mahavira, Gautam Buddha, Asoka, and Akbar made dents in history whereas from nineteenth century onwards social reformers like Mahatma Jotirao and Savitri Phule, Pandita Ramabai and Dr. Bhim Rao Ambedkar have been on the frontier to resist it. The point here is this that they also provide us with some leadership models.

Deriving from models of leadership from the above personalities I have identified four types of leadership within the church which were modelled either on monarchy or management or service.[2] These are *ministerial, magisterial, managerial* and *transformational* models of leadership. Let us study each of these below.

Ministerial Model: Leadership of Emperor Asoka

Let us take the example of Emperor Asoka to understand this model of leadership. Asoka defeated the three Kalinga Kingdoms in about 256 BCE. The famous thirteenth Rock Edict declared that the victory was overwhelming and losses among the defeated people were devastating. Asoka was profoundly moved by the casualties, privations and suffering of the conquered people. The cause of his regret was "because" as he said "the conquest of a country previously unconquered involves the slaughter, death and carrying away captive of the people. That is a matter of profound sorrow and regret to His Sacred Majesty".

From this time till the end of his reign in 232 BCE Asoka never waged any war. Subsequently he converted to Buddhism and led a pious life. He introduced his *Dhamma* which was based on the Buddhist discipline of life and piety. Unlike the caste system where honour was reserved exclusively for the so called upper castes, *Dhamma* required that reverence be paid to those it was due e.g. teachers, elders, parents and relations. Irrespective of caste it required respect and sanctity of all animate life, and humane and just treatment of sentient beings, including backward and uncivilized peoples both inside and outside the empire. The *Dhamma* treated all people as equal and thus there were injunctions and prohibitions against vices such as envy, indolence and injustice. The imperatives and prohibitions of the *Dhamma* formed a network of righteous relationships between all sentient and inanimate beings affecting public, social and familial relationships, and affecting relationships between peoples of different levels of development and between humans and animals. No one was outside the ambit, not even Asoka or the Empress. No one was treated exceptionally or exclusively as privileged by virtue of belonging to the so called upper castes. At the centre was the Emperor Asoka himself who had assumed the burden of ensuring the propagating and enforcing of the *Dhamma*.

Asoka not only became a minister of *Dhamma* but he served or ministered his subjects through it using the absolute authority of his kingship. He sets a desirable model of ministerial leadership.

Magisterial Model: Leadership of Emperor Akbar

An example of this model of leadership is Akbar the Great (1542-1605). He was Humanyun's son. When he ascended the throne, only a small portion of the Mogul Empire was intact, so set out to recover this loss. Realising that subduing the Rajputs would not be economically viable Akbar wooed them by diplomacy. For instance he succeeded in a matrimonial alliance with the Rajput rulers of Amber (Jaipur). By setting up a roaming camp to administer his empire he sidestepped the building of a Capital City. To encourage commerce, he had the land surveyed, which facilitated a better precision for taxation. He gave strict orders to prevent extortion by the tax collectors. Akbar abolished the *jizya* tax levied on the non-Muslims in the empire.

Akbar's initiatives were not in accordance with the caste norms. For instance no one was excluded from the religious discourse at the *Ibadat Khana* (House of Worship) he had constructed. He tried to establish an inclusive religion called the *Din-I-Ilahi* (The Divine Faith), which was syncretistic incorporating both Islam and Hinduism with elements of Christianity and Jainism. His attempt to liberate knowledge from the grip and monopoly of Sanskrit and Arabic is evident from the fact that he invited scholars of different faiths to discuss matters of theology and philosophy with him. He engaged Feizi to translate many scientific works from Sanskrit into the Persian language and Abdul-Fazel to compile the *Akbarnama*, i.e., the records of the emperor's reigns. It is also held that Akbar employed Jerome Xavier, a Jesuit missionary, to translate the four gospels into Persian and used to pray before the picture of Christ. Akbar's leadership in military campaigns, diplomatic endeavours and practice of tolerance was aimed to maintain the unity of the empire in a magisterial role.

Managerial Model : Leadership of Pandita Ramabai

The third model I like to put forward is of Pandita Ramabai whose contribution towards the emancipation and progress of women in India is praiseworthy. She was the youngest daughter of a liberal and progressive Brahmin family of Mangalore. Against the traditions of those days, her father taught her Sanskrit and the Hindu *Shastras*. She married a Bengali gentleman of non-Brahmin caste but their happy marriage came to a sudden end when in 1892 her husband died.

Among the collection of her husband's books she came across the gospel of Luke, which she read. Subsequently in Pune where she had settled she met Fr. Nehemiah Goreh, an Indian Anglican priest whose instructions convinced her of the truth of the Christian faith. While in England she stayed at the Wantage Convent and was baptized on 29th September 1893 in the Anglican Church. Eventually the revivalist form of Church would satisfy her spiritual cravings. Gifted with learning languages she translated the Bible into Marathi from the original Hebrew and Greek. As a nationalist she was the first woman to address the Indian National Congress.

From England she travelled to America where here raised considerable interest in her vision of uplifting the Indian women from adverse social condition. After her return in 1899 to Mumbai she established Sharada Sadan for women of all caste communities and a number of schools to educate women. Earlier in 1896, during a severe famine Ramabai had toured the villages of Maharashtra with a caravan of bullock carts and rescued thousands of outcaste children, child widows, orphans and other destitute women and brought them to the shelter of Mukti Mission and Sharada Sadan. She is now remembered as a nationalist, educationalist and an emancipator of women. In the work and life of Pandita Ramabai we see a great organizer of relief work, administrator of projects and manager of institutions. She sets the example of a managerial model of leadership.

Transformative Model: Leadership of Dr Ambedkar

Dr B R Ambedkar is my fourth model who unlike Asoka and Akbar did not possess absolute authority and unlike Pandita Ramabai he did not belong to the so-called upper caste. He led and organized active protests against untouchability and was rightly acknowledged leader of the Dalits. In 1923 he founded *Bahishkrit Hitkarini Sabha* to encourage the untouchables to educate themselves and to improve their economic condition. He caused a stir in 1927 by publicly burning *Manusmriti*. His march at Mahad to assert the right of Dalits to taste water in the

Public *Chawdar* Lake, traditionally prohibited to them, marked the commencement of the anti-caste movement; and at *Kalaram* Temple in Nasik in 1930 he started the case for allowing untouchables to enter the Hindu temples.

He was appointed as the first Law Minister in Nehru's government. He was the Chairperson of the committee which drafted the Indian Constitution. The mark of his hand is clear in that monumental work. He knew that 'political power alone could not be a panacea for the ills of the depressed classes. Their salvation lay in their social elevation.' He challenged his followers by advising them,

> My final worlds of advice to you are educate, organise and agitate have faith in yourself. With justice on your side I do not see how we can lose our battle. For ours is a battle not for wealth or for power. It is a battle for freedom. It is a battle for the reclamation of the human personality.

To ensure justice and dignity for the Dalits Ambedkar included the Fundamental Rights and Directive Principles of the State Policies in the Indian Constitution. This provision protects Dalits and minorities from disabilities caused due to social degradation and economic disadvantage.

The model of leadership that Dr Ambedkar established climaxed with the Yeola Declaration in 1935. Underscoring the poor initiative of the caste Hindus to bring about any change, he embarked upon the task of taking a definite step. Noting that it was from within the Hindu fold and not from the outside that Dalits were being stripped of their dignity and endured humiliation, the required course of action seemed clear: conversion to an egalitarian religion. He said that he was born a Hindu and there was nothing he could do about that, but he could do something! Taking a deep breath he boomed "I solemnly assure you, I will not die a Hindu!"[3] In his conversation with Bishop Picket on 24th November 1936 he expressed his inability at that time to choose which religion he would espouse because 'it would risk alienating some who were friendly to him', but he could never remain a Hindu. He held that,

Hinduism is not a religion but a disease. People of every caste should flee from it as from the plague. When Hindus have extracted nectar from poison, let them begin to talk of extracting salvation from Hinduism.[4]

McPhee records what Ambedkar thought of missionaries who had come under the influence of Hindu propagandists like Gandhi and Natarajan. "He pitied them especially C.F. Andrews."[5] From the notes of the November meeting that Bishop Picket wrote, Ambedkar seemingly felt that his life was not his own, that he had been given the privilege of an education and other advantages for a reason for some special destiny. 'He believes', wrote Bishop Picket, 'that the hand of God is upon him.'[6]

Some thought that Dr Ambedkar might embrace Christianity, however, on 14th October 1956, he along with 365,000 followers converted to Buddhism. He continued the crusade for social revolution until the end of his life. He was posthumously honoured with the highest national honour *Bharat Ratna* in April 1990.

Dr Ambedkar set a model of transformational leadership. The aim of transformation was not only to bring a change in the human behaviour but also in the human society.

Are We Correctly Oriented?

I have put forward four types of leadership models in the Indian context i.e. the *Ministerial,* the *Magisterial, the Managerial* and the *Transformational.* The above models were in an era before independence, the rise of free press and Human Rights. The present Indian church was also established in that era. Initially, Saint Thomas the Apostle had established the Community in AD 52. Then came the Orthodox Church in the third century under the Patriarch of Chaldea. Later in 1498 Vasco De Gama and the Portuguese established the Roman Catholic Church. Finally the Protestant Missions arrived from eighteenth century onwards. Due to their endeavour Christian communities across the Indian sub-continent were established. Now the question is this, is the leadership of the Indian Christian Community, which was established at various turns of this country's history, correctly oriented? To answer our query let us study just one Christian community namely the Church of North India.

The Church of North India

The Church of North India (CNI) draws 90% of its membership from the Dalit and Adivasi (tribal) people of India. The Indian Church has been an integral part of the Indian society. The first response of the Church in India was the indigenisation of its governance. Accordingly after forty years of ecclesiastical Round Table Conferences to negotiate between major Protestant denominations the CNI was inaugurated on 29th November 1970 at All Saints Cathedral grounds in the city of Nagpur in central India.

The CNI is a post-denominational, united and indigenous church governed by democratic process at local, regional and national levels by Pastorate Committees, Diocesan Councils and the Synod. Although the emphasis of ordained ministry is equality, and therefore it is described as threefold, instead of three tier, ministry of deacons, presbyters and bishops, nonetheless it is a functional hierarchy. Moreover as the ordained ministers are set apart to do the sacred ceremonies like the sacraments, they are fenced off to a degree from the laity. This is so due to the rite of ordination which bestows on them the permanent legitimacy on theological grounds to make things sacred. To assess the merits and demerits of this arrangement is beyond the scope of this paper. However, a glimpse into the CNI Constitution can be helpful for us which says,

> The ordained ministry of the Church has descended from Christ and His apostles, and under the guidance of the Holy Spirit continues to derive its authority in the Church from Christ. The minister is in his own charge the representative of the Church as a whole, and also represents his own charge to the Church as a whole.[7]

Therefore, leadership that entails shepherding and governing of the community, albeit with the cooperation of the laity, is in the hands of the privileged few. Ordination confers on the ecclesiastical ministers a representational authority derived from the absolute authority of Christ. No doubt the ordained minister is often compared to the captain of the ship who is expected to know 'his men'. Mr N K Biswas, a prominent lay person in Delhi, wrote concerning what is expected from an ordained minister. He is to be a 'keen observer of people's talents and look for opportunity to allow these talents to be used for the good of the church' typically expresses this sentiment. To cite the CNI Constitution, 'the authority of the whole church shall be represented in ordination' further establishes this status.[8]

The relevance of citing the Constitutional text of the CNI is to point out the fact that provisions which intend to preserve the historicity of the Church's ministry through ordination nevertheless renders leadership to be understood and exercised as possession of *authority* dispensed through the hand of a few clerics and lay leaders. Functionally the CNI operates like a pyramid of authority. The ordained minsters who cannot be de-titled occupy the tip at the top of this pyramid as sacred personals in a descending order of authority i.e. moderators, bishops, presbyters, deacons and licensed lay leaders and lastly the laity.

This is exactly how the Indian society operates on the caste structure which is in descending order of purity and authority. The results are disastrous. Oppression, high handedness, corruption, hegemony, nepotism, monopolization of public resources, inefficiency and social stagnation has become terrible realities. The people have suffered the loss of empowerment to such an extent that instead of identifying, nurturing and electing befitting leaders they yearn for benevolent dictators. The Dalit church has alas, emulated the characteristics of the caste society surrounding it.

In this sense the leadership of the church is expected to be experts in magisterial and managerial roles. So also are the so-called upper caste landlords. Such roles are further reinforced in the contemporary management roles of young executives in the multi-national companies. So why should not a presbyter or a bishop of the church see him/herself in similar roles in the ecclesiastical establishment? As a leader, a bishop and a presbyter not only have to minister or serve to their congregations but also manage the administration of the church, institutions and property on which thousands of Christians live. It conjures up the rural picture of landless Dalits and peasants living on the landlord's property. Naturally the ecclesiastical leaders too expect subordination and subservience of the church tenants.

It is clear that the magisterial, the managerial and the ministerial models of leadership within the CNI do not seek social transformation in the country. It is mainly concerned with the maintenance of the social order administration of the institutional character of the church and running the show, so to say, of the church as an established institution. Major undertakings as mission within the church are in the field of relief, development and charity. In the last decade the relief interventions in the Tsunami affected remote islands of Car Nicobar had been commendable. Similarly the work to raise awareness of HIV/AIDS was also extremely relevant in its time. However, undertaking the project of relief, development and charity are all within the ambit of *managerial* and *ministerial* leadership. In as much as they are significant and cannot be done away with, they do not bring about social transformation. The question before us is this, what should now be done?

The answer to this query is to rediscover Dr Ambedkar as a prophetic figure to understand the social realities and renew our commitment as leaders of God's mission to bring social change. What then us his relevance for the Christian church? The answer lies in understanding the issues he raised with the Christian leaders of those times. In his conversation with Bishop Picket in 1935 he pointed out that the Christian missionaries were poor representatives of Jesus in India for at least three reasons,

> Firstly, many missionaries had compromised, giving Brahmins a respect it did not deserve. Instead of listening to them, they should have, like Jesus, been attuned to the cries of the oppressed.

> Secondly, Christians in India were too otherworldly. In contrast Jesus was interested in all kinds of human needs, but missionaries seemed more concerned with salvation of souls from hell.

> Thirdly, missionaries had not adequately adapted their methods to (challenge) the Indian social order and had, thus, produced leaders with little social conscience.[9]

From what we have studied we can say that the Indian Christian community and the church is not oriented to reform the larger society by endeavouring to annihilate the caste-system or to stem corruption. Instead it has shaped itself to fit in the frame of the dominant culture of caste. This is what Dr Ambedkar had also concluded. In this regard what bishop Picket had entered in his diary of his conversation with Dr Ambedkar in 1935 in essence is correct as it is similar to what he wrote in 1937 in 'The Condition of the Convert'.[10] Dr Ambedkar was candid in his observation saying that the church leaders in Maharashtra were self-centred with no sense of duty of anyone, 'not even to their Christian fellows in the villages.' He was clear that he wanted 'equality and removal of all discriminations based on caste.'

THE CHALLENGE OF DR AMBEDKAR ENTAILS SOCIAL CHANGE. He had asked Bishop Picket,

> I want to know what Christianity can do and is prepared to do to remove the disabilities under which my people live.[11]

The point is this that the root of all injustices is the caste system. On the anvil of this challenge we need to measure the life and witness of the Church and with courage prophesy the annihilation of the caste system from our country. This means that the church should inspire, make people aware of justice and enable people to raise movements to advocate, procure and protect their fundamental, constitutional and human rights.

Endnotes

[1] CNI Constitution Part-I.

[2] Monodeep Daniel, *Models of Leadership in the Indian Church: An Evaluation* (2007) published in Studies in World Christianity Volume-13 Part-1 of The Edinburgh Review of Theology and Religion. Edinburgh University Press.

[3] McPhee. Arthur,G., *Road to Delhi: Bishop J Waskom Pickett Remembered 1890-1981* (2005) SAIACS Press. Bangalore. p. 240.

[4] *Ibid* McPhee (2005)   p. 245.

[5] *Ibid* McPhee (2005)   p. 246.

[6] *Ibid* McPhee (2005)   p. 247.

[7] Constitution of the CNI Part-I Chapter-1 Section-VIII Clause-11.

[8] *Ibid* Constitution of the CNI.

[9] *Ibid* McPhee (2005) p. 244.

[10] B. R. Ambedkar, *Writings and Speeches* Volume-5. Vasant Moon *et al* (Editors) Mumbai: Education Department, Government of Maharashtra, 1989.

[11] *Ibid* McPhee (2005) p. 245.

Chapter 6

Christians

On 5th January 1938 at a Christian gathering in Sholapur Dr Ambedkar said,

> "I have had a great impact on my mind of two great personalities, Buddha and Christ. I want a religion which could teach us to practice equality, fraternity and liberty".

James Massey, a well-known figure in Dalit theology, observed that 'Dr. B.R. Ambedkar probably was the first person who though not a Christian, yet looked at Christianity and its message seriously. This was the reason he used in his writings both directly and indirectly, the illustrations from the Bible to clarify a number of his beliefs.'[1]

Dr Ambedkar's interest in Christianity was attested by the late Revd Ian Charles Weathrall the vicar of St James Church, Delhi at that time. He recalled that through the winter of December 1952 and January 1953 Dr Ambedkar made several visits to him. He could do this as his residence at Alipur Road was close to the Church. Despite the Vicar's advice for the alternative Proposed Prayer Book, he insisted to read the 1662 Prayer Book that contained the 39-Articles of Faith (Anglican). He used to read it in the Lady Chapel of the Church and sometimes sitting in his car.[2]

Dr Ambedkar had many Christian friends. Some of these were well known personalities like Waskom Pickett a Methodist Bishop who recorded in his diary that Dr Ambedkar twice asked him for baptism, Bishop Samuel Azariah of Dornakal, Ms Mildred Drescher an American Methodist missionary, Lady Fanny Fitzerald in London with whom he shared his insights on Biblical passages.[3] Despite the fact that Dr Ambedkar sternly noted the disinterest of Indian Christians to fight social injustice,[4] the impact of Christianity on him was so great that throughout the volumes of his works he cited examples from the Christian world. For instance in the presentation speech of the Draft Constitution for India to the first Constituent Assembly of India in 1949 Dr Ambedkar cited a discussion of the Protestant Episcopal Church of the United States of America whether they could pray for the nation. This was the quote:

> Some years ago the American Protestant Episcopal Church was occupied at its triennial convention in revising its liturgy. It was thought desirable to introduce among the short sentence prayers a prayer for the whole people, and an eminent New England divine proposed the words, "O Lord, bless our nation". Accepted one afternoon on the spur of the moment, the sentence was brought up next day for reconsideration, when so many objections were raised by the laity to the word 'nation' as importing too definite a recognition of national unity, that it was dropped and instead there were adopted the words 'O Lord, bless these United States.[5]

Dr Ambedkar observed that 'there was so little solidarity in the U.S.A. at the time when this incident occurred that the people of America did not think that they were a nation. If the people of United States could not feel that they were a nation', Dr Ambedkar mused, 'how difficult it is for Indians to think that they are a nation'. It is not within the scope of this paper to discuss Dr. Ambedkar's views on nation and nationalism, but this citation is to prove his sense of association with the Christian world.

Inspiration from Moses

Biblical narratives were source of inspiration to Dr. Ambedkar. One example is the leadership of Moses. If not the figure of Moses, certainly his leadership was a source of inspiration and hope to Dr Ambedkar.[6] This is what he wrote in 1941, which has been regarded as a masterpiece of a small essay,

> The story of the Jews told in the Old Testament is a moving tale. It has few parallels. It is told in a simple but thrilling language. The pathos inherent in the subjugation and ultimate emancipation of the Jews cannot, but affect the emotions of those who are as depressed as the Jews were in Egypt in the days of Pharaoh. But the heart of everyone who is working for emancipation of a depressed people is bound to go to Moses, the man who brought the emancipation of the Jews.

> What did Moses not do for the Jews? He led them out of Egypt, out of bondage; he laid the foundation for their religion by bringing the Ten Commandments from Mount Sinai. He gave them laws for social, civil and religious purpose and instructions for building the tabernacle.

> What did Moses not suffer at the hand of the followers? When the children of Israel left Egypt and were pursued and attacked by the army of Pharaohs they were sore and said unto Moses, "(Is it) because there were no graves in Egypt, hast thou taken us away to die? It had been better for us to serve the Egyptians than that we should die in wilderness."

> The marching Israel came to Elim and camped there. There was not sufficient water for them all. They all shouted, "Give us water wherefore is this that thou hast brought us out of Egypt to kill us and our children and our cattle with thirst?" They were ready to stone him because there was no water.

> Moses went up to Mount Sinai and delayed to come down. Immediately the Jews went to Aaron and said to him. "Make for us Gods, which shall go before us; for as for this Moses, the man that brought us out of Egypt, we know not what has become of him."

> Even the leadership was challenged. The Old Testament records the Miriam and Aaron spoke against Moses because of the Ethiopian woman he had married and they said, "Hath the Lord indeed spoken only Moses. Hath he not spoken also by us?" Yet Moses bore their calumny, their abuse, tolerated their impatience and served them with the fullness of his heart.

As the Old Testament truly says there arose not a Prophet since in Israel like unto Moses, whom the Lord knew face to face. Moses was not merely a great leader of the Jews. He is a leader whose birth, any downtrodden community may pray for. Whatever interest others may have felt in the story of the Exodus and leadership of Moses they have been to me a source of perennial inspiration and hope.[7]

The inspiration of Exodus narrative lies in its compelling storyline of liberation and unwavering role of Moses not to yield to any pressure from within or without. He saw in this story all that he had experienced for over the years as he struggled for the rights of the Dalits, namely the yearning of the slaves to remain under bondage rather than to come to terms with the risks involved in freedom, temptation to worship idols of oppressive deities and exclusion of aliens for instance Moses' wife.[8] It would not be difficult to notice the underlying analogy of the Israelites to the Dalits, and Moses to Dr Ambedkar.[9] It is in this light that his comment, 'Moses was not merely a great leader of the Jews. He is a leader whose birth, any downtrodden community may pray for' becomes clear of its meaning.[10] Moreover he underscored the relevance of Moses—a prophet who gave egalitarian laws to a society in its antique stage, as an inspirational figure not only for the contemporary Jews but for the Dalits and their leaders in India too. But what may come as a surprise is a curious but concrete statement,

'I believe that just as there was a land of promise for the Jews, so the Depressed Classes must be destined to have their land of promise. I trust that just as the Jews reached their land of promise, so will be the Depressed Classes in the end reach their land of promise.'[11]

It is very interesting to note that Dr. Ambedkar did not use the well-known term 'promised land' which means the land which God had promised to the Israelites; instead he used the phrase the 'land of promise' which was indicative of prospects of progress and prosperity. A nuance of this could be *Begampura* a city without sorrow.[12] This is where, he envisioned the destiny of Dalit community was and it was here that it should reach. Was this 'land' geographic or was it metaphorical? We could examine both options before we draw some conclusion. *Firstly*, did Dr Ambedkar in his mind saw a possibility of Dalits having their own geographical space? In view of the fact that his book *Pakistan of the Partition of India* was published in December 1940,[13] his inclination in this direction, it could be argued, be taken as plausible. Although it was under compelling political conditions that he admitted to partition, his reasoning could support a movement of Dalits in this direction as well.

Be that as it may, the *second* option is to examine whether the phrase 'land of promise' was metaphorical? This leads us to another query. If so then what did he mean by this metaphor? For Christians the nuance can be the *heavenly Jerusalem*. However, it cannot be denied that by the term 'land of promise' he meant the new state of Israel established by the pioneering efforts of the Jews particularly "in respect of the Social order that was being created there"[14] that was to be governed on democratic principle and egalitarianism. These options indicate that he used the phrase 'land of promise' metaphorically for egalitarian society. However, unless the social turn would compel, he would not have advocated territorial division of India because fragmentation of India held no promise of prosperity, which in his view was the key for the restoration of *selfhood* of Dalits.

Now let us study Dr. Ambedkar's methodological content. I have grouped his methods as four 'tools' or components to give a shape to his method for assessing religions. I have called these as *Ambedkar Assessment Apparatus*.[15] These components have biblical content. Let us study them in the section below.

AMBEDKAR ASSESSMENT APPARATUS

Dr Ambedkar's life was a journey of a soul seeking a faith-community as a home, both for himself and for his people. He understood religions as good or bad, not as right or wrong. He was looking for a good religion. Therefore, he assessed major religions whether they upheld justice, were beneficial and rational. He developed an Assessment Apparatus for this purpose. This Apparatus has four components: *first,* Definition of religion; *second,* Ten-shifts Hypothesis; *third,* Two Regimes of Religion; and *fourth,* Norms to assess Religions.

The *Assessment Apparatus* could be used for assessing a religion whether or not it fulfilled the condition of being useful, just, and rational. God and deities, miracles and faith in the unseen world for him were not essential for religion. However, this does not mean that he neglected the transcendent aspect of religion, rather he identifies its foundational principles as important . The point to bring this to fore is to underscore the fact that the bible had a profound impact on how he developed this *Assessment Apparatus.*

The first component: Definition of Religion

I must admit that Dr. Ambedkar nowhere presents us with his complete scheme of method. He developed his methods approximately over a period of ten years i.e.1936-46, analyzing and writing on religion and society. To present this as *Ambedkar's Assessment Apparatus* is purely my way of coherently compiling his methods. Accordingly I have placed the definition of religion as the first component of the apparatus which he defined it as,

> I take religion to mean the propounding of an *ideal scheme of divine governance,*
> the aim of which is to make the social order in which men (*sic*! people)
> live a moral order.[16]

His point in the above definition is that religion sanctioned and sacralised social order as moral order. Deity was not, in his view, the central aspect of religion. Scholars like Larbeer agree to accept this as Dr. Ambedkar's definition of religion.[17] That he was consistent in this view is clear from his speech to the Mahars at Mumbai in 1936 where he had described religion as 'that which governs people'. Though in this instance he had attributed this definition to Mr. Tilak—'the foremost leader of Sanatani Hindus'[18] as he had described him, but this understanding in fact was taken from Robertson Smith's Burnett Lectures 1888.[19] If we examine some words here it is clear they are nuanced with biblical ideas. For instance 'an ideal scheme' could mean the Torah; 'divine governance' could mean God's Reign as set out by Jesus in the gospel. Similarly the 'social order' of Torah is egalitarianism and the 'moral order' is justice. We may recall God's instruction to his people in the Torah,

> Justice and justice alone you shall follow.[20]

But in this definition he radically discontinued with the bible as well. As noted above there was no place for God in this definition. Religion for him was purely social.

The second component: Ten-shifts Hypothesis

The second component of the Apparatus is the *Ten-shifts hypothesis*. Dr. Ambedkar identified ten shifts marking revolutionary transitions in religion from antiquity to modernity. Interestingly the time line that begins from antiquity extraordinarily stretches to the second millennia of the Common Era. These shifts that changed the norms of religion I have called as the *Dr. Ambedkar's Ten-shifts hypothesis*.[21] These are as below:

- The 1st shift was the elimination of God from the social composition. This was over and against the antique society where gods formed a socio-political and religious whole.

- The 2nd shift was the perception of God as universal. This was a complete change from the idea of parochial divinities in antiquity.

- The 3rd shift replaced the notion of the physical fatherhood of God with the idea of God as the creator. Consequently God as a governor of the universe was credited to be good.

- The 4th shift replaced proselytizing into a religion from naturalization into a society. Consequently change of religion no more entailed change in citizenship.

- The 5th shift distinguished between acquiring knowledge of divine laws in order to obey them, from engagement in speculative exercise to gain understanding of the nature of the deity.

- The 6th shift placed theoretical working out of the system of belief, prior to the   performance of fixed tradition of practices.

- The 7th shift placed individual conviction, prior to the observance of religious rituals. Unlike the antique society, the individuals in the modern society prefer to work out their convictions and reason out their beliefs prior to their engagement in their religious practices.

- The 8th shift removed religion from public domain to private. No more public ceremonies were compulsory to appease gods for harvest or victory.

- The 9th shift related God to each individual rather than to meet collective need. This was over and against the idea that God had an indifferent attitude to individual as long as *his* community flourished. In fact the sufferings of an individual were perceived as a sign of deity's displeasure with that person.

- The 10th shift involved God, albeit privately, to sort out personal problem or even help out in situation where a person was in conflict with the state. This shift was over and against the perception that God could not be appealed for the vindication of a righteous cause if it collided with the collective interest.[22]

Using this hypothesis he explained how deity's role had changed in the modern society. However, that these theological shifts were already made in the biblical literature is striking as the people-of-God evolved from primitive social stage to more advanced stages. Following Dr. Ambedkar's line of thinking, it is possible to see traces of henotheistic phase in the Jewish religion as recorded in the Bible. Henotheism was a mark of antiquity. The pointers of this are the gods of Laban's house hold (Gen. 31.19). Similarly the mention of the deities like Molech (Lev 20.3), Rimmon (2 Kings 5.18) and Baalzabub (2 Kings 1.6) are such instances. In this sense Yahweh was accepted exclusively as the God of Israel (Lev 26.12). The idea is that Yahweh was responsible for securing the protection of Israel, his own people, in as much as other deities were responsible for theirs.

Gradually, local deities were replaced by a moral God over all people and the idea that human beings were created in God's image was also incorporated in religion. Attention should also be drawn to the fact that for him religion and society were inseparably associated. In as much as the above ideas were shaped by the sociology of his times, they also reflected the human understanding of God as recorded in the Bible.

As far as sociological ideas about evolution of society are concerned, Dr. Ambedkar affirmed the idea that society evolved into three stages, namely, savage, antique and modern. Each progressive stage had its priorities. In the context of these three stages of society religion sanctioned three social priorities respectively. In the first stage of savage society the priority was to conserve life; in the second stage of antique society it was to preserve community and in the third stage of modern society it was to protect individual's interest. Religions approved and sanctified the priorities of each social stage. The questions to ask here is this which religion preserve the traits of a religion of antique society? Dr. Ambedkar found these were preserved in Judaism. An example of this is in what he wrote in 1945 to Fanny Fitzerald on the first chapter of the book of Ruth,

> I know how, when we used to read the Bible together, you would be affected by the sweetness and pathos of this passage. While you will be glad to read it again you will, I am sure, ask me what made me recall it in this connection. I wander if you remember the occasion when we fell into discussion about the value of Ruth's statement,

> Thy people shall be my people and thy God my God.

> I have a clear memory of it and can well recall our difference of opinion. You maintained that its value lay in giving expression to the true sentiments appropriate to a perfect wife. I put forth the view that the passage had a sociological value and its true interpretation was the one given by Prof. Smith, namely, that it helped to distinguish modern society from ancient society. Ruth's statement "Thy people shall be my people and thy God my God" defined ancient society by its most dominant characteristic namely that it was a society of man plus God while modern society was a society of men only (pray remember that in men I include women also). My view was not acceptable to you. But you were interested enough to urge me to write a book on this theme. I promised to do so. For as an oriental I

> belong to a society which is still ancient and in which God is a much more important member than man is. ...[23]

The reason I have included a larger portion in this excerpt is to bring out the human side of Dr Ambedkar. He had friends whom he cherished but to note the relevance he found of this biblical text is more important. The relevance was sociological.

The third component: The Two Regimes of Religions

The third component is a classification of religions into two regimes. According to Dr. Ambedkar, religions fall into two regimes, namely, Religions-of-Rules and Religions-of-Principles. According to his *Assessment Apparatus* every religion has to be assessed to which regime it belongs. He was of the view that the religions of rules were detrimental to establish a just society, partly because they were outdated and largely because they propounded hierarchical form to establish society, the worst of this was the society established on the caste-system. He held that under rules, people acted without thinking whereas with principle as their guide people had to think about why and how they were to act. Therefore, such actions had to be responsible acts.

> Doing what is said to be good by virtue of a rule and doing good in the light of a principle are two different things. The principle may be wrong but the act is conscious and responsible. The rule may be right but the act is mechanical. A religious act may not be a correct act but must at least be a responsible act. To permit this responsibility, Religion must mainly be a matter of principles only. It cannot be a matter of rules. The moment it degenerates into rules it ceases to be Religion, as it kills responsibility which is the essence of a truly religious act.[24]

The idea of this excerpt can be explained by a lively folklore of demons that live on trees. Let us regard the two regimes i.e. the religion of rules and the religion of principles, like two demons that lived on a tree. They would descend each night to quarrel with each other till the break of the day. Then they would ascend the tree and sleep the whole day long. Again at night they would descend from the tree to resume their fight. Similarly the religion of rules and the religion of principles, like two demons, live on the same tree. The tree is our society where these two may either quarrel or live with indifference to each other. However, both have survived into our modern society.[25] Dr Ambedkar stood alongside with the *religion of principles* and did his best to exorcise the demon of the *religion of rules*. He held that the religion of rules in the Indian context was Manu's *dharma*.

Interestingly biblical influence is evident here. The legalistic observance of the Sabbath as obedience to God's command to Moses is the religion of rules, whereas Jesus' disregard for rule by restoring the withered hand of a man on a Sabbath day points to the religion of principles.[26] The instance underscores the fact that Jesus acted in a responsible, not mechanical, manner. That is why Jesus defended his action by saying,[27]

The Sabbath was made for human beings, not human beings for the Sabbath.

The principle is that God's ultimate concern was not cessation of work on the Sabbath but the happiness and wholeness of human beings by enjoying leisure once a week. Needless to say that leisure is best enjoyed when a person is wholesome in health.

The fourth Component: Norms to Assess a Religion

For Dr. Ambedkar bible provided the fundamental norm for a good religion. It was justice. He found justice had several aspects of which equality and fraternity and fidelity were based on sound biblical principles.

Justice

He contended that the *ideal-scheme-of-divine-governance* which religions propounded offered one of the two schemes. Either it emphasised hierarchical social order where individual's interest was overlooked;[28] or it promoted individual's good in a free and just social order. The former was incompatible with modern society because, as he had pointed out in his *Ten-shifts hypothesis*, the focus of modern religion to do justice i.e. to protect individual's interest, had reached an irreversible point.[29] Justice for individuals was possible only in a free and equal social order where distinctiveness and worth of every individual was recognized. This meant that individuals were to be awarded what they had merited. Accordingly unmerited disadvantages and sufferings would be unjust as these would reinforce social injustice. In this line of thinking it would be unjust for a person to suffer by virtue of belonging to a disadvantaged class. Here Dalit would be the obvious case in point. It would also be unjust not to undertake initiatives to alleviate the socially disadvantaged people from their sufferings under the pretext of their ancestral sins. Let us study the various aspects of justice for which Dr. Ambedkar found biblical basis.

Equality

We know that in his *Ten-shifts hypothesis* Dr Ambedkar had held that the deities in the antique society were thought to have physically given birth to their respective ethnic communities. This however changed when religion evolved into modernity where people instead of being perceived as physical descendents of God were considered as created in the image-of-God.

> In modern society the idea of divine fatherhood has become entirely dissociated from the physical basis of natural fatherhood. In its place man is conceived to be in the image of God; he is not deemed to be begotten by God.[30]

This change in Dr Ambedkar's view was moral.[31] What he underscored was that in its *ideal-scheme-of-divine-governance* a religion of modern society perceived God not as a father but as its moral governor. Accordingly God came to be revered as supreme moral being 'capable of absolute good and absolute virtue'.[32] In other words God was absolutely just. The question that now begs an answer is this, how did Dr Ambedkar explain God's justice specifically his goodness and his virtue? In answer Dr Ambedkar pointed out that God treated all human beings as equal. He used the Hebrew Bible to show that God did this in two ways, firstly by creating them in his own image so that no one was inferior to another. This is how it reads in the New Revised Standard version,

> Then God said, "Let us make humankind in our image, according to our likeness, and let them have dominion over the fish of the sea, and over the cattle, and over all the wild animals of the earth, and over every creeping thing that creeps upon the earth". So God created humankind in his image, in the *image of God* he created them male and female he created them.[33]

Secondly, God showed this by treating each personality as sacred[34] so that no one was to suffer for the iniquity for another. He found a passage in the Hebrew Bible to support his view.

> As a starting point for the discussion of the subject one may begin by referring to the words… where Jehova says to Ezekiel, 'Behold, all souls are mine; as the soul of the Father, so also the soul of the son is mine; the soul that sinneth, it shall die ... the son shall not bear the iniquity of the Father, neither shall the father bear the iniquity of the son; the righteousness of the righteous shall be upon him, and the wickedness of the wicked upon him.[35]

Here Dr Ambedkar emphasised individual's worth and privileges which he/she merits.[36] Anything less than this would be unjust. Clearly in his view justice required that society, despite the economic and political disparities must be prepared at least to treat people equally and with dignity.

Attention should be drawn here to the obvious that is to say Dr Ambedkar had discovered the moral principle of *justice* in the bible. This was the foundational principle to modernize the Dalits. The advantage was that Bible was written when the society was in its antique stage and therefore any hierarchical scheme propounded by another religion of antiquity to create an unequal social order could be adequately challenged of its authenticity. Antiquity of a religious text, in the light of the biblical fear of antiquity, was no basis to justify unequal society. There was no excuse to support social order at the cost of individual liberty and there was no reason to advocate social inequality as a pretext to maintain social order.

So we have seen in this section that in Judaism Dr Ambedkar not only found trails of antique society and its religion, but also identified ingredients for a good religion suitable for modern society. This was in his line of thought. He did not believe religions to be true or false; rather he assessed them to be good or bad.[37] It must be stated here that in Ambedkar's view the marks of a good and lay in its inherent nature to be rational, useful and just.

Fraternity

According to Dr. Ambedkar a society of equals will be manifested in the free intermingling of people with one another. The caste based society does not allow this by prohibiting inter-marriages and inter-dining between different castes. In his monograph 'Philosophy of Hinduism' Dr. Ambedkar explains two trajectories of human relationship which run in opposite directions. One trajectory is individualism. Those who live by this view are self cantered. Every individual regards him/herself as an end itself and look after their own interests thereby developing a non-social and even an anti-social self. The opposite is the fellow feeling or fraternity. Those who hold this view identify themselves with others and seek to bring benefit to others.[38]

To underscore his point Dr Ambedkar gave a direct citation from the New Testament and from the writings of Pilgrim Fathers. This is what he wrote,

> Fraternity is the name of the disposition of an individual to treat men as the object of reverence and love and the desire to be in unity with his fellow beings. This statement is well expressed by Paul when he said, 'of one blood are all nations of men. There is neither Jew nor Greek, neither bond nor free, neither male not female, for yet all one in Christ Jesus.' Equally well was it express when the Pilgrim Fathers on their landing at Plymouth said: 'We are knit together as a body in the most sacred covenant of the Lord...by virtue of which we hold ourselves tied to all care of each other's' good and of the whole.' These sentiments are of the essence of fraternity.[39]

Fidelity

Dr Ambedkar made use of the story of Daniel to bring out the theme of fidelity.[40] His interest in this story was due to his *Ten-shifts hypothesis*.[41] It primarily demonstrated faithfulness of the Israelites to their God *YHWH*,[42] which showed that each antique society had its own deity which bestowed on its people prosperity and abundance.[43] However, for Dr Ambedkar fidelity of a community to its God helped its adherents to proceed in the right direction. We know that fidelity to God means reposing one's faith in God and on nothing else. Here Dr Ambedkar uses the story of Nebuchadnezzar and the Three Young Men of the Jewish tradition.[44] He wrote,

> Indeed the Brahmins have made religion a matter of trade and commerce. Compare with this faithlessness of the Brahmins the fidelity of the Jews to their God even when their conqueror Nebuchadnezzar forced the Jews to abandon their religion and adopt his religion.

Then he follows the narrative of the book of Daniel chapter 3,

> Nebuchadnezzar, the king, made an image of gold...And these three men, Shadrach, Meshach and Abednego, fell down bound into the midst of the burning fiery furnace.

And he ended with a sharp question,

> Can the Brahmins of India show such steadfast faith and attachment for their gods and their religious faith?[45]

He showed that fidelity of these young men was primarily to their God.[46] Scripture do not take the place of God. This approach opens up the possibility to critically test the worth of scriptures on the anvil of justice. For Dr Ambedkar a religion that taught its adherents to place their trust on the scriptures instead on its God halted human progress.[47] This may sound difficult for bible believing Christians. But if this is understood in the context of religious pluralism we will appreciate Dr. Ambedkar's view. He showed the advantage that was derived from the narrative of Daniel, i.e. it encourages the adherents to be bold to doubt and to inquire their scriptures and tradition using his Assessment Apparatus.

DR. AMBEDKAR'S CRITIQUE OF CHRISTIANITY

Notwithstanding his use of Bible to build his ideas, values and inspiration, he was critical of some aspects of Christianity. The picture will be incomplete if we fail to take this into consideration.

Doctrine of Original Sin

Dr Ambedkar regarded the doctrine of Original Sin of the traditional Christian theology as a drawback. The reason for his criticism of this doctrine was that he regarded it as wholly inappropriate for the Untouchable converts to Christianity in the Indian context. But to say that Dr Ambedkar denied the doctrine of the fall of humankind from righteousness will be a hasty conclusion. What he did was to differently explain the cause of fall. He argued that a person does not fall due to Adam's sin but due to wrong unjust environment.

> The Christian church teaches that the fall of man is due to his original sin and the reason why one must become Christian is because in Christianity there is promise of forgiveness of sins. Whatever may be the theological and evangelistic basis of this doctrine there is no doubt that from a sociological point of view it is a doctrine which is fraught with disaster. This Christian teaching is a direct challenge to sociology which holds that he fall of man is due to an unpropitious environment and not to the sins of man. There is no question that the sociological view is the correct view and the Christian dogma only misleads man. It sets him on a wrong trail. Instead of being taught that his fall is due to a wrong social and religious environment and that for his improvement he must attack that environment he is told that his fall is due to his sin.[48]

It is obvious that his argument has advantage for Dalits. Unlike the doctrine of original sin that blames the victims for their adverse condition, Dr Ambedkar argues to shift the blame away from them. He pins down the cause of injustice of social environment to the systematic operation of the caste system. Belief in the doctrine that Adam, a remote ancestor, had originally committed sin had consequences in the way people behaved. As it was impossible to recede into the past to correct the remote ancestor, who committed the original sin, it was impossible to avert the predetermined consequence that falls on the descendents of Adam. Resultantly the Indian Christians were indifferent towards social justice. He observed that,

> The consequence is that the untouchable convert instead of being energized to conquer his environment contents himself with the belief that there is no use struggling, for simple reason that his fall is due to the sin committed not by him but by some remote ancestor of his called Adam. When he was a Hindu his fall was due to the sins of his ancestor. In either case there is no escape for him. One may well ask whether conversion is a birth of a new life and a condemnation to the old.[49]

If we venture to juxtapose two doctrines with which he dealt i.e. Image-of-God and Original Sin, what comes out is a paradox which explains to a degree Dr Ambedkar's uncertainty with Christian theology. If the former empowered people with dignity, the latter made them weak interiorly. Dalits are not sinners, as the logic of original sin imputes, rather they are sinned against by the dominant oppressors. But this position will be a contradiction to those who hold to the idea of original sin. Such instances of contradictions set a challenge before the theologians to reorient their theological understanding of sin and salvation especially in connection with doing theology from Dalit perspective. The question should be: If the Dalits have been sinned *against* then what does salvation mean to them? Salvation then should be understood as emancipation from the dominant oppressors in this world here and now.

Understanding of Christ

Another issue that drew Dr Ambedkar's attention was Christology. Instead of writing directly about it he preferred to quote from the book[50] of a person called Winslow[51] who had underscored Christological propositions unacceptable to the Hindus. The first was that Christ was divine in a unique way. The second that he alone was God incarnate. The third was that Christ exclusively was the means to salvation. These in Winslow's view made Christianity repulsive to Indians which explained their low numerical turnover to Christianity. Dr Ambedkar did not commit himself to approve or disapprove these ideas at this juncture in 1937; however, later in 1956 he plainly rejected the affirmation of Christ as the divine incarnation and the sole saviour of this world.

> Christ claimed to be the prophet of Christianity. He further claimed that he was the Son of God. Christ also laid down the condition that there was no salvation for a person unless he accepted that Christ was the Son of God. Thus Christ secured a place for himself by making the salvation of the Christian depend upon his acceptance of Christ as the Prophet and Son of God.[52]

He could not accept that a person had to depend on someone else for his/her salvation. Such doctrines placed the saviour at an unequal pedestal vis-à-vis the saved. And yet earlier in 1949 he had used the Christian doctrine of Trinity which ascribes divinity to Christ, as a model for social democracy. This is how he explained it,

> What does social democracy mean? It means a way of life which recognizes liberty, equality and fraternity as the principles of life. These principles of liberty, equality and fraternity are not to be treated as separate items of a trinity. They form a union of trinity in the sense that to divorce one from the other is to defeat the very purpose of democracy. Liberty cannot be divorced from equality; equality cannot be divorced from liberty. Not can liberty and equality be divorced from fraternity.[53]

Attention should be drawn to the fact that it was not the doctrine of *trimurti* or *dattatray*, but the Christian theological doctrine of Trinity that offered a suitable concept for social side of democracy. The unified relationship of the three divine persons of the Trinity was key to understand the unified relationship of the three aspects of justice. Justice was that substance which blended the three aspects—liberty, equality and fraternity—in democratic society. In other words, the trinitarian relationship of freedom, egalitarianism and kinship were three aspects of justice which maintained the equilibrium between the three. This was fundamental for a true democratic society to constitute a genuine government-of-the-people. From the above excerpt it is clear that for

Dr. Ambedkar, society could only be just if the Constitution of the country held the three—liberty, equality and fraternity—unified and related in all aspect of its dealings. We not only should appreciate his attentiveness to detect the social aspect of Trinity but also the fact that nothing else except this doctrine could offer him the concept to explain the social aspect of democracy.

Sublimation of Poverty

His moral critique of Christianity is embedded in his defence of Buddhism to the Communist critique of religion. He wrote,

> But to communist Religion is anathema. Their hatred to Religion is so deep seated that they will not even discriminate between religions which are helpful to Communism and religions which are not. The communists have carried their hatred of Christianity to Buddhism without waiting to examine the difference between the two.[54]

This observation, however, cannot be taken for granted as a full rejection of Christianity. In fact in his article *Buddha or Karl Marx* which he wrote in 1956 he is unclear whether or not he should accept this critique of the communists against Christianity as valid. Nonetheless it seems that he did to a degree agreed with the communists. This is evident in his remark which appears in the same paragraph that, 'the sermon on the Mount sublimates poverty and weakness. It promises heaven to the poor and the weak'.[55] Dr Ambedkar underscored two criticisms of communists against Christianity. The first was to make the poor voluntarily accept poverty and the second was to offer them false security of heaven.

> The charge against Christianity levelled by the communists was two-fold. Their first charge against Christianity was that they made people other worldly and made them suffer poverty in this world. ... The second charge levelled by communism against Christianity ... is summed up in the statement that Religion is the opium of the people. This charge is based upon the Sermon on the Mount which is to be found in the Bible.[56]

Dr Ambedkar agreed with both these charges and at this juncture he was in no mood to defend Christian doctrines. Here it is important to take into consideration Dr Ambedkar's predicament to piece together what he saw in the gospels as two extreme poles. These were its liberating message on the one hand and on the other the glorification of poverty as an ideal. The former was just but the latter unjust because poverty made people unequal.

Deficient for developing intellectual culture

One of the reasons for Dr. Ambedkar to adopt Buddhism was his view that Christianity was anti-intellectual. To support his view he cited Prof. W. T. Stace who alleged that 'knowledge has never been any part of the Christian ideal man. Owing to the unphilosophical character of its founder in the Christian scheme of thought the moral side of man has been divorced from the intellectual side.'[57] It is with this in view that he wrote in 1956, a day after his conversion to explain his act,

> There is a difference between buffalo, bull and man. Buffalo and bull need fodder every day. Man also needs food. But the difference in between the two is that buffalo and bull have no mind; man has body and mind too. Therefore, both should be pondered over. The mind should be developed. The mind should be cultured. It should be made cultured.[58]

"Christianity will denationalize the Depressed Classes." Could he say that?

We have seen in our discussion above that Christianity confronted Dr Ambedkar with irresolvable paradoxes. Under these circumstances his ambiguity to consider Christianity can be expressed in his unspoken question was this, should Christianity be propagated in India? Surprise may well be expressed on a statement that was released on 24th July 1936 in the *Times of India* supposedly as Dr Ambedkar's view. As it seems to offer an answer to the above query we need to read it in detail,

> Conversion to Islam or Christianity will denationalize the Depressed Classes. If they go to Islam the number of Muslims will be doubled and the danger of Muslim domination also becomes real. If they go to Christianity, the numerical strength of Christians becomes five to six cores. It will help to strengthen the hold of the British on this country. On the other hand if they embrace Sikhism they will not harm the destiny of the country but

they will help the destiny of the country. They will not be denationalized.
On the other hand they will be a help on the political advancement of
the country.[59]

The words '*denationalize*' and the phrase '*strengthen the hold of the British on
this country*' were unduly hard against Christians of whom Dr Ambedkar
always spoke with sympathy and tenderness. This is surprising. To
examine this text we need to examine its source. Vasant Moon gives
the context of this text in the paragraph preceding the text in the 17th
Volume of Dr Ambedkar's *Writings and Speeches*:

> 'Regarding conversion, "Dr. B.R. Ambedkar, consulted his colleagues
> from different provinces in the matter of choosing the proper religion
> for conversion. He had now decided to embrace Sikhism. His friends and
> colleagues felt that Dr Ambedkar should seek the support of the Hindu
> Sabha leaders in their conversion to Sikhism; for the Hindu Sabha leaders
> believed that Sikhism was not an alien religion. It was an off-spring of
> Hinduism and therefore the Sikhs and the Hindus intermarried and the Sikhs
> were allowed to be members of the Hindu Mahasabha. Accordingly, Dr
> Moonje, the spokesman of the Hindu Mahasabha was invited to Bombay,
> in the presence of two other friends; Dr Ambedkar had a talk with Dr
> Moonje at Rajgriha, on June 18, 1936, at half past-seven that night. Dr
> Ambedkar cleared all issues and had a free talk with Dr. Moonje. Next day
> the *purport* of Dr Ambedkar's views was *reduced to a statement* and was given
> to *Dr. Moonje who approved* it personally.'[60] (emphasis added)

What has been published above is questionable for various reasons.
Firstly, it is not known who wrote out this 'purport of Dr Ambedkar's
views' for the press release and it is improbable that it was presented to
Dr Ambedkar for pre-view. Secondly, how much of this text is accurate
recording of the actual words uttered by Dr Ambedkar cannot be
determined. For it appears that Dr Ambedkar did not respond to this
press release. It is possible that some words were fed into the mouth of
Dr Ambedkar by the reporter. Thirdly, the statement could have been
composed by a person with a degree of prejudice against Christians.
Fourthly, Dr Ambedkar had criticized Christians of tolerating caste
but never becoming denationalized. Here it appears as a new word
in his vocabulary in the sphere of his dealings with Christianity! This

word does not fit into the normal 'Ambedkar language'. Fifthly, this was not a recording of the whole conversation but a reduction. In other words it is only the essence of what was discussed. Sixthly, the word 'denationalize' and the phrase 'strengthening the hold of the British' are in line with the Hindutva ideology which was not the line that Dr Ambedkar would tow.

Juxtaposing Christianity with Islam in this text betrays a similar colour of prejudice. It is unlikely that Dr Ambedkar keen on Sikhism at this phase could have embraced ideas resonating Hindutva ideology of Vir Damodar Sarvarkar of which he was so critical. He was not a type of politician who could have said things to please people. This is evident in the 'formula for amicable settlement' on the question of conversion. Clearly Sikhism was preferred over Islam and Christianity, but in his view it was Muslims not Christians who needed to be checked in converting the depressed classes.[61] Seventhly, in the light of Dr Ambedkar's statement[62] on 5th January 1938 reiterating the great impact of Jesus Christ on his mind, the reliability of the above 1936-press note seems to be doubtful. Keeping in view the above facts one could consider this statement as unreliable in details. In value and authenticity it weighs less than the articles which Dr Ambedkar wrote himself. Accordingly it would be misleading to construe conclusions on this text.

Considering the question we had raised at the beginning of this section, obviously Dr Ambedkar was unclear whether Christianity in India should be propagated or not. Nonetheless, it will be apt to recall his most moving conclusion at the end of his article on Christians: *The Condition of the Convert*. He had realized the utility of Christianity for Dalits which was evident in their conversion to it. He expressed his deep interest for Christians, that he was their friend and that he wanted them to be aware of their weaknesses in order to overcome them. He wrote,

'I am deeply interested in the Indian Christians because a large majority of them are drawn from the Untouchable classes. My comments are those of a friend. They are not strictures of an adversary. I have drawn attention to their weaknesses because I want them to be strong and I want them to be strong because I see great dangers for them ahead. They have to reckon with the scarcely veiled hostility of Mr. Gandhi to Christianity taking roots in the Indian social structure. But they have also to reckon with militant Hinduism masquerading as Indian Nationalism.'[63]

For none else did Dr Ambedkar write a postscript with a touch of affection and tenderness as this. He who wrote this could not have said what the 1936-press note had released. Although he on no occasion spared them wherever he found them at fault, this addendum demonstrates his inclination to Christianity. Yet he did not choose Christianity as a home for his Dalit community.

A few things should be noted in the conclusion. In his own words Dr. Ambedkar wrote the narratives of three biblical personalities. In 1941 he wrote about Moses, in 1945 about Ruth and in 1956 about the three young colleagues of prophet Daniel. They were useful for inspirational as well as for theoretical purposes. It is interesting to note that these three were from the Hebrew Bible. However, with regard to the New Testament he had serious disagreements which he disclosed only in 1956, the year he converted to Neo-Buddhism. These were the divine status of Christ, sublimation of poverty and unphilosophical approach of Christ. It must be admitted that these critiques were directly pointed to Christ. The detailed discussion on this is beyond the scope of this paper.

So what did he mean when in 1938 he said that Christ had made a great impact on his mind? As a matter of fact he never explained what this impact was. Keeping in view that in 1932 he had entered the Poona Pact with Gandhi promising not do anything that would harm the interest of the Hindus he had distanced himself from Christians. However, after his disagreements with Mahatma Gandhi resurfaced in 1947, it can well be that in the years following 1932 he changed his thinking. If on the one hand he recovered his appreciation of Christianity then on the other he disapproved some of its aspects. Three of which we have brought to fore above. So what was the impact of Christ on him?

It must be admitted that there is no evidence of any impact except that in passing he wrote a line in his article 'Reformers and their Fate' of 1956,

> [Buddha's] time was divided between feeding the lamp of his own spiritual
> life by solitary meditation, just as Jesus spent hours in lonely prayer. ...[64]

The mention of Jesus praying in seclusion for long hours is in the gospel of Mark 6.46. This indicates that Dr. Ambedkar was reading the gospels. Obviously the seclusion of Jesus in prayer struck him as resonating with the solitariness of Buddha in meditation. The reason for him to read the gospel was to acquaint himself with its style with the intent to recast the Buddhist scriptures for the Neo-Buddhists. This he did and called the book "The Buddha and his Gospel" but later renamed it as "The Buddha and his Dhamma".

Christianity: A Model for Ambedkar's Neo-Buddhism

The events of Dr. Ambedkar's life after 1950 show that he was now seriously studying Buddhism and he felt no hesitation to openly express his dissatisfaction with Christ's claim to be God's Son.[65] Over and against this he found Buddha's insistence to be nothing more than one who showed the way to salvation as more convincing.[66] Yet attention should be drawn to his admittance that Buddhists should regard Christians as their role model. This advice was not in passing rather its seriousness can be gauged from his insistence on it in his writing in 1954 and 1955 and also after his conversion in 1956. At the second instance Ambedkar while insisting in having a Buddhist initiation ceremony like Christian baptism and ordination, firmly stated that 'in this respect the new movement for the propagation of Buddhism in

India must copy Christianity'.[67] In this matter he considered no other religion or organization as appropriate.

> Bhikku Sangha must borrow some of the features of the Christian priesthood particularly the Jesuits. Christianity has spread in Asia through service—educational and medical. This is possible because the Christian priest is not merely versed in religious lore but because he is also versed in Arts and Science. This was really the ideal of the Bhikkus of olden times.[68]

In this line of reasoning he mapped some specific details of ways in which this would be done. In our list of these features below we will use *dhamma* in Pali for the Buddhist ideal to highlight its distinctiveness from *dharma* its Sanskrit equivalent.[69]

i.   A *dhamma* of Buddha, like the gospel of Jesus Christ, should be concise containing his moral and social teachings.

ii. A Buddhist initiation ceremony for the laity like the Christian baptism.

iii. Appointment of lay preachers like Christian catechists.

iv. Establishment of a Buddhist Religious Seminary like Christian Seminaries for priests.

v.   Sunday Worship in *Vihara* should have a sermon.

vi. Establishment of High Schools and Colleges, on the pattern of Christian institutions, under Buddhist management.

vii. Literary works, like inviting people to write essays on Buddhist topics, in order to increase interest of the people in Buddhism.[70]

Dr. Ambedkar carefully followed up each proposal. He succeeded to prepare a concise edition of Buddha's life and teachings. Initially he called it *The Buddha and His Gospel*. This book patterned on the scheme of the Christian gospels started with Buddha's genealogy, his birth and childhood stories, his temptations and going out as a seeker till he attains enlightenment and becomes a Buddha. Then he preaches his philosophy and gains disciples, finally his death. Subsequently Dr. Ambedkar changed the title of this book to *The Buddha and His Dhamma*. In a similar proposed pattern he designed a ceremony of initiation, like the Christian baptism, for Buddhists. The conversion ceremony had no rituals but three components, namely ascription in praise of Buddha with the Intention, the Resolve and the Promises. The first component started with an attribution of praise was followed by a recitation of *Trisharan* i.e. seeking refuge in *the Buddha, the Dhamma and the Sangha*. The second component was the recitation of the famous *Pancha Sila*. This was the recitation of the resolve to follow the five precepts of Buddha and finally the Promise to abide by a list of twenty directives. This list was drawn up by Dr. Ambedkar. It is very interesting to note its resemblance to the Ten Commandments of Moses in the Judeo-Christian tradition.

The reason Dr. Ambedkar suggested that the Monks should be trained to become preachers of *dhamma* was due to his realisation of the imperative to impart Buddhist teaching not only to the unconverted but also to thousands of Dalits who had embraced Buddhism with him on October 14, 1956 at *Deeksha Bhoomi* Nagpur. A fortnight later in a letter to Valisinha, he suggested two ways to do this. The first model was the Roman Catholic missionaries and social preachers.[71] The idea was to train the monks after this pattern. The second model was the Protestants. Keeping in view that celibacy had a limited appeal to Indian youth his idea was to have an order of married priests too.[72] Similarly, a year earlier on January 11, 1955, he had announced the starting of a Buddhist seminary in Bangalore, obviously after the pattern of a Christian theological seminary. For this he had obtained help from the World Buddhist Mission, Myanmar.[73]

Be this as it may, his own intellectual conflicts arising out of the contentions he saw between Christianity and Buddhism needed to be addressed. Was there a possible way to hold the two traditions together? He did in a way to address the conflict of his conscience. How he did this is clear in his article which he wrote in 1950 for the Fourth Conference of the World Fellowship of Buddhists at Kathmandu. He claimed that Christianity freely borrowed from Buddhism, therefore, now Buddhists should liberally take from it. It is very interesting to see that he wouldn't allow Buddhists to borrow ideas from any other religion except Christianity. Obviously if he claimed Christianity to be almost wholly based on Buddhism then it was legitimate and safe for Buddhists to be close to Christians and none other. Significantly he stated this soon after his conversion to Buddhism.

> 'You will be probably surprised to know that 90 percent of Christianity is copied from Buddhism both in substance and in form ... There is so much to it, I think time has turned and we must now copy some of the ways of the Christians in order to propagate our religion among the Buddhist people.'[74]

But if we accept Dr Ambedkar's position, can we consider Christianity as anything but an extension of Buddhism? In view of the discussions that surround close resemblances between certain stories of Christ and the Buddha, Dr Ambedkar could have maintained a neutral stand. Now while it is certainly true that an encounter between Buddhism and Christianity is afforded by many similarities in their narratives, such as the visitation of the wise sages at Christ's as well as at Buddha's birth, Simeon's and Asita's story surrounding the birth narratives of the two, the conversion of Zacchaeus the tax collector by Christ and the conversion of Angulaimala the robber by Buddha, and temptations of Christ by the tempter and of Buddha by a woman, but that does not erase the possibility of parallel development of two entirely independent religious traditions.

However, it is remarkable that there were no borrowings of Buddhist philosophical ideas in the New Testament. For instance John's gospel employed *logos* and *theos* Greek concepts but not *nirvana* as was the case with the *Bhagavada Gita*.[75] Now while it is true that religious and philosophical ideas do get disseminated across the globe, still, the Jewish root of Christianity is an undeniable fact. Keeping this in view Dr. Ambedkar's assertion that Christianity had mostly borrowed from Buddhism was farfetched and wrong.

However, the unstated point of his claim was to appropriate the best of these two traditions to deploy it for the emancipation of Dalits and restoration of their *selfhood*. In a curious but concrete way he perceived the relationship between these two religions as if one facilitated the other in order to flourish. In this way he reached an intellectual reconciliation at the end of his life where he could hold and cherish both religions, Christianity and Buddhism, together in his mind. The former had deeply inspired him and the latter had ideologically convinced him.

In more recent times, neo-Buddhism has established itself as a religion across the country but mostly in the Maharashtra State in central India. It is estimated that the three million Hindus who had turned to neo-Buddhism, were mainly from the Dalit communities of *Mahars, Jatavs, Chamars* spread all over U.P., Punjab, Maharashtra, Jammu and Kashmir. Its remarkable growth was noted in census records also. The percentage jumped from 0.05% (1951 census) to 0.74% (1961 census). However a drop to 0.70% was noted in the 1971 census. The reason being that in several places large numbers of neo-Buddhists were reconverted back to Hinduism. Interestingly 12,000 neo-Buddhists from Kolhapur (south of Mumbai) had approached the Church of North India seeking baptism in 1971.[76] Presently the neo-Buddhists have established numerical stability.

As we have seen above Christianity had continued to inspire Dr. Ambedkar even after he had decided to convert to Buddhism. To no other religious sources he went to find models and ideas except Christianity. It is evident that Dr. Ambedkar derived ideals, values and inspiration not only from the bible but from the larger Christian tradition as well. His ideals were social and he aimed to make them relevant and for benefit to the society. We have seen that justice is not merely personal but also social. This is evident from his insistence that justice was another name for liberty, equality and fraternity. For him these were not words of the French revolution but were biblical.

The point for us to learn from Dr. Ambedkar is that religion and their scripture have an important role in establishing a society. The social structure of the society can be just or unjust. If the society is established on egalitarianism it is just. Conversely if it is hierarchical it is unjust of which the caste system is the worst form. This depends what is the worldview of the dominant religion.

DR. AMBEDKAR HAD GRASPED THAT BIBLE PROPOUNDED EGALITARIANISM AS THE FOUNDATION OF SOCIETY WHICH WAS FUNDAMENTAL FOR JUSTICE. The challenge before us is to propagate the biblical worldview and its social values to advance justice in our society. One reason for this should be to reckon with the fact that Christianity is the oldest minority in India with a continuous history. It is, therefore, the right of every Indian to be informed about this faith.

Endnotes

[1] James Massey, '*Dr. B.R. Ambedkar: A Study in Just Society.*' Centre for Dalit/Subaltern Studies. Manohar. 2003. p. 43.

[2] I was told this verbally by Revd Weathrall on 29th March 2008 at his residence i.e. the Brotherhood House, 7-Court Lane, Rustamji Sehgal Marg, Delhi-54.

[3] The references to these people are strewn in many books. Some of these references that I used are from the following books: Stephen Neill. *Men of Unity.* London: SCM Press. 1960, p. 57; Arthur G. McPhee. *Road to Delhi: Bishop J Waskom Pickett Remembered 1890-1981.* Bangalore: SAIACS Press, 2005, p. 240-247; Nanak Chand Rattu *Little Known Facets of Dr Ambedkar.* Focus Impressions, 2001, pp 124-152.

[4] Vasant Moon, *Dr Babasaheb Ambedkar* (Translated by Asha Damle) New Delhi: National Book Trust of India, 2007, p. 122.

[5] B.R. Ambedkar, 'Closing Speech in the First Constituent Assembly of India' in *Great Speeches of Modern India* (Editor: Rudrangshu Mukherjee) New Delhi: Random House, 2007, p. 219.

[6] Glora Becher, 'Dr Ambedkar and The Jewish People' (1941) *Writings and Speeches* Vol. 17.1. 2003, p. 343.

[7] Glora Becher, *idem.*, pp. 342-43.

[8] Glora Becher, *idem.*, p. 343.

[9] Glora Becher, *idem.,* p. 518.

[10] Glora Becher, *idem.,* p. 343.

[11] Glora Becher, *idem.,* p. 343.

[12] The term "Begampura" was coined and used by Sant Ravidas (c. 1450-1520) who was a bhakti radical saint. The term is a utopia but different from Mahatma Gandhi's utopia of *Ram Rajya. Cf.* Gail Omvedt. *Seeking Begampura: The Social Vision of Anticaste Intellectuals.* Navayana. New Delhi. 2008. p.7.

[13] B.R. Ambedkar, 'Pakistan or the Partition of India' (1940), behind the title page.

[14] Glora Becher, 'Dr Ambedkar and the Jewish People' (1941) *Idem., Writings and Speeches* Vol. 17.1. p. 342.

[15] Monodeep Daniel, *'Faith on the Anvil of Justice.'* Vrije Universiteit. Amsterdam. 2013. p. 58.

[16] B.R. Ambedkar, 'Philosophy of Hinduism'. (1941) *Idem., Writings and Speeches* Vol.3. 1941.

[17] Mohan P. Larbeer, *'Ambedkar on Religion: a Liberative Perspective.'* ISPCK. New Delhi. 2003. p. 160.

[18] *'What way Emancipation?'* (1936) in Writings and Speeches Vol-17. Part-III. p. 121.

[19] This is was Smith said in his lecture-1, 'If we were called upon to examine the political institutions of antiquity, we should find it convenient to carry with us some general notion of the several types of government under which the multifarious institutions of ancient states arrange themselves. And in like manner it will be useful for us, when we examine the religious institutions of the Semites to have first some general knowledge of the types of divine governance, the various ruling conceptions of the relations of the gods to man, which underlie the rites and ordinances of religion of different places and at different times. Robertson W. Smith. *Lectures on the Religion of Semites.* First Series. London: Adam & Charles Black. 1907. p. 22.

[20] *Cf.* Deuteronomy 16.20.

[21] Monodeep Daniel, *'Faith on the Anvil of Justice: Dr. Ambedkar's Response to Religions in India.'* Vrije Universiteit. Amsterdam. 2013. p. 36.

[22] B.R. Ambedkar, 'Philosophy of Hinduism' (1941) *Writings and Speeches* Vol-3. Mumbai,1987. pp. 14-20.

[23] B.R. Ambedkar, 'What Congress and Gandhi have done to the Untouchables.' (1945) *Writings and Speeches* Vol-9. Govt. of Maharashtra. 1990. Dedication page.

[24] B.R. Ambedkar, 'Annihilation of Caste.' (1936) *Writings and Speeches* Vol-1. Govt. of Maharashtra. 1989. p. 75.

[25] B.R. Ambedkar, *Ibid.,* p. 75.

[26] Compare Exodus chapter 20 with Mark chapter 3.

[27] *Cf.* Mark 2.27.

[28] B.R. Ambedkar, 'The Hindu Social Order' (1946) *Idem.,* p. 99.

[29] B.R. Ambedkar, 'Philosophy of Hinduism' (1941), pp. 19-20.

[30] B.R. Ambedkar, 'Philosophy of Hinduism' (1941), *Idem., Writings and Speeches* Vol.3. p. 16.

[31] B.R. Ambedkar, *idem.,* p. 16.

[32] B.R. Ambedkar, *idem.,* p. 16.

[33] Book of *Genesis* Chapter-1 verse 26-27.

[34] B.R. Ambedkar, 'The Hindu Social Order' (1946), *Idem.,* Vol. 3. p. 99.

[35] Ezekiel 18.4 & 20.

[36] B.R. Ambedkar, *idem.,* p. 99.

[37] B.R. Ambedkar, 'Philosophy of Hinduism' (1941), *Idem.,* p. 22.

[38] B.R. Ambedkar, *idem.,* p. 44.

[39] B.R. Ambedkar, 'The Hindu Social Order' *Idem.,* (1946), p. 97.

[40] The Bible: The Book of Daniel Chapter 3.

[41] B.R. Ambedkar, 'Philosophy of Hinduism' (1941), *Writings and Speeches* Vol.3. pp. 14-20.

[42] B.R. Ambedkar, 'Riddles in Hinduism' (1956), *Writings and Speeches* Vol.4. p. 6.

[43] B.R. Ambedkar, 'Philosophy of Hinduism' (1941), *Idem., Writings and Speeches* Vol.3. p. 19.

[44] The Book of Daniel in the Hebrew Bible.

[45] B.R. Ambedkar, 'Riddles in Hinduism' (1956), *Idem.,* Vol.4. pp. 6-8.

[46] B.R. Ambedkar, *idem.,* p. 6.

[47] B.R. Ambedkar, *idem.,* p. 8.

[48] B.R. Ambedkar, 'The Condition of the Convert' (1937), pp. 472-73.

[49] B.R. Ambedkar, *idem.,* p. 473.

[50] The book identified by the Compilers of Vol-5 of *Dr Babasaheb Ambedkar: Writings and Speeches* [1989] is "On Christianity in India" by Mr. Winslow is appended in the list of other books used by Dr Ambedkar in the articles compiled in this volume.

[51] B.R. Ambedkar, 'The Condition of the Convert' (1937), *Idem.,* Vol.5. p. 453.

[52] B.R. Ambedkar, 'The Buddha and His Dhamma' (1956) *idem.,* Vol.11. Mumbai: 1992, p. 215 (Book-III. Part-1, Section-1).

[53] B.R. Ambedkar, *'Closing speech of the first Constituent Assembly of India'*(1949) in Great Speeches of Modern India. Rudrangshu Mukherjee, Random House. New Delhi. 2007. p. 218.

[54] B.R. Ambedkar, 'Buddha or Karl Marx' (1956) *idem., Writings and Speeches* Vol-3. Mumbai: 1987, p. 460.

[55] B.R. Ambedkar, *idem.*, p. 460.

[56] B.R. Ambedkar. *idem*, p. 460.

[57] B.R. Ambedkar, 'The Buddha and His Dhamma.' (1956) *idem., Writings and Speeches* Vol-11. Mumbai: 1957. p. 598.

[58] B.R. Ambedkar, 'The Buddha Dhamma will be the Saviour of the World.' (1956) *idem., Writings and Speeches* Vol-17.3. Mumbai: 2003. p. 537.

[59] B.R. Ambedkar, 'Hindus should not be Indifferent to Conversion of Depressed Classes' (1936) *idem., Writings and Speeches* Vol-17. Part-1. Mumbai, 2003, p. 241.

[60] B.R. Ambedkar, 'Hindus should not be Indifferent' (1936), *Ibid.*, p. 239.

[61] *Idem., Writings and Speeches* Vol-17 Part-I. Appendix-X. Pg. 476. The 'formula' was cited in a letter dated 30th June 1936 as a response to the reactions to this Statement Dated 19th June 1936. The wording of the 'formula' and the content of Dr B.S. Moonje's letter seems to express the spirit of Dr Ambedkar genuinely. However, in the light of the above discussion the title of the Appendix-X of Volume-17.1 (2003) of the *Writings and Speeches* attributing the Statement, issued to the press, solely to Dr Ambedkar is not correct. Compare it with the details in the Chapter-11 of Volume-17 (2003) p. 239, it is stated that the anonymous composer had this Statement approved by Dr Moonje (President of the Hindu Mahasabha) the next day for Press Release. Therefore the title of Appendix-X of Vol-17 (2003) is misleading.

[62] Vasant Moon, *Dr Babsaheb*, 2007 p. 122.

[63] B.R. Ambedkar, 'The Condition of the Convert' (1937), p. 476.

[64] B.R. Ambedkar, 'Reformers and their Fate' (1956). p. 166.

[65] B.R. Ambedkar,'Buddha and the Future of His Religion' (1950), p. 95.

[66] B.R. Ambedkar, *idem.*, p. 95.

[67] B.R. Ambedkar,'Buddhism Disappeared from India Due to Wavering Attitude of the Laity' (1955) p. 430.

[68] B.R. Ambedkar, *Buddha And The Future Of His Religion* (1950), p. 107.

[69] To deconstruct the preeminence of Sanskrit language Braj Ranjan Mani has argued that in the literature of the Vedas the word *dharma* does not occur. However, its use was popularized only after Buddha's time. He writes that, 'Brahman priests and grammarians may well have fashioned the word in imitation of the Pali term, dhamma'. *Cf.* Mani. *Debrahmanising History*, p. 418. Also read HaBir Angar Ee. *Pali is the Mother of Sanskrit.* Nagpur: Tarachand Chavhan, 1994.

[70] B.R. Ambedkar, 'Buddhist Movement in India: A Blue Print' (1954) *idem., Writings and Speeches* Vol-17 Part-3. Mumbai: 2003, p. 508.

[71] B.R. Ambedkar, 'Bhikkhus Should Serve the Buddha by Becoming Preachers of His Dhamma' (1956) *idem., Writings and Speeches* Vol-17 Part-1. Mumbai: 2003, p. 446.

[72] B.R. Ambedkar, *idem.,* p. 447.

[73] B.R. Ambedkar, 'Buddhist Seminary to be Started in Bangalore' (1955), *Writings and Speeches* Vol-17 Part-1. Mumbai; 2003, p. 428.

[74] B.R. Ambedkar, 'Buddha or Karl Marx' (1956), p. 557.

[75] B.R. Ambedkar 'Krishna and His Gita' (1956), p. 369.

[76] *World Christian Encyclopaedia Vol-1.* (2nd edition) David B Barrett et. al. (editors)

SECTION THREE

MANUSMRITI · CASTE · VIOLENCE

The third section consists of three essays. These are on *Manusmriti*, Caste System and Violence. The thread of concern underlying these essays is about the forced submission of Dalits to the dominant castes. This forced submission is visible, structural and mute; but situation ferociously erupts when the order of caste is defied. Then the thunder of violence against the untouchables is heard which normally remains unheard. This connection in these three essays must be kept in mind by the readers.

The first essay on *Manusmriti* (the Laws of Manu) brings to fore the practical way in which the depressed castes were forced into submission. This was done with the help of law. The principle is simple i.e., by dividing up the whole society into four castes in a descending order of purity. The caste is determined by the birth of a person in a particular *jati* and family. Thereafter, the penalties for offences also follow a similar pattern; i.e. the harshness of punishment increases down the line of caste. However, there is a fifth section of populace who are religated as untouchables. They have been casted out from the social order of the fourth tier caste system.

From a Christian perspective this is unacceptable because it teaches to include in our generosity the poor, the widows and the orphans. In our context the untouchables will also be included. In Old Testament the leading principle in the Law of Moses was egalitarianism. This is evident in the principle which the Lord God had told Moses that the degree of penalty for an offence should not be diminished for the poor or enhanced for the rich. No one was to be favoured but all were to be treated equally under the God's law (Deut. 16.19).

The second essay "Caste System" underscores the fact that whatever may have been the classification of society, the brahmanical scriptures i.e. the Vedas and *Manusmriti* gave it a legitimacy of excellence and declared it to be a sacred system. Dr Ambedkar rightly argues that the unique feature, which distinguished Hinduism from other religions, was the caste system. In this situation the role of the British to aggravate and reinforce caste system for the advantage of their own establishment is also brought to fore. This occurred by default. They needed to employ people at various levels. Accordingly they did this by following caste-like arrangement in civil administration, army, mills, railways and construction of infrastructures. So for instance the janitors were the Untouchables and the accountants were the *saukars*.

The third essay deals with "Violence". The essay aims to expose the fierce approach of the so called upper castes to dominate over others. Interestingly violence in the caste-based society is both structural and active. It is structured in the laws of Manu to protect the supremacy of Brahmins and the caste system. Dr Ambedkar pointed out that the practice of boycott of the Untouchables by others was the worst kind of violence without shedding a drop of blood. The point is to grasp that the nature of structural violence is such that it does not require the violation of life or ferocity of destruction but it leads its victim to silently surrender. It is so deeply ingrained in the culture and legitimised by religion that it is unquestioningly tolerated even by the victims.

Chapter 7

Manusmriti

Dr Ambedkar fiercely protested against *Manusmriti* or The Laws of Manu. He did this by burning this book in full public view on the Christmas day of 1927.[1] The day made sense demonstrating the influence of the Judaeo-Christian tradition on him i.e. Christ's fulfilment of the Old Testament and the displacement of the Law of Moses by his gospel. While the nationalists were mobilizing the masses to protest against Simon Commission Dr Ambedkar mobilized Dalits to protest against Manu.[2] It was definite that the old ordinance of Manu was now to be supplanted by a constitution for modern democracy in India. The one who was destined to do this was to be none other than Dr Ambedkar. His influence on the Indian Constitution is so definite that by virtue of it he became the founder of the modern democratic republic of India.

But before we explain what the *Manusmriti* is we must recall who Ambedkar was? More than adequate information is uploaded on the internet however for our purpose we must bring to fore some facets of his personality.

Dr Ambedkar was born in Mhow, a town well known for its large garrison. He was a nationalist and a contemporary of Mohandas Karamchand Gandhi (1869-1948), Mohammed Ali Jinnah (1876-1949), Vallabhbhai Patel (1875-1950), Abdul Kalam Azad (1887-1958) and Pandit Jawaharlal Nehru (1889-1950).

It was rare in those times but he was fortunate to obtain the highest academic credentials both in economics and in law. However in India, he was never spared of being degraded for being an Untouchable, which turned him to become a revolutionary reformer and to take definitive initiatives to challenge the caste system. He wrote volumes against it, he started social movements for social equality and founded political parties to organize the Untouchables and a new religion *Navabaudh* or Neo-Buddhism to assimilate the Dalit converts into Buddhism. He became the law minister of independent India and ensured incorporating legal equality for the Scheduled Castes in the Indian Constitution.

An icon and inspiration to millions in the heartland of India, on whose insistence the *ashokachakra* was embossed on the Indian national tricolour, yet at his death Dr Ambedkar's body was not wrapped in it. Neither was he honoured with the twenty-one gun salute nor the sounding of the Last Post and Reveille at his funeral, yet millions have come to honour him every year since 1956 at *Chaitya bhoomi* in Mumbai. This shows that Dalits will remember him and will continue to draw inspiration from him.

This is evident as I write this article today.[3] It is *Bharat Bandh* called by Dalits against the decree of the Supreme Court of India which revoked the provision of FIR and arrest of those who would address Dalits with derogative words. The marches and rallies were replete with slogans of *Jai Bhim*! i.e. the first name of Dr Ambedkar namely "Bhimrao". Even Lutyens' Delhi today has come to a standstill at midday.

In Dr Ambedkar's view the Indian society was governed by the values of the dominant culture of Bhraminical Hinduism. This meant that neither its scripture nor its doctrine or its philosophy were the pivot to regulate the personal behaviour of its adherents, instead it was the codes of Manu which did this. This may sound farfetched particularly in view of the fact that people do draw inspiration and lessons from various characters of mythologies and legends. For instance, *Sita* examplifies a wife, *Rama* for perseverance in sufferings and *Hanumana* for devotion and self-control. But Dr Ambedkar was convinced that the Indian society for all practical purpose was founded on the doctrine of inequality of Caste system as propounded in the Law of Manu. He wrote,

> Is there then no principle in Hinduism which all Hindus … feel bound to render willing obedience? It seems to me that there is and that principle is the principle of Caste. There may be difference of opinion as to which matters constitute matters of essence so far as Hinduism is concerned. But there can be no doubt that Caste is one and an essential and integral part of Hinduism. Every Hindu—if he is not merely a statutory Hindu believes in Caste and every Hindu—even one who prides himself on being a statutory Hindu—has a Caste. A Hindu is as much born into caste as he is born in Hinduism. Indeed a person cannot be born in Hinduism unless he is born in a Caste. Caste and Hinduism are inseparable.[4]

In Dr. Ambedkar's view it was caste system that directed the social behaviour of his co-religionists. Therefore, he proceeded to explore that most important thing in Hinduism which directed the behaviour of its adherents which was *Manusmriti.*

Promulgation of *Manusmriti*

Manusmriti is a corpus of ordinances in metrical form which propounds the law for all the social classes. Dr Ambedkar draws a line under its revolutionary impact affirming that "the *Manusmriti* is a record of the greatest social revolution that Hindu society has undergone."[5] He also notes that *Manusmriti* was promulgated by *Pushyamitra* as embodying the principles of Brahminic Revolution against the Buddhist state of the Mauryas. This is what he argued in the light of the history,

> Ashoka made Buddhism the religion of the state. This of course was the greatest blow to Brahminism. The Brahmin lost all state patronage and were neglected to a secondary and subsidiary position in the Empire of Ashoka … for the simple reason that Ashoka prohibited all animal sacrifices which constituted the very essence of Brahminic Religion. … they lost their occupation which mainly consisted in performing sacrifices for a fee which was substantial. The Brahmin therefore lived as the suppressed and

Depressed Classes for nearly 140 years during which the Maurya Empire lasted. A rebellion against the Buddhist state was the only way of escape left to the suffering Brahmins and there is special reason why Pushyamitra should raise the banner of revolt against the rule of the Mauryas.

Pushyamitra was a Sung by Gotra. The Sungas were Samvedi Brahmins, who believed in animal sacrifices and soma sacrifices. The Sungas were therefore quite naturally smarting under the prohibition on the animal sacrifices throughout the Maurya Empire proclaimed in the Rock Edict by Ashoka. No wonder if Pushyamitra who as a Samvedi Brahmin was the first to conceive the passion to end the degradation of the Brahmin by destroying the Buddhist state which was the cause of it and to free them to practice their Brahminic religion.

That the object of the Regicide by Pushyamityra was to destroy Buddhism as a state religion and to make the Brahmin the sovereign rulers of India so that with the political power of the state behind it Brahminism may triumph over Buddhism is borne out by two other circumstances. The first relates to the ... his performance of the Ashvamedha Yajna or the horse sacrifice, the Vedic rite which could only be performed by a paramount sovereign. And the second is his launch of a violent and virulent campaign of persecution against Buddhists and Buddhism. How pitiless was the persecution by Pushyamitra can be gauged from the Proclamation which he issued against the Buddhist monks ... by setting a price of 100 gold pieces on the head of every Buddhist monk.[6]

After this slaughter of Buddhists and destruction of Buddhism, Pushyamitra who ascended the throne as a sovereign, promulgated *Manusmriti* as a code of law on his subjects.[7] So the question is this what is *Manusmriti*?

What is *Manusmriti*?

Prof G Bühler in his "Introduction" to the Laws of Manu[8] gives both its mythological origins as well as Max Muller's theory of its origin. The Myth is fascinating which claims the divine origin of these ordinances.

Its opening versus narrate how the great sages approached Manu, the descendent of self-existent Brahman, and asked him to explain the sacred law. Manu agrees to their request and gives to them an account of the creation as well as of his own origin from Brahman. After mentioning that he learnt 'these institutes from the sacred law' from the creator who himself produced them, and that he taught them to the ten sages whom he created in the beginning, he transfers the work of expounding them to *Bhrigu*, one of his ten mind-born sons. The latter begins his task by completing, as the commentators call it, Manu's account of the creation.[9]

Granted that myth in the antiquity were written to draw the track where history is untraceable, yet even in those texts one can find traces of sensible thinking.

In the case of *Manusmriti* it is similar. If one were to understand the first verse of this book as commented by Govindaraga, Narayana and Raghavananda in its modified form[10] then the meaning is that these Laws were not communicated by one person but by several. Buhler contends that "*Manusmriti* does not contain the original words of Bhrigu, but a recension[11] of his recension such as it had been handed down among his pupils."[12]

Having discussed this Bühler gives a summary of Prof Max Müller's explanation of the origin of the *Manusmriti*. This is what he writes,

The systematic cultivation of the sacred sciences of the Brahmanas began and for a long time had its centre in the ancient Sutrakaranas, the schools which collected the fragmentary doctrines, scattered in the older Vedic works, and arranged them for the convenience of oral instruction in Sutras or strings of aphorisms. To the subjects which these schools, chiefly, cultivated, belongs besides the ritual, grammar, phonetics and the other so-called Angas of the Veda, the sacred law also.[13]

This clearly is a rational explanation of the origin of *Manusmriti*. However Dr Ambedkar concluded something different. He discovered that this work was composed by a man named Sumati Bhargava.[14] This point of authorship was earlier in 1886 noted by scholars like Buhler who observed that "the original law-book of one hundred thousand verses were not composed by Pragapati and abridged by Manu and others, but alleges that its author was Manu Pragapati, and that Narada and Sumati the son of Bhrigu summarized it."

However, in a monograph which Dr Ambedkar wrote sometime after 1941 he debunked the claim of supernatural origin of *Manusmriti* contended in the light of the latest finding in this field at that time that "the claims made in the *Manusmriti* regarding its authorship is an utter fraud and the beliefs arising out of this false claim is quite untenable."[15] Thereafter he goes on to say that,

> The code itself is signed in the family name of Bhrigu as was the ancient custom. "The text Composed by Bhrigu (entitiled) "The Dharma Code of Manu" is the real title of the work. The name Bhrigu is subscribed to the end of every chapter of the code itself. We have therefore the family name of the author of the code. His personal name is not disclosed in the Book. All the same it was known to many. The author of Narada Smriti writing about the 4th century AD knew the name of the author of the *Manusmriti* and give out the secret. According to Narada it was one Sumati Bhargava who composed the Code of Manu. Sumati Bhargava is not a legendry name, and must have been historical person for even Medhatithite the great commentator on the Code of Manu held the view that this Manu was a 'certain individual'. Manu therefore is the assumed name of the Sumati Bhargava who is the real author of *Manusmriti*.[16]

The *Manusmriti* translated in 1794 by Sir William Jones thereafter it became known to the western academicians. It must also be noted that this ancient book relies on two sources which predated it, firstly, the *artha-shastra* which was the state-craft and secondly the *Grihya Sutra* which dealt with the ideas connected with duty, conduct, virtues, rights and laws. The view that *Manusmriti* was a modified version of an earlier code titled *Dharma Sutra* has been discarded as there has been no trace of any such work.[17]

Having said that about its origins attention should further be drawn to the text. The text itself can be divided into four sections. These are creation of the world, source of *dharma*, the *dharma* of the four castes and the law of *karma* and final liberation. The date of origin of this book is difficult to ascertain. Earlier Sir William Jones and Karl Schlegel, well known eighteenth century orientalists, deduced it to be written around 1250 BCE and 1000 BCE. However, this has been revised and scholars now assign it to be a work composed between 200 BCE to 200 CE.

Dr Ambedkar had accepted that the *Manusmriti* was composed sometime between 170 BCE and 150 BCE and that *Pushyamitra* had overturned the Buddhist regime in C. 185 BCE after which this code was imposed.[18]

Manu's Vision versus Ambedkar's Vision of Society

For Dr Ambedkar the significance of *Manusmriti* was in its prescriptions of what was to be done as one's duty in society. He showed how this treatise regulated both ethical action and social behaviour of people. Care should be taken in reading what Dr Ambedkar writes and what he does not write about the Hindu ethics. If this is so then, we may say that he would agree that what Manu considered as non-injury (*ahimsa*), truth (*satya*), non-stealing (*asteya*) and control of senses (*indryia-nigraha*) was moral. But these could be observed even by those who followed *sadharana-dharma* or ordinary duty of human beings. Therefore, Dr Ambedkar was keen to test this treatise from the caste-cum-stage scheme of governance i.e. *vern-ashrama-dharma* which prescribed proper duties associated with one's station in life i.e. stations determined by one's *verna* or caste and one's *ashrama* or specific stage in life.[19]

In Dr Ambedkar's line of reasoning all laws were to be tested on the anvil of justice. Accordingly Manu's Laws which were not only a treatise on duties, but it also laid down penalties for offences were to be tested on the same scale. The scale of justice is straight forward i.e., to serve exactly what a person deserves with partiality to none. But Dr Ambedkar found that *Manusmriti's* penalties were based on caste system and not on justice as such. This was so because the system of caste was regarded as the divinely ordained law of society promulgated to protect the world-order by means of castes and to make it prosperous "*varnair lokarakshanasam vardhanartham*" (*Manusmriti* 1, 31). This is evident from how Manu argues in defence of the divine origin of castes in the first chapter of his book *Manusmriti*,

As at the change of the seasons each season of its own accord assumes
its distinctive marks, even so corporeal beings (resume in new births) their
(appointed) course of action.(I.30)

"For the sake of the prosperity of the worlds; he caused the Brahma*n*,
the Kshatriya, the Vai*s*hya, and the Shudra to proceed from his mouth, his
arms, his thighs, and his feet." (I.31)

Dr Ambedkar underscores the fact that as Manu had propounded the
belief of the divine origin of Castes; therefore its maintenance was of
key importance for him. In other words to uphold the caste system,
in Manu's view, was tantamount preservation of the social order.

"To the Brahmins he (swyambhu Manu) assigned the duties of reading
the Veda, of teaching it, of sacrificing, of assisting other to sacrifice, of
giving alms, if they are rich, and if indiquent, of receiving gifts," (1.88)

"To defend the people, to give alms, to sacrifice, to read the Veda, to shun
the allurements of sensual gratification are in a few words, the duties of
a Kshatriyas." (I.89)

"To keep herds of cattle, to bestow largeness, to sacrifice, to read the
scriptures, to carry on trade, to lend at interest, and to cultivate land are
prescribed or permitted to a Vaishya." (1.90)

"One principal duty the supreme Ruler assigns to a Shudra, namely, to
serve the before mentioned classes, without depreciating their worth." (I.91)

However, the point that Dr Ambedkar makes is that Manu had
amended the older codes. He observes that Manu was so intent "on
the maintenance of the system of *Chaturvernya* (caste system) that he
did not hesitate to make fundamental changes in it."[20]

Having said that I will now highlight a few features of Manu's
Laws as exposed by Dr Ambedkar. His aim was to demonstrate that
Manu's law was not in line with the best understanding of justice i.e.,
surveying without partiality exactly what a person derserved.

Firstly, the severity of penalty :

The unique feature of the penalties in *Manusmriti* on the offenders
was progressively increased in the descending order of castes. Let us
take the penalty of defamation,

"A soldier (Kshatriya), defaming a priest, shall be fined *a hundred* panas; a merchant (Vaishya) thus offending *two hundred*; but for such an offence, a mechanic or servile man (Shudra) shall *be whipped.*" (VIII 267)

Similarly in case of assault, Manu provides

"If a man of the lowest class should spit on him (the one superior to him) through price, the king shall order both his lips to be gashed; should he urine on him, his penis; should he break wind against him, his anus." (VIII.282)

Secondly, the penalty was harsh :

The harsh aspect of Manu's Laws was particularly explicit in the cases when the sexual alliances regulated by caste rules were ignored. For instance in case of adultery Manu laid down that,

"A man of servile class, who commits actual adultery with the wife of a priest, ought to suffer death; the wives indeed, of all the four classes must be most especially guarded." (VIII.359)

"A low man, who makes love to a damsel of high birth, ought to be punished corporally; but he who addresses a maid of equal rank shall give the nuptial present and marry her, if her father please," (VIII.366)

Thirdly, the caste system was reinforced :

The caste system was reinforced by extreme penalties but chiefly by excluding Brahmins from punishments. For instance,

"Manu, son of the Self-existent, has named ten places of punishment, which are appropriate to the three lower classes, but a Brahman must depart the realm unhurt in any one of them." (VII.124)

These ten points of punishment were in the parts of physical body, as below,

"The sex organs, the belly, the tongue, the two hands, and, fifthly, the two feet, the eye, the nose, both ears, the property, and, in a capital case, the whole body." (VIII.125)

"No greater crime is known on earth than slaying a Brahman; and the King, therefore, must not even form in his mind an idea of killing a priest." (VIII 381)

Fourthly, the disarming of Shudras :

In an overall assessment of *Manusmriti* it is noticeable in that except for the Kshatriya or rulers, it did not provide possibility for the Shudras to take up arms. This was a precaution to curb any possibility of rebellion against those who enjoyed a social advantage by virtue of their caste.

Fifthly, the rearming of Brahmins :

According to Dr Ambedkar this was a fundamental change that Manu had brought in the Law. Its objective was to maintain or to restore social order by reinforcing caste system especially when a ruler disregarded the caste arrangement in society.

> "The twice-born may take arms, when their duty is obstructed by force; and when, in some evil time, a disaster has befallen the twice-born classes." (VIII.348)

It is clear that only the three privileged castes had the right to rebel but not the Shudra. This was natural because these three would benefit by the maintenance of caste system. But what if the Kshatriya had joined the King in destroying the system? What was to be done? Manu gives the authority to the Brahmins to punish all and particularly the Kshatriyas. This is what the Law of Manu lays down,

> "A priest, who knows the laws, need not complain to the king of any grievous injury; since, even by his own power, he may chastise those who injure him." (XI.31)

> "His own power, which depends on himself alone, is mightier than the royal power, which depends on other men; by his own might, therefore, may a Brahman coerce his foes." (XI.32)

> "He may use, without hesitation, the powerful charms revealed to Atharvan, and by him to Angiras; for speech is the weapons of a Brahman; with which he may destroy his oppressors." (XI.33)

> "Of a military man, who raises his arm violently on all occasions against the priestly class, the priest himself shall be the chastiser; since the soldier originally proceeded from the Brahman." (IX.320)

Dr Ambedkar quires "How can the Brahmans punish the Kshatriyas unless they can take arms? Manu knows this and therefore allows the Brahmans to arm themselves to punish the Kshatriyas. Accordingly Baudhayana, Manu's successor, further improved this law by laying down that,

> "For the protection of the cows, Brahmins or in the case of the confusion, Brahmins and Vaishya also should take up arms out of consideration of the Dharma." (II.24,18)

"This was to maintain the caste system at any cost" thus asserted Dr Ambedkar. Moreover, to him it was clear that the caste system could only be maintained by treating people unequally, by favouring the *suvarna* and discriminating against the untouchables. This was a clear case of perverting justice.

Democracy as Dr Ambedkar's Vision of Society

In contrast to the social inequality established by the caste system, vision of Dr Ambedkar was democracy and justice. In other words if democracy was an associated way of living in a society, then it was not only to be a political arrangement but a social pursuit too. What did this mean for Dr Ambedkar?

It meant that that society should enable all people to be free and equal. Accordingly if democracy brings freedom then justice brings egalitarianism. In fact justice is an inseparable aspect of democracy. The inspiration for him came from the French Revolution. He identified the three words "liberty, equality and fraternity" as three aspects of justice.[21] He identified these three words as emerging from within the Judaeo-Christian tradition. Now while the possibility for establishing equality may also be asserted by other political institutions, for Dr Ambedkar democracy was best suited to facilitate it. The reason why Dr Ambedkar emphasised democracy was because it valued all people equally by virtue of one-person one-vote. Such political equality of democracy was essential for all people to enjoy freedom. At the same time democracy was rooted in good religion. This is what he wrote,

> What sustains democracy? Some would say that it is the law of the State which sustains equality and liberty. This is not a true answer. What sustains equity and liberty is fellow-feeling. What the French Revolutionists called fraternity ... without fraternity liberty would destroy equality and equality would destroy liberty. If in democracy liberty does not destroy equality and equality does not destroy liberty it is because at the basis of both these is fraternity. Fraternity is therefore the root of democracy ... Wherein lie the roots of fraternity without which democracy is not possible? Beyond dispute, it has its origin in religion.[22]

For Dr Ambedkar fellow-feeling or feeling of kinship was rooted in two religious traditions—one was Christian and the other was Buddhist. In Christian tradition it is known as "fellowship" and in Buddhist "friendship". It was from within these two cultures, which were remarkably influenced by Greeks, as Roger Osborne has put it, that thinkers arose 'to address questions left unanswered by other forms of cultural expression such as, how to live the good life, how to act justly and how to balance the demands of freedom and order.'[23] Other traditions fell short of the standard.[24]

Dr Ambedkar identified two essential features of a democratic society. *Firstly*, the absence of stratification of society into castes and classes, and *secondly*, the social habit of people to re-adjust in reciprocation of interest. Dr Ambedkar pointed out that mere election to constitute a government was no democracy, rather,

> A government for the people can be had only where the attitude of each individual is democratic which means that each individual is prepared to treat every other individual as his equal and is prepared to give him the same liberty which he claims for himself. The democratic attitude of mind is the result of socialization of the individual in a democratic government.[25]

Dr Ambedkar points out that without this attitude of mind the foundations of democracy would be laid on shifting sands. In his discussion on the democratic values of equality, liberty and fraternity, he contended that the central concern of these three values was not the French Revolutionists but religion. This shows that his affinity to Judaeo-Christian ideas was exceptional. I had noted in my earlier study,

> The inspiration of the Exodus narrative lies in its compelling storyline of liberation and the unwavering role of Moses not to yield to any pressure from within or without. Dr Ambedkar saw in this story all that he had experienced for over the years as he struggled for the rights of the Dalits, namely, the yearning of the slaves to remain under bondage rather than to come to terms with the risks involved for freedom; temptation to worship idols of oppressive deities; and exclusion of aliens from instance Moses' wife. It would not be difficult to notice the underlying analogy of the Israelites to the Dalits, and Moses to Dr Ambedkar. It is in this light that his comment, 'Moses was not merely a great leader of the Jews. He is a leader whose birth, any downtrodden community may pray for'[26] becomes clear of its meaning.[27]

IT IS CLEAR FROM THE ABOVE DISCUSSION THAT DEMOCRACY WAS DR AMBEDKAR'S ALTERNATIVE TO *VERNA-ASHRAMA-DHARMA*. Against the social order of the Caste system which fragments people by propagating graded inequality, fixity of occupation and fixation by birth, Dr Ambedkar propounded social egalitarianism, freedom and fellowship. Attention should be drawn to the fact that democracy is as ancient as any other political system. In fifth century BC Athens had it and it was practiced in Buddhist communities; it emerged among Protestant Christians i.e. in Congregationalist and Presbyterian churches; and thereafter Dr Ambedkar reinvented democracy for the Indian republic in 1950 with typical institutions of representational government, parliamentary system, embedded opposition, free media, adult franchise, separation of power between parliament, bureaucracy and judiciary, after the pattern of other modern democracies of the world. Indeed Ambedkar emerges, the first ever in the history of India, a decisive opponent of Manu.

Endnotes

[1] Monodeep Daniel, *Religions in India: The Vision of B.R. Ambedkar* (2016) ISPCK-DBS. New Delhi. p. 6.

[2] Bidyut Chaktrabarty and Rajendra Kumar Pandey, *Modern Indian Political Thought: Text and Context.* (2009) Sage Publications. New Delhi. p. 285.

[3] 2nd April 2018.

[4] B.R. Ambedkar, 'The Morals of the House' (1941) in *Writings and Speeches* Vol-3. Mumbai 1987. p. 336.

[5] B.R. Ambedkar, 'The Triumph of Brahmanism' (1941) in *Writings and Speeches* Vol-3. Mumbai. 1987. p. 270.

[6] B.R. Ambedkar, 'The Triumph of Brahmanism' (1924?) in *Writings and Speeches* Vol-3. Mumbai. (1987) pp. 268-69.

[7] *Ibid.,* B.R. Ambedkar, 'The Triumph of Brahminsm' (1924?) p. 270.

[8] G Buhler (trans.) *The Laws of Manu* (1886) Clarendon Press. Oxford. p. xii.

[9] *Ibid* Buhler. p. xii.

[10] The first verse of the Laws of Manu is "The great sages approached Manu, who was seated with a collected mind, and, having duly worshipped him, spoke as follows:" Kull. Thinks that *pratipugya* 'having worshipped' may also mean 'after mutual salutations' and he connects, against the opinion of the other commentators, 'duly' with 'spoke'. Govindaraga, Narayana and Raghavananda and Kull. as well as various MSS begin with *Samita* with the following verse, omitted by Medh. Kull. and Nand. 'having adored the self-existent Brahman, possessing immeasurable power, I will declare the various eternal laws which Manu promulgated.'

[11] The word "recension" means "revised text". *Cf. Ibid* Buhler. p. 01.

[12] *Ibid.,* Buhler. p. xiii.

[13] *Ibid.,* Buhler. p. xviii.

[14] Monodeep Daniel, *Religions in India: The vision of B.R. Ambedkar* (2016) ISPCK-DBS. New Delhi. p. 93.

[15] B.R. Ambedkar, 'The Triumph of Brahmanism' (1941) in *Writings and Speeches* Vol-3. Mumbai. (1987) p. 270.

[16] B.R. Ambedkar, 'The Triumph of Brahmanism (1941) in *Writings and Speeches* Vol-3. Mumbai. 1987. p. 270.

[17] B.R. Ambedkar, 'The Triumph of Brahmanism" (1941) in *Writings and Speeches* Vol-3. Mumbai. 1987. p. 270.

[18] B.R. Ambedkar, 'Literature of Brahmanism' (1956). p. 240 & 'The Triumph of Brahmanism' (1941) p. 271 in *Writings and Speeches* Vol-3. Mumbai. 1987.

[19] Monodeep Daniel, *Religion's in India: The Vision of B.R. Ambedkar* (2016) ISPCK-DBS. New Delhi. p. 93.

[20] B.R. Ambedkar, 'The Morals of the House' (after 1941) in *Writings and Speeches* Vol-3 (1987 edt). p. 356.

[21] B.R. Ambedkar, 'Brahma is not Dharma' (1956) *Writings and Speeches* Vol-4. (1987) p. 284.

[22] B.R. Ambedkar, 'Brahma is not Dharma' (1956) *Writings and Speeches* Vol-4. (1987) p. 284.

[23] Roger Osborne, *Of the People by the People: A New History of Democracy* (2011) The Bodley Head. London. p. 19.

[24] Later he identified the exception of Sikhism but his interest in it was short-lived.

[25] B.R. Ambedkar. 'Brahma is not Dharma' (1956) *Writings and Speeches* Vol-4. (1987) p. 281.

[26] B.R. Ambedkar, 'Dr Ambedkar and the Jewish People (1956) *Writings and Speeches* Vol-17.1. (2003) p. 343.

[27] Monodeep Daniel. *Religions in India* (2016) ISPCK-DBS. New Delhi. p. 215.

Chapter 8

Caste System

In whatever way caste system may be explained[1] it was of key importance to Dr Ambedkar to distinguish Hinduism from other religions.[2] He highlighted that the social order of Hinduism resulted in unequal social stratification.[3] In another way we can say that caste system has been sustained by untouchability and social exclusion.[4] Indeed certain underpinnings even in *Manusmriti* which, in Lipner's words aimed "to draw the sting out of the hereditary view of caste"[5] demonstrate its indispensability for the Hindu way of life. So the question before Dr Ambedkar was this, how the caste system originated in India?

As early as in 1916 he wrote a paper titled *Castes in India: Their Mechanism, Genesis and Development*[6] whose standard manifests an astonishing intellectual ability in spite of his young age. In the understanding of caste he disagreed with the scholars of his time except Dr. Ketkar contending that they had either overstated or underestimated the case.[7] Following Dr. Ketkar's line of thinking he underscored the prevalence of exogamy in the Indian society. He observed,

> 'The various *Gotras* of India are and have been exogamous: so are the other groups with totemic organizations. It is no exaggeration to say that with the people of India exogamy is a creed and none dare infringe it, so much so that, in spite of the endogamy of the Castes within them, exogamy is strictly observed and that there are more rigorous penalties for violating exogamy than there are for violating endogamy.'[8]

This posed a problem, namely, what explanation could be offered for the endogamy of castes over and against the exogamy of *gotras*? Arguing for the case of overlapping of endogamy with exogamy Dr. Ambedkar gave his famous dictum for the genesis of caste: "the superposition of endogamy on exogamy means the creation of caste."[9]

As he was well aware of the tendency of close lying groups to assimilate and amalgamate to forge a homogeneous society, he pointed out the existence of an outer circle beyond which people were not allowed to contract marriages.[10] This explanation, however, gave rise to another problem. It was the problem of surplus women and men who were single. He contended that this problem was addressed by three mechanisms which he called as singular uxorial customs, namely, girl marriage, *Sati* or the burning of the widow on the pyre of her deceased husband, and enforced widowhood by which a widow is not allowed to remarry. Along with this he also noted the popularity of *Sannyasa* (renunciation) on the part of the widower.[11]

However, his line of thinking despite its clarity has failed to convince the scholars. Whereas, Susan Bayly, a social anthropologist in Cambridge University, underscores an alternative mechanism of modes of existence and conduct that aggravated the reinforcement of the caste system since the nineteenth century. Bayly argues that although till the nineteenth century the three modes namely, the man of prowess, the service provider and the settled man of worth, lived in uneasy synthesis, a very large populace lived and conducted themselves in a very uncastelike manner.[12] However, at the time when Dr. Ambedkar wrote, he did not think that the iron hand of caste was any less in the pre-colonial era as it was during his time in the colonial era.

It was, therefore, logical in continuation of his own line of reasoning to raise a third question, namely, how did the caste system spread in among various groups in society. In Dr. Ambedkar's opinion caste system in other groups spread by way of imitation of the Brahmins. He pointed out that,

> [The] subdivision of a society is quite natural. But the unnatural thing about these sub-divisions is that they have lost the open-door character of the class system and have become self-closed unites called castes. The question is: were they compelled to close their doors and become endogamous or did they close them of their own accord? I submit that there us a double line of answer: *Some closed the door; others found is closed against them.* The one is a psychological interpretation and the other is mechanistic; but they are complementary and both are necessary to explain the phenomena of caste-formation in its entirety.[13]

His point of imitation brings him close to what later Susan Bayly was to say in 1999. To this we will turn later in our discussion, but to the question how did the Brahmin justify this system led him to the scriptures. He started his probe with the Vedas.

He found the oldest deposit of this idea in *Purushukta* in the Rig Veda where caste system said to have originated at creation in a cosmic sacrifice. He noted its omission in the Sam Veda with a degree of curiosity, but more interestingly was his astonishment at alternative explanations in the Yajur and Atharva Vedas.[14] Dr Ambedkar's query was why had the exponents of scriptures taken note only of the Rig Veda text and ignored the alternative stories in Vedas. This is what he wrote,

> Stopping for a moment to take stock so to say of the position it is quite clear that there is no unanimity among the Vedas on the origin of the four castes. None of the other Vedas agree with the Rig-Veda that the *Brahmin* was created from the mouth of the *Prajapati*, the *Kshatriyas* from his arms, the *Vaishyas* from his thighs and the *shudras* from his feet.[15]

This excerpt viewed that the exponents aimed to reinforce the hold of the Brahmins over the rest in society. Highlighting this Dr Ambedkar pointed out how people's behavior, both individually and collectively, of domination and of submission was to reinforce this social inequality continuously.

However, it is surprising to note that Dr. Ambedkar despite his incisive power of analysis failed to develop what Susan Bayly would do much later. Although her observations about the expansion of the caste system do not contradict Dr. Ambedkar's theory of its expansion by method of imitation what Dr. Ambedkar failed to elaborate was the role of the British in developing and reinforcing the caste system.

She pointed out that under the British colonial rule the casteist practices were aggravated due to imposing of taxes in agrarian sectors, expansion of civil administration, establishment of army, founding of mills, and construction of infrastructure and extension of railways. In all these sectors labour was needed of unskilled work and removing waste for which the pollution-removers were identified and employed. The castes crystallized in a legal way particularly with the exercise of census where people were identified, named and classified as castes.

Nevertheless, the British were not the sole contributors to this phenomenon; they merely took advantage of the trait that easily was available in culture. For example when East India Company that had decisively removed the Brahmin rulers from the former Maratha realms of the Deccan, used the caste logic to justify their decision when they were in danger to reverse it. James Grant Duff, Company's chronicler, argued that 'the Peshwas were not and never had been rightful rulers; they were Brahmins, whose proper sphere in life was that of priest and scribe. So it could only have been through guile and subversion that their line had achieved power at the expense of the descendents of Shivaji Bhonsle.'[16]

Under this political situation, since the nineteenth century, different versions of caste system developed. This uncaste like populace was either absorbed into a caste or excluded as untouchables. In Bayly's research—*Caste, Society and Politics in India*—we can identify three, namely the Brahmin, the Kshatriya and the Vaishya versions respectively. One common feature all versions shared was to subordinate Dalits to work for the priestly Brahmin and the thread-wearing warrior dynast as pollution-removers of organic waste with no enjoyment of human rights as such.

The Brahmins, as service providers, had a well known version of caste where social segregation was ordered to the advantage of the priestly castes in a descending order of purity. According to this version, the various *jati* or communities are placed into four levels of descending order of purity. The Brahmin caste was placed on top. From among their diverse *jati* various kinds of priests are prepared, some to teach, others to cremate the dead, still others to do the rituals or *karmakanda*. At the second level under them is the *kshatriya* caste. These are the warriors. At the third level is the *vaishya* caste. These are business communities, for instance, the *bania* community. At the fourth level is the *shudra* caste. These are the servile people who are made to serve those above them. The rest were the untouchable Dalits unfit for associating with the three top clean castes.

The Kshatriya, as men of prowess, also had a version of caste for themselves. If purity was the anxiety of the Brahmins, legitimacy was for Kshatriya. Both had to do with possessing social and political power. The Kshatriya version was for legitimizing themselves as rulers and defenders. This was acutely felt by Shivaji Bhonsle (1630-80) who needed to be rescued from his rustic non-dwija (i.e. non-twice-born) background and accommodated in a caste which would legitimize him as a Maratha ruler. This was done by Brahmins who were linked with Banaras and Mewar. They performed the ceremony of investiture of Shivaji with the sacred thread, anointing his body with sweet and transforming essences of Brahminical rituals particularly milk, curds and *ghee* which were the all nurturing gifts of the holy cow.[17]

The accommodation of non-*dwija* as Kshatriya did not end with legitimizing kingship. Groups that wanted to be recruited as soldiers were willing to follow their patrons who willingly vested them a *jati* title and other casteist designations. Some recent caste formations bear the titles Jat, ahir, Koli, and Kanbi. Reengaging into arms-bearing groups such castes over a period of time started to behave like a caste except that did not worry about attaching significance to the Brahmins or standards of purity.[18]

The settled men of worth associated themselves as the third caste i.e. Vaishya develop their version of caste system. These communities were variously known as *bania* or *mahajan or saukar.* During the depression of 1830s and with the eclipse of Mughals and the incoming of East India Company, many emerged as traders and specialists in handling money. Some consolidated their hold on State and military finance while others became revenue collectors and money-lenders. Many increased their fortunes by grabbing the land rights from the original land owners.

Be this as it may, Dr Ambedkar argued that there were specific inbuilt features of caste system that gave it unique character, none like it existed in any other social system in the world. In particular he underlined three features. The first was the principle of graded-inequality.[19] The second was the principle of fixity-of-occupation. He found that Manu had fixed the occupational continuance of every person by his/ her heredity. He instructed that 'in order to protect the universe the most resplendent one assigned separate (duties and) occupations, to those who sprang from his mouth, arms, thighs and feet'.[20] The third was the principle of fixation-of-people. It meant that people were permanently fixed from the day of their birth in their respective caste-groups. These three reasons also explained the restrictions on inter-dining and inter-marriages across the caste lines. He accepted that there was no society without classes[21] but in the caste system there was something more. It created isolated groups in such a manner that a permanent gap was retained between the forward and the depressed castes.

> What a free social order aims to do is to prevent isolation and exclusiveness being regarded by all classes as an ideal to be followed. For so long as the classes do not practice isolation and exclusiveness they are only *non-social* in their relations towards one another. Isolation and exclusiveness make them *anti-social* and inimical towards one another. Isolation makes for

rigidity of class consciousness, for institutionalizing social life and for the dominance of selfish ideals within the classes. Isolation makes life static, continues the separation into privileged and underprivileged, masters and servants.[22] (emphasis added)

This excerpt demonstrates Dr. Ambedkar's insight that despite the fascinating uniqueness of the endogamy of caste and exogamy of gotras, the caste system is basically an antisoicial institution.

FROM THE ABOVE DISCUSSION IT IS CLEAR THAT IN DR AMBEDKAR'S VIEW THE NON-NEGOTIABLE CORE OF HINDUISM WAS THE *VERNA-VYAVASTHA* OR THE CASTE SYSTEM. The impact that this had on people was seen in how it made them behave in society both individually and collectively. Clearly those who perceived themselves of a legitimate origin held an attitude of superiority and behaved condescendingly towards those who were perceived as low or illegitimate origin. Not only this but thre subjugation and exploitation was not regarded to be anti-social and unethical by the so called upper caste.

Endnotes

[1] The only difference that Dr Ambedkar makes between Verna and Caste is that the first does not fix occupation by birth but the second does. For all practical purpose the meaning of the two terms is the same which entails ordering of society into four levels in hierarchical manner.

[2] B.R. Ambedkar, 'Riddles in Hinduism' (1956), *Writings and Speeches* Vol.4. (1987). p. 189.

[3] Klostermair, *A Survey of Hinduism.* p. 47.

[4] Doniger, *The Hindus: An Alternative History.* pp. 17-40.

[5] Lipner, *Hindus*, p. 112.

[6] Dr. Ambedkar presented this paper at the Dr. A. A. Goldenweizer Anthropological Seminar in Columbia University, New York, on 19th May 1916 and was published in *Indian Antiquity Vol.XLI* in May 1917.

[7] B.R. Ambedkar, 'Castes in India: Their Mechanism, Genesis and Development' (1916), *idem., Writings and Speeches* Vol.1. (1989). p. 9.

[8] B.R. Ambedkar, *idem.*, p. 7.

[9] B.R. Ambedkar, *idem.*, p. 9.

[10] B.R. Ambedkar, *idem.*, p. 10.

[11] B.R. Ambedkar, *idem.*, p. 13.

[12] Bayly. Susan, *Caste, Society and Politics in India from Eighteenth Century to the Modern Age* in The new Cambridge History of India Vol. IV.3. (1999) Cambridge University Press. Cambridge. p. 95.

[13] B.R. Ambedkar, 'Castes in India: Their Mechanism, Genesis and Development' (1916), idem *Writings and Speeches* Vol.1. (1989). p. 18.

[14] Dr Ambedkar observed that the *Sama-Veda* neither included the *Purushukta* in this collection nor gave any explanation of the Caste. The next under consideration was the *Taitterriya Sanhita* of the 'black' *Yajur Veda*. According to it the Brahmin and the Kshatriya originated from *Vratya* [*Cf.* B.R. Ambedkar, 'Riddles in Hinduism' (1956) Idem *Writings and Speeches* Vol-4. Mumbai: 1987, p. 191]. Whereas *Vajasaneya Sanhita* of the 'white' *Yajur Veda* holds that the four castes were created by the *Prajapati* [*Cf.* B.R. Ambedkar, 'Riddles in Hinduism' (1956) *Idem., Writings and Speeches* Vol-4. Mumbai: 1987, p. 191-192]. These texts do not endorse the claim of the divine origin of castes as propounded in the *Purushasukta*. The last in this section are the two citations from the *Atharva Veda*. The first citation suggests that the Brahmin is the first-born and has the power to liberate others[15] [*Cf.* B.R. Ambedkar. 'Riddles in Hinduism' (1956) *Idem., Writings and Speeches* Vol-4. Mumbai: 1987, p. 192]. The other suggests that the whole human race descended from Manu. [*Cf.* B.R. Ambedkar. 'Riddles in Hinduism' (1956), p. 193].

[16] Op cit. B.R. Ambedkar. 'Riddles in Hinduism' (1956), p. 193.

[17] Grant. Duff, James Cuninghame. (1826). *A History of the Mahrattas.* London. 1921. p. 531. (cited in Bayly 1999: p. 88).

[18] Op cit. Bayly. Susan. 1999. p. 60.

[19] Op cit. Bayly. Susan. 1999. p. 62.

[20] B.R.Ambedkar, 'The Hindu Social Order; Its Essential Principles' (1946), p. 106.

[21] *Manusmriti* I.87 and I.88-91.

[22] B.R. Ambedkar, 'The Hindu Social Order: Its Essential Principles' (1946), p. 113.

[23] B.R. Ambedkar, *idem.*, p. 113.

Chapter 9

Violence

Dr Ambedkar had a remarkable insight in the connectivity of law, society, religion and morality. This is what he wrote,

> In all societies law plays a very small part. It is intended to keep the minority within the range of social discipline. The majority is left and had to be left to sustain its social life by the postulates and sanction of morality. Religion in the sense of morality, must therefore, remain the governing principle in every society.[1]

But what happens when the Law discriminates? What happens when the religion justifies inequity? And what happens when morality is skewed? In India the result was not anarchy. She is too civilized for that! But violence was institutionalized and structured. Its delivery was measured with precision and heartlessly conveyed. All this has been manifested for centuries in the violation of the Human Rights of two million Dalits who have silently endured subjection and deprivation.

In this essay we will discuss structured forms of violence under following sections, namely: law, religion, dogma and ideology. Needless to say that customs and culture in society emanate out of these and in turn are justified by these. Moreover violence can have three forms: one, it can be *active* in forms of killing, burning, beating, ridiculing by parodies; two, it can also be *passive* by way of ignoring, isolating, dumping, non-cooperating, boycotting and neglecting. Dalits face both forms of violence. A third form of violence that must be taken into cognisance is what I call as the *structured* violence. By this I mean institutionalised violence. This condition is another name for a persistent state of injustice in social relationship of people. It is an ordered situation that comes into existence and is sustained by the socio-cultural structure.

LAWS: ANCIENT AND MODERN

Under Manusmriti

In as much as violence can be curbed through law it can also be structured through it. A classic example of it in India is the *Manusmriti* meaning the codes of Manu. It is the brahmanic law and is held in great reverence by them. Earlier the scholars assessed its composition to be around 5th century BCE[2]; But Dr Ambedkar after an authentic research fixed it after 185 BCE by Sumati Bharagava.[3] Needless to say that it has involved several revisionists and a long period of time to take its full and present form. Its worldview and jurisprudence has not only made a deep impact on Indian mind but it has permanently tailored the cultural traits of this subcontinent. The most important thing to note in its prescriptions and proscriptions is the presupposition on which it rests. The assumption is the preservation of *Dharma* in all aspects of human life. This includes the *ashramas* i.e., phases of life as a student, a householder, a recluse and finally ascetic. The law of Manu directs people to keep to the Dharma which means to maintain the purity of *Chaturverna* i.e. the four-tier caste system.

In this ancient Law of Manu, the justification of caste is based on the Rigvedic *Purushukta* in the following verse,

"But for the sake of the prosperity of the worlds, he caused the Brahmana, the Kshatriya, the Vaisya, and the Sudra to proceed forth from his mouth, his arms, his thighs and his feet" (Manusmriti I.31)

It was for this reason that the sages who approached Manu had asked him,

"Deign, divine one, to declare to us precisely and in due order the sacred laws of each of the (four chief) castes (varna) and of the intermediate ones." (Manusmriti I.2)

Once the divine origins of *Chaturverna* were accepted, then the reasonable duty was to preserve it. However, the question before us is whether the case of such preservation is just?

According to Dr Ambedkar, the *Chaturverna* is a system of graded inequality which dispossesses those at the lowest social rung. The transformation of *verna* into caste was gradual. The process involved fixing occupation by heredity instead of ability.[4] This Caste system relegated whole masses of people as low castes *sudra* and utterly rejected other as casted out. Unequal castes stand unequally before the law and are penalized unequally for the same crime. The result of this is structured injustice. This is obvious in social, punitive and economic laws. A few examples would suffice here,

"Let the first part of a Brahmana's name (denote something) auspicious, a Kshatriya's be connected with power, and a Vaisya's with wealth, but a Sudra's (express something) contemptible." (*Manusmriti* II.31)

"Let him (a caste householder) not stay together with outcasts, not with Kandalas, nor with Pukkasas, nor with fools, nor with overbearing men, nor with low-caste men, nor with Antvavasavins". (*Manusmriti* IV.79)

"Let him not give to a Sudra advice, nor the remnants (of his meal), nor food offered to the gods; nor let him explain the sacred law (to such a man), nor impose (upon him) a penance." (*Manusmriti* IV.80)

"Manu, son of the self-existent, has named ten places of punishment, which are appropriated for the three lower classes but a Brahmin must depart from the realm unhurt in any one of them." (*Manusmriti* VII.124)

'No collection of wealth must be made by Sudra, even though he be able (to do it); for a Sudra who had acquired wealth, gives pain to Brahmanas'. (*Manusmriti* X.129)

The list of such codes endlessly goes on. The fundamental point of Manu's jurisprudence is to uphold the caste-ordered society which he contended could only be kept intact by the fear of punishment (*Cf. Manusmriti* VII.22). However, the punishment for the same crime for the Sudra exceed far more in degree than for a Brahman. The reason is this, that the jurisprudence of *Manusmriti* is not founded on truth and justice; instead it aims to preserve the *Dharma* in and through a caste-ordered society for the realization of the ultimate-universal Self (*Cf. Manusmriti* XII: 118-126).

Under the British

The British not until 1919 gave India a Constitution. This was a relief from the centuries of religious laws. However, there were controversies regarding this. Accordingly various statutory commissions were sent to India to find a possible solution to these objections by hearing the voice of the people. The British aimed to give justice to the people through the rule of law; however, the objection from the Indians to it was that it failed to represent the interest of the various interest groups. Broadly the major groups were the Hindu, the Muslim, the Untouchables and the minorities. Among the minorities were the Parsees, the Indian Christians, the Europeans and the Anglo-Indians.

Simon Commission: As per their commitment, the British Government was to appoint a Royal Commission at the end of ten years to revisit the Constitution. This they did in 1928 which became famous as the Simon Commission chaired by Sir John Simon. It was not their intention to violate the feelings of any group; instead it was to tone down the feeling of violence. This concern should be appreciated. But what transpired subsequently was a history of violence directed against the Untouchables.

The Simon Commission was opposed by the Congress on the grounds that it had excluded Indians from its composition. To assuage the feeling of opposition His Majesty's Government announced a round of discussion with the Indians after the work of this Commission was completed. Accordingly on 12th November 1930 King George-V inaugurated the Indian Round Table Conference to settle a new Constitution for India.

The Round Table Conference: The Conference was divided into nine Committees. The most important of which was the minorities committee which was assigned the task to settle the communal question. It was chaired by the Prime Minster, Ramsay MacDonald. The memorandum submitted by Dr Ambedkar to this Committee reveals the features of structural violence on the Dalits. The opening sentence of Condition No. 1 sets forth the political context of its times. This is what it states,

> The Depressed Classes cannot consent to subject themselves to majority rule in their present state of hereditary bondsmen. Before majority rule is established their emancipation from the system of untouchability must be an accomplished fact. It must not be left to the will of the majority. The Depressed classes must be made free citizens entitled to all the rights of citizenship in common with other citizens of this State.[5]

Politically India was at the throes of Independence. New if democracy was characterized by the rule of majority, then the Untouchables and minorities would not be free. It is clear from the above excerpt that this fear of Dr Ambedkar was that freedom from the British rule would not mean freedom for all people of India; rather the Dalits would be under the rule of privileged castes.

With Dalits as bondsmen within the caste-system, the fact of structural violence already was in place. Passively it was by exclusion of the Dalits from all social intercourse with other groups of privileged castes and actively it was done in the practice of forced labour and untouchability. For this reason in this memorandum Dr Ambedkar sought to abolish untouchability though the instrument of law. What he proposed under the clause *Infringement of Citizenship* which was to be added to the Part-XI of the Government of India Act-1919 reveals how structural violence actively operates. This is what his proposed injunction was,

> Whoever denies to any person, except for reasons by law applicable to persons of all classes and regardless of any previous condition of untouchability, the full enjoyment of any of the accommodations, advantages, facilities,

privileges of inns, educational institutions, roads, paths, streets, tanks, wells and other watering places, public conveyances on land , air, or water, theatres, or other places of public amusement, resort or convenience whether they are dedicated to or maintained or licensed for the use of the public shall be punished with imprisonment of either description for a term which may be extended to five years and shall also be liable to fine.[6]

What this injunction indicates is the prevailing condition of active violence against the Dalits by debarring all public places for them to access. Violence does not cease by declaration of Human Rights; rather the tyranny of the strong has to be controlled by fear of law and infliction of penalties.

It must be noted that in every Indian village the Dalits constitute a minority, residing in a segregated area, under the fear of a numerically strong caste groups. This majority resorts to any means to protect their benefits and dominance. The ferocity of active violence comes to fore when the police sides with the privileged castes and inflicts violence on Dalits. Numerous cases on records prove that this and other government departments instead of protecting the minorities and Dalits begin to harass them.[7]

Another example how structural violence actively occurs is revealed in the clause *Offence of Boycott* which Dr Ambedkar proposed to be added to the Part-XI of the Government of India Act 1919. This is what he proposed as the Clause,

A person shall be deemed to boycott another who—(a) refuses to let or let use or occupy any house or land, or to deal with, work for hire, or do business with another person, or to render to him or receive from him in service, or refuses to do any of the said things on the terms on which such things should commonly be done in the ordinary course of business, or (b) abstains from such social, professional or business relations as he should having regard to such existing customs in the community which are not inconsistent with any fundamental right or other rights of citizenship declared in the Constitution ordinarily maintained with such person, or (c) in any way injures, annoys or interferes with such other person in the exercise of his lawful rights.[8]

The background of this injunction is the violence caused due to economic systems especially in the villages, where the Dalits are totally dependent on the landed castes for their subsistence. As a result when the Dalits dared to exercise their constitutional rights the landed orthodox castes have mercilessly 'evicted them from their lands, stopped their employment and discontinued their remunerations as village servants'.[9] At other times violence was passive by way of boycotting i.e. stopping sale of essentials of daily use by the village *bania* to the Dalits. Concerning social boycott against Dalits Dr Ambedkar observes,

> We do not know of any weapon more effective than this social boycott which could have been invented for the suppression of the Depressed Classes. The method of open violence pales away before it, for it has the most far reaching and deadening effects. It is more dangerous because it passes as a lawful method consistent with the theory of freedom of contact. We agree that this tyranny of the majority must be put down with a firm hand.[10]

The proposed clause for *Protection against Discrimination* is another example of protection of the Dalits from infliction of violence. This is what the clauses say,

> (4) to be deemed fit for and capable of sharing without distinction the benefits of any religious or charitable trust dedicated to or created, maintained or licensed for the general public or for persons of the same faith and religion. (5) to claim full and equal benefit of all laws and proceedings for the security of person and property as is enjoyed by other subjects regardless of any previous condition of untouchability and be subject to like punishment pains and penalties and to none other.[11]

The above clauses 4 and 5 of this injunction indicate the extent to which of violence was practiced against the Dalits in the society. Violence against Dalits, whether structured, planned or sporadic, in the pre-independence era took dangerous proportions as listed below,

1) Bring false cases in village court and in the criminal courts.
2) Obtain, on application, waste lands from Government lying all-round the *paracheri*, as to impound the Pariah's cattle or obstruct the way to their temple.
3) Pull down huts and destroy the growth in the backyards.

4) Forcibly cut pariahs' crops and on being resisted charge them with theft and rioting.

5) Under misrepresentations, get them to execute documents by which they are afterwards ruined.

6) Cut off the flow of water from their fields.

7) Without legal notice have the property of sub-tenants attached for the land-lords' arrears of revenue.

What was true during the British era is true even to this day. It was, therefore, important that Dalits were not only to be empowered to turn the tide of politics but also to have adequate representation at all levels of the government to duly influence its actions and policies in the interest of Dalits. It was this concern that Dr Ambedkar represented at the Round Table Conference (1930-1931). Accordingly Dr Ambedkar proposed separate electorate for the Depressed Castes.

If these are active aspect of violence then there is a passive aspect too. This is the system of caste. It is characterized by *graded inequality, fixity of occupation* and *fixation of people* within their respective caste-groups.[12] All the three were fixed at the birth of a person. The root of this problem has been the caste system. The constitutional provisions under the British Governance and subsequently in the Independence era aimed to remove these disabilities of the Dalits. The task before us is to explore whether this was achieved.

Defeat of the Demand for Separate Electorate: A Historical Case of Structural Violence

The provisions inherent in the modern constitutional to curtail violence against untouchables or scheduled castes cannot be understood apart from what happened in 1931 Round Table Conference [RTC] culminating in 1932 Poona Pact. What needs to be taken into account is that Dalits suffer double fold i.e., by segregation and marginalization. In this sense Dalits truly are the minority of this country.

To understand the issue surrounding RTC one should know that in those times there were three types of electorates: the general, the joint and the separate.[13] The Ambedkar-Gandhi controversy was over the separate versus joint electorates for to the Depressed Classes. The fiasco in 1932 RTC came to light when Prime Minister Ramsey McDonald took a written undertaking from all the Indian delegates, including Gandhi, to accept his verdict as final and binding, and later gave his unilateral decision to grant the privilege of separate electorates to the Depressed Classes.

Of course Gandhi did not accept this verdict despite his signing on the paper. He had to undertake fast-unto-death the threat of which he thought would work on the British.[14] It did not, and so being honour-bound could not withdraw but was forced to continue the Epic Fast.[15] At the end of the day Dr Ambedkar had to save Gandhi's life by reluctantly signing the Poona Pact (September 1932). In return the Depressed Classes had an increased number of Reserved Seats in the Legislative Assemblies but lost 'political weapon beyond reckoning'.[16] The violence of it he described in vivid terms. This is what Dr Ambedkar wrote,

> The Poona Pact was only the first blow inflicted upon the Untouchables and that the Hindus who disliked it were bent on inflicting on it other blows as and when circumstances gave them a occasion to do so.[17]

The fig leaf offered to the Dalits in the Poona Pact of reservation in principle has continued to operate even in the present Indian Constitution.

Under the Indian Constitution

The present Constitution of India provides what Gandhi promoted, namely, a caste based society but free of untouchability. His thoughts became a school of Gandhism. In Gujarati Journal called *Navajivan* 1921-22 Gandhi elaborated his views stating that "If Hindu Society had been able to stand it is because it is founded on the caste system".[18] As it could be accepted, he further stated that 'interdining or intermarriage is not necessary for promoting national unity'.[19] These points though unacceptable are understandable, but the surprising element in it is his line of reasoning. This is what Gandhi wrote,

> Taking food is as dirty an act as answering the call of nature. The only difference is that after answering the call of nature we get peace while after eating food we get discomfort. Just as we perform the act of answering the call of nature in seclusion so also the act of taking food must be done in seclusion.[20]

Truth indeed is stranger than fiction! So also the present Indian Constitution though it has outlawed untouchability (Article-17) it does not proscribe caste system. In other words social segregation and inequality are not viewed as unlawful per se. Consequently, passive violence through structured system of caste continues unchallenged and unabated till now.

The Constitution of independent India, drawn under the Chairmanship of Dr Ambedkar, ensured that all citizens of the country were treated equally. Hence, one person one vote and one vote one value was put in place. However, the Constitution did take into consideration that unequal people could not be treated equally under the law. Accordingly provisions were made for compensatory discrimination through Reservations and quota for the Scheduled Castes and Tribes. Such discrimination was fair.

Surprise may well be expressed on the Presidential Ordinance of 1950 which deleted those converted to Buddhism, Sikhism, Islam and Christianity from the schedule. Subsequently the Sikhs in 1956 and then the Buddhists in 1990 were included, but Muslims and Christians have not been included till date. What does this mean? Only that, that restrictions on freedom have been placed on Dalits to choose and practice a religion they desire. This also is a situation of violence as there is no protection against this discrimination.

RELIGION AND CULTURE: ANCIENT AND MODERN

Hindus

It goes without saying that the core of Hinduism is caste system. Unlike Christianity Hinduism is not an organized religion, but it is an *organizing* religion. It organizes society into castes. The idea of caste is rooted in Verna. Some people like to make a distinction between the two by saying that *verna* is occupation based concept of the division of society which is determined by innate qualities; whereas caste detracts by making occupation hereditary. In the *verna* system each person could do what was innate in him/her from among the four castes: Brahmin, Kshatriya, Vaishya and Shudra. Thus educating, defending, trading and serving could be chosen according to a person's capability or as handed by the family. In contrast to *verna*, the caste-system had fixed occupations by birth.

However, the situation gets more complicated when besides fixing occupation by birth, the status of castes is graded unequally. Here the Brahmin is at the top of the social pinnacle and Shudra at its base. Consequently Dalits, even below the Shudra, become segregated *bahishkrit* and untouchable *achoot*. In this way violence gets permanently structured. In due course of time Manu's Laws added extraordinary violence to the already existing situation. It consistently imposed discrimination in prescriptive and proscriptive laws. In order to show the superiority of the Brahmin, the penalty awarded to the Shudra was greater and to a Brahmin less.

Muslims

As such Islam is an egalitarian religion. However in the Indian subcontinent Muslims adapted their community to the social context by imitating caste-like practices. This in effect causes a condition of violence to exist. Dr Ambedkar found out this caste based character of Indian Muslim community from Census Records of 1901 for Bengal.

The fundamental point that he highlighted was the three social divisions in the Muslim society: *Ashraf*, *Ajlaf* and *Arzal*. The conventional division of Sheikh, Saiad, Moghul and Pathan were of no consequence in Bengal. The *Ashraf* are the noble class of Muslims which includes Saiads, Sheikhs, Pathans, Moghul, Mallick and Mirza. The *Ajlaf* are lower classes of cultivating Sheikhs, Darzi, Jolaha, Dhobi and Hajjam. The *Arzal* are the degraded classes of Hijra, Halalkhor, Lalbegi, Mehtar and Mocha.[21] At the same time the three Muslim groups Sunni; Shia and Momins are segregated in many castes-like groups that do not intermarry.[22] The result is that the Indian Muslim community is afflicted with the same disabilities as the Hindus; but Dr Ambedkar observed that there was something more that added to this already existing violent social situation. It was the system of Purdah.

He observed that the violence of *purdah* system was like perpetual social boycott. The women were segregated from the males. Even within the family they were confined to live in the annexes, garden and backyards. Many women have to share in single rooms causing lack of privacy. Dr Ambedkar's study of the consequences of the purdah system is revealing indeed. This is what he wrote,

> These burka (veil) women walking in the streets is one of the most hideous sights one can witness in India. Such seclusion cannot but have its deteriorating effects upon the physical constitution of Muslim women. They are usually victims of anaemia, tuberculosis and pyorrhoea. Purdah deprives Muslim women of mental and moral nourishment.[23]

Dr Ambedkar is quick to add that purdah is not only confined to Muslims but is observed in the Hindu society too. Fortunately the condition in our times has improved due to the spread of modernity and medical care.

Sikhs

If caste system is the condition of violence in the Indian society then even the Sikh community is not immune from this. It is well known that social segregation is imposed on the Mazabhi Sikhs of the Scheduled Caste origin. Similarly the Ramdasis are Sikh by religion but are listed as Scheduled Castes. Dr Ambedkar had noted that in the Light Sikh Infantry the Sikhs of scheduled Caste origin were recruited in the ranks whereas the Officers were Jats. The only difference is that the Sikhs do not believe in the divine sanction of Caste system, but this does not halt the condition of social violence affected by the replication of casteist practices within the Sikh community.

Christians

The Christian community is not immune from the structured violence either. It is silently present in their community. The Catholics and Protestants are divided into caste Christians and non-caste Christians who not only hesitate to eat together but avoid intermarriages and in many instances maintain separate churches.[24] This does not mean that there is no inter-dining but it is only in community-gatherings of church functions; however inter-caste marriages remain rare. Here it is a matter of casteist attitude. Such attitude certainly is not sanctioned by any Christian dogma or the Bible, but sustains the passive condition of violence by encouraging social status.

DOGMAS: ANCIENT AND MODERN

It is never quite clear what came first, a social practice or the scriptural injunction. In some instances scriptural injunction was an attempt to incorporate the normal social custom of those times.

Rig Veda

Over a period of time this scriptural texts came to be used to justify unjust practices. The *Purushukta* is a case in point. This is how it has been translated,

> When (the gods) divided Purusha, into how many parts did they cut him? What was his mouth? What arms (had he)? What two objects) are said (to have been) his thighs and feet? The *Brahman* was his mouth; the *Rajanya* was made his arms; the being called *Vaishya*, he was his thighs; *Shudra* sprang from his feet.[25]

This text now in Rig Veda Chapter-X became the scriptural evidence to justify the dogma of Verna *Vyavastha* i.e. the Caste system in the subsequent brahmanical literature for example, *Manusmriti*. It starts with the section on the method of laying down laws to maintain the caste distinctions. Manu based this on the *Purushasukta* text of the Rig Veda. The caste based organising of society and the proscriptive, prescriptive and penal injunctions are indicative of an oppressive system actively imposed and passively accepted by all. This in other words is a situation of structured violence.

Bhagwat Gita

The line of reasoning in the Bhagwat Gita is caste system. The violence of battle against one's own family is justified as caste duty. So Arjun being a *kshatriya* was coerced to fight. Not to fight would be to play the effeminate which was unbecoming of a *kshatriya*. Grief was unjustified because all things were perishable and to kill a human being was no killing because the *atman* is imperishable.[26]

Gita is clearly following the fixity of occupation and fixation of person in a group. Once this is accepted as a religious dogma then everyone is coerced to follow this as a religion. As a result of this emerges structured violence where the social relationships are constructed in silence on the brutality of caste practices of untouchability and segregation. Such coercion even at the point of infringement of Human Rights is not perceived as wrong. This dogma was also reinforced in the *Puranas* and the *Ramayana*.

IDEOLOGIES

The Challenge of Lal Salaam or the Christian offer of Shalom

The horrendous memories of Kandhamal have gone down in the annals of history of Christianity in India. Mayhem and arson against Christians in Orissa started on 23rd August 2008 when Swami Lakshmananda and four other Hindus were killed at their ashram admittedly by the

Maoists at Jalespata district of Kandhamal. The pogrom unleashed by the *Kandhas* continued for months directly aimed at the *Panas* who were Christians. Though both the groups are tribal, but the Panas have been treated as the untouchables as Kandhas became increasingly Hindu. Although, the Maoist took responsibility of Swamiji's gruesome murder, but no one believed and the killings of Christians and their forced re-conversion to Hinduism went on unabated.[27]

Maoists who belong to the Communist Party of India (Maoist) were responsible of the 1969 Naxalite uprisings. The party was subsequently banned and the Maoist liquidated. It is true that ideologically they oppose the inherent structural inequality of Indian society and therefore they advocate violent overthrow of the Indian State in order to re-establish a new society of equality. Now even if we disagree with their strategy of violence, yet the Maoist popularity among the masses in tribal belts of Bengal, Jharkhand, Orissa, Andhra Pradesh and Chhattisgarh is a fact to reckon with. Their other incarnations were the Maoist Communist Centre (MCC) and People's War Group (PWG).

Arundhati Roy in her insightful article *Mr Chidambaram's War* presents plausible reason for this situation.[28] This is what she writes,

> Right now in central India the Maoists' guerrilla army is made up almost entirely of desperate poor tribal people living in conditions of such chronic hunger that it verges on famine of the kind we only associate with sub-Saharan Africa. They are people who, even after sixty years of India's so-called independence, have not had access to education, health care or legal redress. They are people who have been mercilessly exploited for decades, consistently cheated by small businessmen and moneylenders, the women raped as a matter of right by police and forest department personnel.[29]

The truth of this analysis has been known for a long time; what is of interest, however, is her conclusion. Analysing the violent scenario in the tribal areas this is what she writes about the tribal people,

> Their journey back to a semblance of dignity is due in large part to the Maoist cadre who have lived and worked and fought by their side for decades. If the tribals have taken up arms, they have done so because a

government which had given them nothing but violence and neglect now wants to snatch away the last things they have—their land.[30]

It is not the Maoist who is blamed here but the government's high handedness and insensitivity to the isolated communities. Such people have been treated as dispensable for all practical purposes. In fact the fear of Maoist carders has been hyped by those in authority. It is obvious that their fighters are ragged, undernourished and the majority of their soldiers have never seen a bus or a train. No agency can be absolved of violence, but the fault of legitimate authorities is far greater. Arundhati explains that,

> In order to keep its better-off citizens absolutely safe from these dangerous people, the government had declared war on them. A war, which it tells us, may take between three and five years to win. Odd, isn't it, that even after the Mumbai attacks of 26/11, the government was prepared to talk with Pakistan? It is prepared to talk to China. But when it comes to waging war against the poor, it's playing hard.[31]

Indeed it will be hard for the government forces to distinguish between the Maoist and an innocent tribal in those deep forests. The bow and arrow carrying adivasis will be targeted and killed perhaps in hundreds. Operation Green Hunt is merely a beginning to totally subjugate the tribals in order to hand over their mineral-rich lands and hills to the multinational corporations. It is to this that Lal Salaam of Maoist comes as a challenge.

Understanding the Scope of Violence

To study the nature of military operations and political domination, though significant to understand violence, is beyond the scope of this essay. We have covered what we could under the section of ideology. The aim is to highlight the point that structured violence need not always be through the violation of physical faculties; rather it is deeply ingrained in society and in the thinking of people and institutionalised through cultural practices justified by religion and quietly accepted by victims. The results of this are clear before us. For instance, Dalits have been devalued, discredited and discriminated. So what do we learn from this?

First lesson for us is to change our understanding of violence to widen its scope to include not only action but systems that perpetuate and maintain the social stratification especially of the caste system. Structural violence is a diminished quality of life; rather than ferocity of action. It is an institutionalized social condition; rather than an occurrence. The second thing we must learn is to identify the source that justifies and reinforces it. In the Indian context we have seen that it is the law, religion and culture both in its antique and contemporary expressions that is responsible for this. Thirdly, the challenge before us is to overcome this violence with peace. Here we need to delve into our own Judaeo-Christian heritage of peace *Shalom*, and non-ciolence. This we need to explore and promote as our contribution to the Indian culture and society. The *Lal Salaam* of the Maoist is not red peace but the red salute of the communist comrades who are up in arms against the oppressors. This violence is not of the thugs but of ideologically driven conviction of the Communist Manifesto. Interestingly *Salaam* and *Shalom* have the same root and meaning, namely, peace.

WHATEVER MIGHT BE THE SHAPE OF VIOLENCE, ONE THING IS OBVIOUS THAT DALIT AND ADIVASI ARE AFFECTED BY IT IN A FAR GREATER MEASURE THAN ANY OTHER PEOPLE. The reason for is because our people are already made weak by the structured violence of caste. Centuries of practice against them in the form of untouchability, segregation and isolation has made them poor, helpless and powerless. This should propel our disciplined exercise of theological refection in order to understand God; how he is working among our people in the face of violence. It is in our interest to explore further how faith sustains our people to positively take up the painful challenge of our struggles for justice and at the same time transcend the pain of it in our journey to become human beings in this world.

Endnotes

[1] B.R. Ambedkar, Vol-17. 2003. p. 104.

[2] Classical Dictionary of Hindu Mythology and Religion (1928) p. 201.

[3] B.R. Ambedkar, *Writings and Speeches* Vol-3 'Literature of Brahmanism' (1987) p. 240.

[4] B.R. Ambedkar, *idem.,* 240.

[5] B.R. Ambedkar, *idem.,* Vol.9. p. 42.

[6] B.R. Ambedkar, *idem.,* p. 43.

[7] James Massey, *Minorities and Religious Freedom in a Democracy.* (2003) Manohar Pub. New Delhi. pp. 51-65.

[8] B.R. Ambedkar, *Writings and Speeches.* Vol.9. p. 45.

[9] B.R. Ambedkar, *idem.,* p. 44.

[10] B.R. Ambedkar, *idem.,* p. 44.

[11] B.R. Ambedkar, *idem.,* p. 47.

[12] B.R. Ambedkar *Writings and Speeches* Vol-13. (1987). pp. 106-113.

[13] B.R. Ambedkar *Writings and Speeches* Vol-9 (1991) p. 150.

[14] B.R. Ambedkar, *idem.,* p. 87.

[15] B.R. Ambedkar, *idem.,* p. 87.

[16] B.R. Ambedkar, *idem.,* p. 90.

[17] B.R. Ambedkar, *idem.,* p. 93.

[18] B.R. Ambedkar, *idem.,* p. 275.

[19] B.R. Ambedkar, *idem.,* p. 276.

[20] B.R. Ambedkar, *idem.,* p. 276.

[21] B.R. Ambedkar, *idem.,* p. 229.

[22] B.R. Ambedkar, *idem.,* p. 272.

[23] B.R. Ambedkar, *Writings and Speeches* Vol-8 (1990) p. 230.

[24] B.R. Ambedkar, *Writings and Speeches* Vol-9 (1991) p. 273.

25 Muir's Sanskrit Text: Vol-1 (1872) p. 7.

26 B.R. Ambedkar, *Writings and Speeches* Vol-3 (1987) p. 377.

27 *People's Reporter.* Vol-21 Issue-17. Mumbai Sept. 10-25, 2008.

28 *Outlook* (9th Nov, 2009) pp. 30-31.

29 *Ibid.,* p. 33.

30 *Ibid.,* p. 34.

31 *Ibid.,* p. 34.

CONSTITUTION · DEVELOPMENT · DEMOCRACY

The fourth section contains the last set of three essays. These are on the Indian Constitution, Development and Democracy. The thread holding these together is justice. Here three things must be kept in mind; firstly, in the absence of justice it is not possible to guarantee the delivery of benefits reaped from development to Dalits, women, children, elderly and minorities; secondly, justice can be best sought and preserved by people who benefit from it; and thirdly, the role of democracy in the pursuit and protection of justice should not be underestimated.

In this line of reasoning the first essay is on the Indian "Constitution". Its Preamble declares that it aims to 'secure to all Indian citizens, Justice: social, economic and political'. The Romans in the antiquity viewed justice in Latin as *iustitia* i.e. joining. In the social context it implies fitting people of diverse capabilities suitably in the overall social order. Quite differently the biblical view proposes justice as obedience to the law of God *Torah*. Attention should be drawn to the thumb rule of biblical justice. It is serving what a person deserves. Hence, an eye for an eye and a tooth for a tooth. Nothing more or nothing less than what was deserved was to be served by the judge (Cf. Lev. 24.20). Secondly, justice was to be administered without partiality. Hence, the rich and the poor, the monarch and the peasant, the citizen and the foreigner were to be awarded the same penalties without fear or favour by the judges. (Cf. Lev. 24.22)

It is remarkable that the leading principles of the ancient Torah are still applicable. For instance how should free people behave and deal with others. Similarly all free people are equal under the law, workers have the right of leisure under Sabbath injunctions (Exodus 20); witness must bear truthful testimony before a judge (Exodus 20); the resident aliens have right of food and protection (Exodus 23.9); and workers have the right of wages (Deuteronomy 24.14-15). All these are aspects of human rights. In this light we must appreciate the Indian constitutional provision of the Fundamental Rights, Judicial System and Directive Principles as aspects of justice to sustain human rights.

The second essay on "Development" presents happiness as a result of just development. Here we should understand justice in its Greek form *dikaiosune* or "virtue in action". It is used in the Greek New Testament and translated as righteousness. For Aristotle, justice was not simply the *right order* of the *polis*; instead it was the *right behaviour* of people with one another. This is not a strict compliance to law but the phrase 'the just person justices' sums it up. Similarly, Jesus taught 'Do to others what you want them to do to you' (Matt. 7.12). It means equality. In the Indian context however, the caste system forms the unequal social order where people hold to their dignity only by trampling on the dignity of the other. This injustice is the cause of backwardness of our people. This is because *Manusmriti* the law of the ancients had perverted justice. Development, therefore, is justice which seeks to remove the evil of caste system that brings poverty and backwardness.

The concluding essay on "Democracy" sums up Dr Ambedkar's vision for society where people will be equal, free, secure and happy. This is best insured in a government which is elected by its people and can be dismantled by them. These ideas of society and government are in harmony the vision of the new earth of the Bible. This shared ideal motivates Christians to develop their nation which will be free from caste and where all people can flourish.

Chapter 10

Constitution

It is axiomatic for Christians to hold that those who belong to Christ also belong to his Kingdom. It will be appropriate therefore for us to dwell on the social values of the Kingdom of God and interlace it with the Indian Constitution whose objective is to integrate the people of India as a unified nation. The vision is to see India as a flourishing nation administered by justice. To appreciate the harmonies of the Constitution-of-India with the Kingdom-of-God we must understand the teachings of both who propounded the Constitution and the Kingdom, namely, the Lord Jesus and Dr. Bhimrao Ramji Ambedkar. The question before us is this, what is the future relevance of Dr. Ambedkar's vision?

The Foundational Values of the Kingdom and the Constitution
So first let us scan the teaching of the Lord Jesus about the Kingdom. The point to note is that in Greek *baselia* denotes the sovereign. Accordingly I will use the word 'Reign' instead of 'Kingdom'. In the teachings of Jesus references to the Reign-of-God, which transcends the governments of the world was with the view that God was sovereign over those who accepted his Reign. However, for the purpose of our theme we will focus on social and moral aspects of God's sovereignity orthis reign. Some themes which are social in nature connected with this are—*power of unity* when Jesus refuted the allegation of Beelzebub's

power (Matt 12.28 ff); *fecundity* in his parable of the Sower (Matt 13.23); *beneficence* in the parable of the Mustard Seed (Matt 13.31); *freedom* of to be *generous* and insistence on *equality* in the parable of the Labourers in the Vineyard (Matt 20.1-16); *inclusiveness* in the parable of the Wedding Banquet (Matt 22.1-10); *cultivation of wisdom* in the parable of the Ten Bridesmaid (Matt 25.1-13); *enterprise* in the parable of the Talents (Matt 25.14-30) and *progress* in the parable of the Growing Seed (Mark 4.26-29). These parables pertaining to God's Reign, namely—power, unity, fecundity, freedom, generosity, equality, inclusion, wisdom, enterprise and progress—have social value with which we can also measure justice. Indeed justice is the fundamental feature both of God's Reign and the Indian Constitution. Hence my theme the kingdom and the constitution.

If we seek the antonyms of these values then we will have a collection of words like—divided, barren, selfish, exclusive, weighed by drudgery, exploited and backward. All these words denote the consequence of selfish human desires and indicate resultant injustice and inequality. We may recall that our Lord Jesus reminded his disciples that justice, mercy and faith were the weightier matters of the law (Matt 23.23). Indeed the Law of Moses had instructed to the people of Israel that

> "Justice, and only justice, you shall pursue" (Deut 16.20).

As far as the Indian Constitution was concerned justice rings out right at its start. This is what its Preamble proclaims,

> WE, THE PEOPLE OF INDIA having solemnly resolved to constitute India into a SOVEREIGN (SOCIALIST) SECULAR DEMOCRATIC REPUBLIC, and to secure to all its citizens:
>
> JUSTICE, social, economic and political;
>
> LIBERTY of thought, expression, belief, faith and worship;
>
> EQUALITY of status and of opportunity;
>
> And to promote among them all

FRATERNITY, assuring the dignity of the individual (and integrity of the nation);

In our constituent assembly this twenty-sixth day of November, 1949, do hereby adopt, enact and give to ourselves this constitution.

The basis of the Indian Constitution is justice which resonates with God's Reign and here the hand of Dr. Ambedkar is clearly visible. He held that the other name for justice was liberty, equality and fraternity which the French revolutionists had taken from their Judaeo-Christian tradition. It is very interesting to note here that he steered clear from using the word "truth". Some reasons for this were that for him the inherent nature of justice as truth was axiomatic; secondly, Dr. Ambedkar did not want to recycle what Mahatma Gandhi had popularized, of which "truth" was one. The term "*satyagraha*" is a case in point.

Before we discuss how Dr. Ambedkar understood justice and its three aspects, namely, liberty, equality and fraternity, let us first outline the history of the compilation of the Indian Constitution.

Development of the Indian Constitution

The framing of the Indian Constitution has its own interesting history. India, under the British was governed as a colony under the Government of India Act 1935. In a way the Act was self-contradictory because despite constituting representational government of Indians it curtailed their participation, yet it envisaged their participation by offering a federal instead of unitary form of government. However, a federal union of India remained unfulfilled due to the princely states who wished to assert their autonomy by not joining the Federation. As the participation of Indians in the country's governance under the British was nominal, it was no secret that the actual control of the Indian administration was held by the British government through their Secretary of State, the Governor General and the Governors.

Obviously, this was deeply resented by Indians who began to demand complete independence *purna swaraj* from the British. Eventually in 1946 a Constituent Assembly was setup to draft a Constitution for free India. The work progressed at snail's pace due to political conflict between the Indian National Congress and the Muslim League. In 1947 the Westminster enacted the Indian Independence Act for the emergence of two independent countries, namely, India and Pakistan. On 15th August 1947 India gained her freedom. Thereafter the work of drafting a Constitution for India was taken in right earnest. Accordingly on 29th August 1947 a Drafting Committee was elected by the Constituent Assembly which under the chairmanship of Dr B.R. Ambedkar started its work immediately on 30th August and produced the complete draft of the Constitution consisting of 395 Articles and 8 Schedules. Finally, on November 26th, 1949 the Constitution of India was adopted and subsequently promulgated on 26th January 1950. On that day, "India," in the words of Dr Ambedkar, became "a democratic country."[1]

Having briefly surveyed the history let us return to the three basic themes of justice in the preamble, namely, liberty, equality and fraternity. Dr Ambedkar found that these were basically biblical values and we will do well to see that they can mould the future of our country provided we remain faithful to the Constitution. Dr Ambedkar in his *Closing Speech* had warned of the future,

> Who can say how the people of India and their Parties will behave? Will they uphold constitutional methods of achieving their purpose or will they prefer revolutionary methods of achieving them? If they adopt revolutionary methods; however good the Constitution may be, it requires no prophet to say that it will fail.[2]

At that time communism was in ascendency worldwide. Its influence was being increasingly felt in India too. But Dr Ambedkar did not live long enough to see its decline. With this background in mind let us state three aspects of Preamble of the Indian Constitution, justice, equality and fraternity. In this section we will explore the impact of Christian tradition on Dr Ambedkar's way of thinking.

Justice

Understanding of justice is deeply embedded in Dr Ambedkar's idea of religion and society. As he developed his theory in this field, he contended that the *ideal-scheme-of-divine-governance* which religions propounded offered one of the two schemes of social order. Either a religion offered hierarchical scheme where individual's interest was overlooked;[3] or it promoted egalitarian scheme where individuals right was affirmed. The former was incompatible with modern society because the focus of modernity was justice i.e. to protect individual's interest.[4] This line of reasoning reflected the fact that justice for individuals was possible only in a free and equal social order where distinctiveness and worth of every individual was recognized. This meant that individuals were to be awarded what he/she had deserved. Accordingly undeserved sufferings and disadvantages would be unjust as these would reinforce social inequality. In this line of thinking it would be unjust for a person to suffer by virtue of belonging to a disadvantaged class. We may recall that Jesus also in his Nazareth manifesto addressed injustice of social inequality. Applying prophet Isaiah's utterance to himself he spoke in the synagogue,

> The Spirit of the Lord is upon me,
> Because he has anointed me to
> Preach the good news to the poor.
> He has sent me to proclaim release to the captives,
> And recovering of sight to the blind,
> To set at liberty those who are oppressed,
> To proclaim the acceptable year of the Lord. (Luke 4.18-19).

In the Indian context "poor, captives, blind and oppressed" in the above text is applicable for Dalits as an obvious case in point. Justice would therefore entail reversal of conditions underwhich dalits suffer. It is very interesting to see that for two aspects of justice, namely, equality and fraternity, Dr Ambedkar found direct reference from the Christian tradition.

Equality

What Dr. Ambedkar underscored was that in its *ideal-scheme-of-divine-governance* a religion of modern society perceived God not as a father in any physical sense but as its moral governor. Accordingly God came to be revered as supreme moral being 'capable of absolute good and absolute virtue'.[5] In other words God was just. The question that now begs an answer is this, how did Dr Ambedkar explain God's justice specifically his goodness in the Christian tradition? In answer Dr Ambedkar pointed out that in the Judeo-Christian tradition God was understood as one who treated all human beings as equal. He used the Hebrew Bible to show that God did this in two ways, firstly by creating them in his own image so that none was inferior to the other. This is how the biblical text reads in the New Revised Standard version,

> Then God said, "Let us make humankind in our image, according to our likeness, and let them have dominion over the fish of the sea, and over the cattle, and over all the wild animals of the earth, and over every creeping thing that creeps upon the earth". So God created humankind in his image, in the *image of God* he created them male and female he created them.[6]

Secondly, God showed this by treating each personality as sacred[7] so that none was to suffer for the iniquity of the other. He found a passage in the Hebrew Bible to support his view.

> As a starting point for the discussion of the subject one may begin by referring to the words... where Jehova says to Ezekiel, 'Behold, all souls are mine; as the soul of the father, so also the soul of the son is mine; the soul that sinneth, it shall die ... the son shall not bear the iniquity of the father, neither shall the father bear the iniquity of the son; the righteousness of the righteous shall be upon him, and the wickedness of the wicked upon him.[8]

Here Dr Ambedkar emphasised individual's worth which he/she deserved.[9] Anything less than this would be unjust. Clearly in his view justice required that society, despite economic and political disparities must be prepared at least to treat people equally and with dignity.

This resonates with the parable of the Labourers in the Vineyard in Matthew 20.1-16, where the owner of a vineyard hired labourers to work after every two hours. At the end of the day he paid them all an equal wage. Does the payment of equal hire for unequal labour reflect in justice? We must read the text from the perspective of justice, for instance, the vine-owner hired the labourers even later in the day was an act of compensation and compassion. It was to compensate the fall in demand of their services. This was not their fault. The owner of the vineyard saved the labourers from being unemployed which could seal their fate for the worst. This was compassion.

Another way to look at this parable is to appreciate John Rawl's approach to justice as fairness. Here all labourers were equally paid for unequal input of work. The point is to appreciate the fairness to sustain each labourer by paying a meaningful wage. Granted the rightness of wages in proportion to the input of work by the labourers, but it would be unfair if at the end of the day that amount was inadequate to sustain their life. In a similar way the provision of equality in the Indian Constitution should be understood in the light of fairness and equity.

In the Indian Constitution the provision of Right to Equality in Articles 14 to 18 is legal. It begins by stating that,

> The State shall not deny to any person equality before the law or the equal protection of laws within the territory of India.

In law this principle has to be practiced by the prohibition of discrimination on grounds of religion, race, caste, sex or place of birth as elaborated in Article 15. The next Article 16 allows compensatory discrimination as a fair favour to backward classes. The most important Article-17 abolishes the practice of untouchability downright. It states,

> Untouchability is abolished and its practice in any form is forbidden. The enforcement of any disability arising out of "untouchability" shall be an offence punishable in accordance with law.

Although with legal equality, the provision for every adult citizen to vote procured political equality for all people, yet it failed to guarantee social justice. It must be noted that resistance to this was embedded in the caste system. And so in his *Closing Speech to the first Constituent Assembly* Dr. Ambedkar had said,

> On the 26th January 1950 we are going to enter into a life of contradictions. In politics we will have equality and in social and economic life we will have inequality. In politics we will be recognizing the principle of one man one vote and one vote one value. In our social and economic life, we shall, by reason of our social and economic structure, continue to deny the principle of one man one value. How long shall we continue to live this life of contradictions? How long shall we continue to deny equality in our social and economic life? If we continue to deny it for long, we will do so only by putting our political democracy in peril. We must remove this contradiction at the earliest possible moment or else those who suffer from inequality will blow up the structure of political democracy which this Assembly as so laboriously built up.[10]

One threat to democracy which was perceived as real in those times was communist ideology of violent revolution to overthrow the political system and its replacement by dictatorship of the proletariat till the emergence of the classless society. This ideology with its utopia of justice and peace by means of anarchy and dictatorship had to be evaded.

Fraternity

Another aspect of justice that Dr Ambedkar attributed to the Christian tradition was fraternity. According to Dr Ambedkar a just society will be manifested in the feeling of kingship and free intermingling of people with one another. He wrote,

> "Fraternity means a sense of common brotherhood of all Indians—of Indians being one people. It is the principle which gives unity and solidarity to social life."[11]

This is a vision for future because casteist society does not allow this by prohibiting inter-marriages and inter-dining between different castes. In his monograph *Philosophy of Hinduism* Dr. Ambedkar explains two trajectories of human relationship which run in opposite directions. One trajectory is individualism. Those who live by this view are self-centred. Every individual regards him/herself as an end itself and look after their own interests thereby developing a non-social and even an anti-social self. The opposite is the fellow feeling or fraternity. Those who hold this view identify themselves with others and seek to bring benefit to others.[12] To underscore his point Dr. Ambedkar gave a direct citation from the New Testament and from the writings of Pilgrim Fathers. This is what he wrote,

> Fraternity is the name of the disposition of an individual to treat men as the object of reverence and love and the desire to be in unity with his fellow beings. This statement is well expressed by Paul when he said, 'of one blood are all nations of men. There is neither Jew nor Greek, neither bond nor free, neither male not female, for yet all one in Christ Jesus.' Equally well was it expressed when the Pilgrim Fathers on their landing at Plymouth said: 'We are knit together as a body in the most sacred covenant of the Lord…by virtue of which we hold ourselves tied to all care of each others' good and of the whole.' These sentiments are of the essence of fraternity.[13]

Fraternity as viewed here is not merely social intermingling but more than that. It involves an inner disposition to meet a fellow being with respect and love. Later he also explored a basis of fraternity in the Buddhist tradition of friendship *maitri*.

Seven Merits of the Indian Constitution

The Constitution of India has 395 Articles spread over XXII Parts. Dr. Ambedkar identifies seven merits of the Indian Constitution in his *Closing Speech of the First Constituent Assembly* in November 1949. These merits are like seven valuable gems:

1. Political democracy; 2. Parliamentary democracy; 3. Protection of private property; 4. Fundamental Rights; 5. Facile procedure for

amendment; 6. Federalism; and 7. Overriding power of the Centre. Let us discuss these merits in some detail below.

The first merit in the above schedule is *political democracy* i.e. a government of people's participation by forming and running it. He wrote that India became "a democratic country in the sense that (it had) a government of the people, by the people and for the people."[14] In the same speech he explained it as a "principle of one man (*sic* person) one vote and one vote one value."[15] In other words, India, by adopting the new Constitution had become a democratic republic. But he saw dangers lurking in the future unless people were alert to avoid falling into the trap of undemocratic methods. This is what he said,

> If we wish to maintain democracy not merely in form, but also in fact, what must we do? The first thing in my judgement we must do is to hold fast to constitutional methods of achieving our social and economic objectives. It means we must abandon the method of civil disobedience, non-cooperation and satyagraha. ... There can be no justification for these unconstitutional methods. These methods are nothing but the Grammar of Anarchy and the sooner they are abandoned, the better for us.[16]

His advice was with the view that in the colonial period the constitutional way to achieve social and economic objectives was closed and so unconstitutional measures could be condoned, but with a constitution in place there was no justification for such measures. This was a direct hit to Gandhi's political methods.

The second is the description of *parliamentary democracy* comes out in his exhortation to the members of the Constituent Assembly and, thereafter, to all citizens of India that they should achieve their goals by constitutional methods, through the Parliament. Accordingly the Constitution provided that,

> The Parliament for the Union which shall consist of the President and two Houses to be known respectively as the Council of States and the House of the People.[17]

The Indian Parliament was to be a bicameral body with the upper and lower Houses i.e. Rajya Sabha and Lok Sabha where proceedings would follow democratic rules. It is very interesting to note that the Parliamentary procedure was also there in the antiquity among the Buddhist Bhikshu Sanghas.[18] However, Dr. Ambedkar pointed out that at some point of time India lost this system. Looking into the future with a degree of alarm he wondered whether she might lose it again. He wrote,

> It is quite possible in a country like India—where democracy from its long disuse must be regarded as something quite new—there is danger of democracy giving place to dictatorship. It is quite possible for this new born democracy to retain its form but give place to dictatorship in fact. If there is a landslide, the danger of the second possibility becoming actuality is much greater.[19]

The reason why Dr. Ambedkar forewarned us was because he appreciated the value of democracy as a conference of different and contradictory voices which were given fair chance to be heard in the legislative bodies. Decisions were to be made only after hearing all the voices. Loss of this liberty, which is the hall mark of democracy, would be a death blow to the "down-trodden classes which are tired to being governed; they are impatient to govern themselves."[20]

The third merit was the provision for the *protection of private property*. Originally this meant that citizens had a right to own private property and so the government had to ensure its protection. That is reason why he provided the constitutional principle that acquisition of private property entailed a just compensation.[21] However, this Article was eventually repealed and an amended form of 31 A, B and C was inserted which empowers the government to acquire, take over properties, amalgamate corporations, and abolish or modify Rules of Corporate bodies for public interest. Along with this a new Article—300A—was also inserted which states that no one was to be deprived of property except by the authority of law.

No person shall be deprived of his property save by authority of law.[22]

This was to counter the communist ideology of State ownership of property and also against rouge State which could acquire property without compensation.

The fourth merit was the provision of *Fundamental Rights.*[23] These Articles (12 to 35) which are published in Part-III of the Indian Constitution consists of six Rights. Their advantage is for curtailing cultural domination of the majority, as well as, to protect and nurture the minorities. The value of these six Rights is to cultivate multiculturalism in society and in so doing maintain social and territorial integrity of India where freedom and justice would abound. These Rights pertain to *1.* Social equality (Articles 14-18); *2.* Freedom (Articles 19-22); *3.* Against exploitation (Articles 23-24); *4.* Religion (Articles 25-28); *5.* Culture and Education (Articles 29-30); and *6.* Constitutional Remedies (Articles 32-35). The value of these Articles of Rights is that they are practical applications of justice which Dr. Ambedkar had showed to be equality, liberty and fraternity.

The fifth merit is the *facile procedure of amendment* of the Constituent was to ensure its relevance and drive. He defended this provision of the Constitution by citing Jefferson, a great American statesman who played an important role in making the American Constitution. Jefferson had said,

> We may consider each generation as a distinct nation, with a right, by the will of the majority, to bind themselves, but none to bind the succeeding generation, more than the inhabitants of another country.[24]

Keeping in view that the amendment of the Constitutions of Canada, America and Australia required some extraordinary terms and conditions to be met, he argued that he had provided an easy procedure of obtaining a 2/3rd majority of the members to amend it. The value of this is in updating the relevance of the Constitution for the contemporary generation.

The sixth feature of the Constitution was the *principle of Federalism*. This feature was particularly thought out for the Indian context which was divided into several States with an elected State government. Dr. Ambedkar said,

> The basic principle of Federalism is that the Legislative and Executive authority is partitioned between the Centre and the State, not by any law to be made by the Centre but by the Constitution itself. This what the Constitution does. The States under our constitution are in no way dependent upon the Centre for their legislative or executive authority. The Centre and the State are coequal in this matter.[25]

The careful balance of power to legislate ensures that on the one hand the Central government does not dominate the State governments and on the other the States remain embedded in the Indian union. The Constitution carefully divides the legislative and the executive powers between the Centre and the States by the Constitution, which ensures that the Centre does not function on its own whims and fancies to decide what pertains to the States.

The seventh merit of the Constitution that merits our attention is about the overriding *power of the Centre* over the States. The usefulness of this provision is to address extraordinary situations. This is how Dr. Ambedkar explains it,

> But before condemning the Constitution for containing such overriding powers, certain considerations must be borne in mind. The first is that these overriding powers do not form the normal feature of the Constitution. Their use and operation are expressly confined to emergencies only. The second consideration is: Could we avoid giving overriding powers to the Centre when an emergency has arisen?[26]

Overriding power of the Centre for emergencies is based on the argument that ultimately only the Centre has the authority to command the loyalty of the citizens. Dr. Ambedkar contended that,

> In an emergency [the States] should take into consideration, alongside their own local interests, the opinions and interests of the nation as a whole.[27]

Dr. Ambedkar conceded that the seven merits of the Constitution above were not absolute or that they could not be changed. What he held was that "they are the views of the present generation and of the members of the Constituent Assembly."[28]

Looking ahead into the Future

The Constitution of India stands midway between the "people-of-India" as the present reality and "the-Indian-nation" as a future ideal, like the sacraments which are midway between the 'present' and the 'future' of the Reign of God. We can say that in the Constitution the two Indias, i.e., the present and future—overlap. The point here is that Dr. Ambedkar did not concede to view India yet as a nation; instead for him India was still a people. Therefore, his consistent reference was "People of India". This is obvious in the Preamble of our Constitution written by Dr Ambedkar which starts with the statement "WE, THE PEOPLE OF INDIA". This expression was resented by the politically minded Indians who might have preferred to use "the Indian nation". Against this Dr Ambedkar argued,

> I am of opinion that in believing that we are a nation, we are cherishing, a great delusion. How can people divided into several thousands of castes be a nation? The sooner we realize that we are not as yet a nation in the social and psychological sense of the word, the better for us ... in India there are castes. The castes are anti-national. In the first place, because they bring about separation in social life. They are anti-national; also because they generate jealousy and antipathy between the caste and caste. But we must overcome all these difficulties if we wish to become a nation.[29]

The future of India is to become a nation. Our progress into this will depend on the annihilation of the castes and caste-system. How can this be achieved? In Dr. Ambedkar's view the answer was social revolution. He held that this revolution was not a violent overthrow of the State but conversion to an egalitarian religion.[30] His single argument for this was the need for kinship which he elaborated in various ways. From what he wrote I deduced five reasons for him to advocate conversion of the depressed castes,[31]

One, convert to remove isolation; two, convert to remove inferiority complex; three, convert to remove social discrimination; four, convert to remove a stinking name; and five, convert to remove untouchability. Furthermore in his Dadar Speech on 30th May 1936 he said,

> Unless you establish close relations with some other society, unless you join some other religion, you cannot get strength from outside. It clearly means, you must leave your present religion and assimilate yourselves with some other society. Without that, you cannot gain the strength of that society. So long as you do not have strength, you and your future generations will have to lead your lives in the same pitiable condition.[32]

In his own case he eventually converted to Neo-Buddhism *Navayana* with Mahars and made constitutional provision to profess, practice and propagate it. Very much like the "here-and-now" versus "the Future" coming of God's Reign, we are on the way but not there yet. The adherence to the Indian Constitution is where the integration of the People-of-India overlaps with the future emergence of the Nation-of-India.

Responsibility of Christian Citizens

From the above discussion it is obvious that Dr Ambedkar had discovered the moral principle of *justice* in the biblical tradition and *democracy* in the Buddhist. These two aspects of Constitution were foundational principles to modernize the people of India including Dalits, Adivasi and women. The advantage was that Bible and Buddha belonged to the antique stage and therefore any hierarchical scheme propounded by another religion of antiquity to create an unequal social order could be adequately challenged of its authenticity. There was no excuse to support a social order at the cost of individual liberty and there was no reason to advocate social inequality to maintain social order on the basis of any scriptural injunction however ancient it might claim to be.

The clue for what is expected of Christians, which also is expected of all citizens, is to destroy two demons. Both are described in Dr.

Ambedkar's speech. The first one is infidelity and its twin treachery and the second is caste and its twin creed. Both of these are twin demons which create division, waste, selfishness, exclusion, drudgery, exploitation and backwardness. These retard progress and prosperity of our people which comes with integration, enthusiasm and loyalty. Dr. Ambedkar quoted Abraham Lincoln who had picked a phrase of Jesus "A house divided against itself cannot stand very long." These evils are diametrically opposite to the values of God's Reign, which, as we had seen at the beginning of this paper, are: power, unity, fecundity, freedom, generosity, equality, wisdom, enterprise and progress.

In the present Indian context the emphasis on "culture" for creating a national consciousness is being given greater importance than "justice". There is an increasing discrimination against Christians and Muslims whose religion and practices are perceived as invasion of culture. This has to be countered by the values of the Reign of God which we have to profess, practice and propagate. This is the key for progress and prosperity of the People-of-India and for the emergence of the Nation-of-India as a casteless society. This was the vision of Dr. Ambedkar, which he has enshrined in the Indian Constitution. There can be no negotiation on this at any stage. I leave the slogan with you all,

PROFESS !   PRACTICE !   PROPAGATE !

This is Dr. Ambedkar's gift to us, the founder of the democratic republic of India.

Endnotes

[1] B.R. Ambedkar, *Closing Speech of the first Constituent Assembly of India*, (1949), published in 'Great Speeches of Modern India.' Rudrangshu Mukherjee (ed.), New Delhi: Random House. 2007. p. 216.

[2] B.R. Ambedkar, *idem.*, p. 211.

[3] B.R. Ambedkar, 'The Hindu Social Order', *Writings and Speeches* Vol.3. (1946), p. 99.

[4] B.R. Ambedkar, 'Philosophy of Hinduism' (1941), *Writings and Speeches* Vol.3. pp. 19-20.

[5] B.R. Ambedkar, *idem.,* p. 16.

[6] Book of *Genesis* Chapter-1 verse 26-27.

[7] B.R. Ambedkar, 'The Hindu Social Order' (1946), p. 99.

[8] Ezekiel 18.4 & 20.

[9] B.R. Ambedkar, 'The Hindu Social Order' (1946), *idem.,* p. 99.

[10] B.R. Ambedkar, *Closing Speech of the first Constituent Assembly of India,* (1949), p. 219.

[11] *Ibid.,* B.R. Ambedkar, p. 219.

[12] B.R. Ambedkar, 'Philosophy of Hinduism' (1941) *Writings and Speeches* Vol.3. p. 44.

[13] B.R. Ambedkar, 'The Hindu Social Order' (1946) *Writings and Speeches* Vol.3. p. 97.

[14] B.R. Ambedkar, *Closing Speech of the first Constituent Assembly of India,* (1949), published in 'Great Speeches of Modern India.' Rudrangshu Mukherjee (edt.), New Delhi: Random House. 2007. p. 216.

[15] *Ibid.,* p. 218.

[16] *Ibid.,* p. 217.

[17] *The Constitution of India.* Article 79.

[18] He held that, "(The Sanghas) knew and observed all the rules of the Parliamentary Procedure known to the modern times. They had rules regarding seating arrangements, rules regarding Motions, Resolutions, Quorum, Whip, Counting of Votes, Voting by Ballot, Censure Motion, Regularization, *Res Judicata* etc. Although these rules of Parliamentary Procedure were applied by the Buddha to the meetings of the Sanghas, he must have borrowed them from the rules of the Political Assemblies functioning in the country in his time." B.R. Ambedkar, *Closing Speech of the first Constituent Assembly of India,* (1949), *ibid.* p. 217.

[19] *Ibid.,* p. 217.

[20] *Ibid.,* p. 220.

[21] *Ibid.,* p. 212.

[22] *The Constitution of India.* Right to Property: Article 300 A.

[23] *Ibid.,* Articles 12-25.

[24] B.R. Ambedkar, *Closing Speech of the first Constituent Assembly of India,* (1949) p. 212.

[25] *Ibid.,* p. 213.

[26] *Ibid.*, p. 214.

[27] *Ibid.*, p. 213.

[28] *Ibid.*, p. 212.

[29] *Ibid.*, p. 220.

[30] B.R. Ambedkar, 'Away from the Hindus' (1936) *Writing and Speeches Vol. 5*, 1989, p. 403.

[31] *Idem.*, 418-20.

[32] B.R. Ambedkar, 'What way Emancipation' (1936) *Writing and Speeches Vol. 17.3*, 2003, p. 121.

Chapter 11

Development

What Dr. Ambedkar dealt with was not development as such, but on ideas that would bring about development for all sections of society. He developed at length his ideas of society's evolution and social reform. It will be appropriate that we understand these ideas and then see how we can apply them for development.

At this point of our discussion I need to present my understanding about evolution, development and reform which underlies the way I will use these terms in this essay. Evolution pertains to the inevitable changes from simple to complex stages in the biological life in response to the modification in environment, whereas development involves human intervention in community and environment in response to social problems; whereas reform, if adequately radical, would trigger evolution to advance to the next stage or it could initiate development of the society to a new phase.

As far as development is concerned we must hold on to two things together, namely, people's development and society's development. Both are practically indistinguishable but their distinction is useful for analytical purpose. Development, like evolution, indicates progress of society from simpler to a more complex stage. Having said that it must be clarified that Dr. Ambedkar's foundational position for all aspects of society was justice. This, therefore, should be equally applicable in the field of development. In other words all human interventions in community and environment for progress must be just. In other words justice will ensure that social development is not at the cost of individuals interest; rather the protection of individuals interest would constitute an important index to measure development of society. This is in line with Torah which holds,

> "Justice, and only justice, you shall pursue." (Deut.16.20).

Dr. Ambedkar was clear that the people who required development the most were Dalits. He wrote, "The very untouchability attached to their person is a bar to their moral and material progress."[1]

What is Development?

Development of society has to do with the changes in society for the betterment of the human beings and the environment in which they live. Development in a way is unfolding the potentials which lie latent within a person and the environment. This can be opened up by education, training and scientific endeavours. In Dr. Ambedkar's threefold dictum–educate, organize and agitate–education takes precedence. In as much as education develops the mind, training develops skills for livelihood. Even cultural activities like art and architecture along with music, dance and drama need skills.

This may sound ideal. The truth of the matter, however, is that development often benefits fewer people than what is made out to be the case. In line with Dr. Ambedkar's thinking, this kind of development would be unjust. The fruits of development in any intellectual, scientific, technical and industrial field must benefit every part of society.

Can Development be Just?

Dr. Ambedkar developed his own ideas on the development of society. He held that there were three stages in human society, namely, savage, antique and modern. As society developed from one stage to another its concerns also developed. In the savage stage it was conservation of life, in the antique stage it was preservation of society and in the modern stage it was protection of individual's interest. Social development from Dr. Ambedkar's point of view can be set out in a sequence like this:

1. Society is the given fact where human beings are born, they live till they die. The social nature of human beings and their dependence on one another to meet their needs make society an unavoidable fact.

2. Society inevitably becomes unequal giving rise to economic classes, castes, gender, language, race and colour. Here some gain dominance and others are subjugated.

3. This injustice of inequality results in oppression, rejection, exploitation, subjugation of the powerless and lawlessness of the powerful. Also we may note that the majority makes law so they are the masters of the law and can make them to suit their own advantages which may perpetuate inequality.

4. Dr Ambedkar contended that society and religion were connected. He unveiled the foundational roots of religion's advancement in society over several millennia. These, as we have discussed earlier, were three, namely, conserving life, preserving society and protecting individual. He reduced these to *utility* and *justice* that constituted the basis of religion to govern society.

5. A society constructed on religion's intention to make people free and secure i.e. *utility* and to treat all people equally i.e. *justice*, would constitute a just society. From this Dr Ambedkar had worked out that the slogan of the French Revolutionists—liberty, equality and fraternity—had religious sources.

6. The establishment of the State to make laws and execute them or to punish those who break it is essential. So the State has to make laws for the people so that they live in a society as well as protect the interests of individuals. The State then comes mid-way of seeing society as closed home and individuals as free beings. Here we should highlight the insight that the rules of society are authorized by religions.

7. However, all societies become unjust and differentiate into unequal factions and so do religions especially when they sacralize unjust norms and worldviews, and therefore there arises a need to assess and reassess our religions.

What is Justice?

Dr Ambedkar did not develop a theory of justice like John Rawls (1921-2002) or Amartya Sen (born 1933) but philosophers like Jeremy Bentham (1748-1832), John Stuart Mill (1806-1873), John Dewey (1859-1952) and Karl Marx (1818-1883) had a strong impact on his thinking. They influenced the way he thought about justice. In the Indian side he was inspired by Mahatma Jotirao Phule (1827 –1890) and Mahadeo Govind Ranade (1842 –1901). Both of them were social reformers[2]. Keeping in view that Indian social condition needed reformation it was clear that Indian society needed to be reformed of inequality. Underscoring the urgency of the situation Dr. Ambedkar wrote,

> Turn in any direction you like, caste is the monster that crosses your path. You cannot have political reform; you cannot have economic reform, unless you kill this monster.[3]

Dr Ambedkar was clear that the cause of this condition was the caste system and the religious notions on which it rests and, therefore, this needs to be annihilated.[4] This system had created a mass of servile people who were deemed unfit for any social association. It was obvious that such servile people needed development. The situation, however, entailed that their liberation from the caste system had to be integral to development. Unless this was done development would not be just. It is well known that justice for Dr. Ambedkar was another name for liberty, equality and fraternity. To make this slogan of the French revolutionists more concrete, Dr. Ambedkar elaborated nine aspects to social justice in his evidence before the Southborough Committee were:[5] first, Personal liberty; second, Personal security; third, the Right to hold private property; fourth, Equality before law; fifth, the Liberty of conscience; sixth, the Freedom of opinion and speech; seventh, the Right of assembly; eighth, the Right of representation in a country's government and ninth, the Right to hold office under the State.

Dr. Ambedkar pointed out to the members of Southborough Committee that the British government had gradually conceded to grant these rights to the Indian subjects, but the untouchability of Dalits had put these rights far beyond their reach. He wrote that,

> The principal modes of acquiring wealth are trade, industry or service. The untouchables can engage in none of these because of their untouchability. From an untouchable trader no Hindu will buy. An untouchable cannot engage in lucrative service…the prejudice was so strong that even the non-caste British had to stop recruitment (into Army) from untouchable classes. In like manner, the untouchables are refused services in the Police Force. In a great many of the Government offices it is impossible for an untouchable to get a place. Even in mills the distinction is maintained… Corporation in India has two different sets of schools, one for children of touchables and the other for those of the untouchables…all avenues of acquiring wealth are closed.[6]

For our purpose justice, therefore, would mean removal of those evil conditions that bring about poverty and backwardness. In the Indian context this entails the removal of caste system. Removing this evil is essential for proper development of society.

The insight that we can draw from this discussion is this that development has to be double pronged. It has to be development of people and at the same time development of society. For Dr. Ambedkar people's development can be brought about by education, but society's development can only be brought about by the annihilation of caste system and strengthening of democratic political system. According to him this has to be through a representational form of government i.e. democracy, which means a popular government by the people and for the people.[7]

Dr Ambedkar's Views on Justice

Earlier we drew our attention to Dr. Ambedkar's position about justice. For him another name for justice was liberty, equality and fraternity.[8] This was not a mere revolutionary slogan of the French revolutionists but was rooted in Christian and Buddhist traditions. We also saw in the previous section that Dr Ambedkar's view on justice entailed two concerns. The first was the protection of individual's interest i.e. civil liberty and the second was social equality.

By equality he meant three things, i.e., equal opportunities, equal start and equal dignity. This is easy to understand because a society which seeks genuine development must seek these for its people so that the last can be first and the first last. But can it be gained from developing industry? Or can it be gained from adopting ideals of *khadi*? The answer to this is no. The point is this that development in the sense of equality does not require welfare approach but participation in politics and protection of human rights. It is unjust for Dalits receive the end of the benefits of development that trickles down to them, rather they must enjoy an equal share of it with full participation.

Justice would best be enjoyed under democracy where through the parliamentary systems the voices of all people would be heard and the benefits would reach to those on the social margins. That is why Amartya Sen describes democracy as a government by discussion.[9] Dr. Ambedkar also discussed at length the merits of democracy especially weighing the values of government *for* the people versus the government *by* the people. Keeping in view that the former would only create a section of superior class of rulers he settled in favour of the latter. The reason is simple. The reinforcement of superior and inferior classes in society would be tantamount injustice.

The importance to do justice, in the sense of forging social equality, should be appreciated from the fact that in it's absence the privileged classes would be the first to take undue advantage of development.

There are aspects of justice that Dr. Ambedkar did not realize in his time, chiefly the environmental issues. In as much as we want development of our children, our cultures and ourselves we need to reframe our economies to work within the limits of environment. In other words development has to be framed in the economy of justice where the use of land, water, forest, resources of earth and human labour do not exceed the right of other forms of life to live with us. Today justice demands that hazards against environment must be removed. One good reason to support this is because the first to be hit by environmental degradation are Dalits and Adivasi communities. This is because of their limited financial resources causing their greater dependence on natural resources.

Development as Justice

Developmental approaches whether through industrialization or through *khadi* were not important for Dr Ambedkar. In his view development would fail to alleviate people unless the problem of injustice was addressed. In the Indian context injustice was the caste system. Therefore, elimination of the caste system had to be an integral part of developmental activities. Accordingly we can contend that the Dr. Ambedkar's approach to development as justice will have to have three components, namely, education, community building and struggle for civil liberty.

Let us take the first component for our discussion, namely, education of people which was most important for Dr. Ambedkar. This was to be in the widest sense of the word involving literacy, training, knowledge, information, culture and religion. Education is a form of power which changes the society to become more just. Amartya Sen would hold that its viability would be proven if grave injustices were removed. We have pointed out above that in Dr. Ambedkar's view the caste system was a grave injustice that needed to be annihilated. People have to be educated in order to understand its dynamics and discard its religious endorsement.

For this education needed to be liberated from the monopoly of the dominant castes and be made available to all. Now we know that the ideal is that all children i.e. those below seventeen years of age, must be in school. The fact, however, is that a large number of children are disinterested to go to school. In his times Dr. Ambedkar had observed with dismay that,

> "Following the division of schools (the Municipal Corporation) has divided its teaching staff into untouchables and touchables. As the untouchable teachers are short of the demand some of the untouchable schools are manned by teachers from the touchable class. The heart-killing fun of it is that if there is a higher grade open in untouchable school service, as there is bound to be because of a few untouchable trained teachers, a touchable teacher can be thrust into the grade. But if a higher grade is open in the touchable school service, no untouchable teacher can be thrust into that grade. He must wait till a vacancy occurs in the untouchable service!!!"[10]

The situation has now changed, at least in law, but the mentality of observing separation has not.

The second component in Dr. Ambedkar's approach to development was to organize people. To organize was a way to build community. He promoted that people must be organized to live together for two things, firstly to be associated and secondly to be in solidarity to resist the tyranny of the dominant i.e., to guard their civil liberty. In such a community people would be free, equal and brave. In his line of thinking the associated life must be viewed in two aspects. One aspect of associated life is at the micro level i.e. the community and the second aspect is at the macro level i.e. the society. Several communities join up to constitute the larger society. Dr. Ambedkar pointed out that communities are organized according to the schemes of divine governance which are propounded in their religion. However, what Dr. Ambedkar did not see was the rise of the civil society organizations at the grass root level who would take up community-building programme seriously. Yet, it must be admitted that, these organizations work on the ideals of their members whose ideals are governed by their religious worldviews.

The point that Dr. Ambedkar made was this that a community whose members were adherent of an egalitarian religion would organize their community on the principles of social equality. Having made this point he noted with disappointment that Christianity and Islam despite propounding egalitarianism had failed to achieve it in their communities. The second aspect of associated life is the national society. At this level he envisaged India to develop as democratic and secular society. This, in his view, would forge an egalitarian society at the national level.

Egalitarianism together at micro and macro levels would bring justice to all people to live as free and equal citizens of the nation. This social reform was integral to development. Without social equality the benefits of development would only be reaped by the dominant communities. Keeping in view the deep-seated caste prejudices among people, a way to deal with it would be to enact good laws which would enable the civil society organizations to undertake their activities with democratic and secular approach.

The third component of Dr. Ambedkar was struggle for civil liberty. We know that the struggle for civil liberty is initiated by those who have the courage and confidence to agitate. This begins with people's demand for human rights. Having achieved this people should carry forward their struggle till these rights ensures every individual to enjoy civil liberty. People must demand their civil liberty from the State. This required political action. Therefore, initiatives for development in Dr. Ambedkar's line of thinking should develop human personalities intellectually, morally and physically to be fit for political participation.

We can see an idea of development inherent in Dr. Ambedkar's writings and speeches. These we can put in form of a sequence.

First that People are in pursuit of happiness and contentment;

Second that happiness and contentment will come by improving people's life;

Third that improvement of life involves development of their intellect, health, culture, security and environment;

Fourth that developments in the field of science, technology and industry have direct impact on people's life. In ways this impact is for the better but it also has its backlash e.g. environmental degradation;

Fifth that development in various fields will benefit all people only if there is social justice.

Sixth that with caste system in operation people will be discriminated on the basis of birth, occupation and colour from receiving the benefits of development. Therefore, annihilation of caste system is integral to development.

IT IS CLEAR FROM OUR DISCUSSION THAT EVERY INDIVIDUAL IS IMPORTANT IN THE PURSUIT OF HAPPINESS. For that reason preservation of social order is for the happiness of human beings. If a social order fails to do this it must be dismantled, whether the order is sanctioned by religion or not. Therefore, dismantling and establishing social order anew for the sake of justice is a necessary requirement development.

Endnotes

[1] B.R. Ambedkar, *Evidence before Southborough Committee* (1919). Writings and Speeches Vol.1. 1979. p. 261.

[2] B.R. Ambedkar, *Ranade, Gandhi and Jinnah* (1943). *Idem.,* p. 225.

[3] B.R. Ambedkar, *Annihilation of Caste* (1935). *Idem.,* p. 47.

[4] B.R. Ambedkar, *Annihilation of Caste* (1935). *Idem.,* p. 27.

[5] B.R. Ambedkar, *Evidence before Southborough Committee* (1919). *Idem.,* p. 256.

[6] B.R. Ambedkar, *Idem.,* p. 261.

[7] B.R. Ambedkar, *Idem.,* p. 251.

[8] B.R. Ambedkar, *The Hindu Social Order* (1946). Vol.3. p. 95.

[9] Amartya Sen, *The Idea of Justice.* Penguin Books. London. 2010. p. ix.

[10] B.R. Ambedkar, *Evidence before Southborough Committee* (1919). *Idem.* Vol.1. p. 262.

Chapter 12

Democracy

Through the chapters we studied diverse issues that have been impacting the Indian society since its independence from British rule. Some of these were Constitution, religion, caste, leadership, identity, *Manusmriti*, Christianity and development. In all these and other subjects we studied Dr Ambedkar's social, political and religious ideas. The lingering inquiry in all these chapters was about the shape of society in the line of Dr Ambedkar's vision. In other words how would our society, if shaped after Dr Ambedkar's idea, look like?

The answer is straightforward. It would be democracy where not only every citizens would be free, equal and secure but also that the concerns of all people are heard before a decision is made, hence the significance of the Parliament and Legislative Assemblies. Besides this transperancy democracy allows people to elect their government and to remove it if they so desire. To grasp Dr Ambedkar's position the question to ask is this, how do we govern in the absence of a Monarch?

We must recollect that until India's independence in 1947 we were under monarchs of various regimes whether Buddhistic or Brahmanic, Muslim or British. However, independence not only ended the British colonial rule in India but also monarchy. This paved the way for democracy.

Granted that democracy is a government by people's participation, this does not mean that it was oriented towards justice as we understand it now. However, it did contain seeds of equality, majorities, liberty, rights, peace, justice, toleration, transparency and progress. These features sprouted with the turn of history as citizens pursued democratic values.

Athens

The popularity of democracy in our times is evident, its history, however, stretches back into the antiquity.[1] Cities like Athens without monarch were governed by its citizens. It had the Citizen's Assembly and an elected Council of five-hundred. This gave us the word democracy i.e. *demos* people and *kratos* rule.

The reason why transparency emerged as its leading feature was due to open debates and collective decisions taken by Citizen's Assembly concerning public-works and the manner in which an accused had the chance to counter his opponent in a public. Even among the political philosophers in our times democracy and transparency are subjects of wide discussion.[2]

Rome

The political conception *res publica* or republic emerged from Rome denoting that its people possessed the supreme power of the State. In this sense they were the sovereigns. Although republic is distinct from democracy, in contemporary times the two are knotted.

It is held that Rome was founded in 509 BC when Lucius Junius Brutus supported by powerful families overthrew the last king. In his reign he strengthened the Senate of nobles. But the working-class rebelled. To pacify them their assembly was formally recognized with the right to elect their officials. With this all roman citizens were able to participate in the governance. Consequently the citizens, not rulers, were sovereign which made it a republic.

Republics and democratic States eclipsed with the diminishing of the classical age. But in late medieval Europe it emerged in cities which became independent from the Holy Roman Empire.

Graubünden

In Europe proper democracy after Athens started in Graubünden, a district in the high Alps of Switzerland. It then was populated by 150,000 people who lived in 7000 square kilometre. It declared its independence from the Holy Roman Empire and in five years constituted itself as a sovereign state. In 1524 by an Act of Union it was made a federal republic. Despite its eventual merger with Switzerland it was openly the first democracy.[3]

Democracy made Graubünden a tolerant society where Catholics and Protestants[4] lived in peace while the Thirty Years of War raged in Europe. Faced with the threat of their survival they appealed for help arguing their case of independence,

> The form of our government is democratic; and the election and removal of all kinds of magistrates, judges and officers, both here in our free and ruling lands and in those lands subject us, lies with our common man.[5]

Interestingly the term 'democratic' gains a positive sense unlike previously in Latin which denoted a contemptible form of government. Secondly, this statement shows peasants at the centre of political activity; previously peasants in Europe were faceless except when engaged in some rebellion.

It contributed two unique political principles firstly, the principle of majority and secondly the principle of political goods. The first 'principle of majority' came out of the assemblies that gave their consent by a majority. These decisions were called 'majorities'. This concept is the cornerstone of democracy. The second is the 'principle of political goods'. It denotes positions of power and responsibility which were allocated to everyone in turns. This practice has died out in our current democracies.[6]

Great Britain

Several attempts roughly between 1500 and 1700 by English people to find a direct participation in their country's government failed. In the strife between the Monarch, the Parliament and the Army what succeeded to curb the power of the English monarch was the Parliament. This did not mean that the Parliament was a democratic body as we understand it now. In fact it was a house of nobles loyal to the Monarch. It was only later that the representatives of the common people found their place in it through the general elections.

When in 1603 James-VI, king of Scotland, inherited the English throne as James I from the childless Elizabeth Tudor, he had already become a Protestant and believed in the divine rights of kings. However, the Army and taxation were outside his control. The relationship of the Parliament and the reigning Monarch deteriorated on the issue of increasing taxes. After all it was the nobles in the Parliament who had to bear the taxes. They could not allow the King to increase their financial burden for what they perceived as his extravagance.

Charles I, who inherited the throne from this father James-I needed money for war against Spain as a part of the Thirdly Years of War. The Parliament sanctioned an insufficient amount of £140,000. As a result the government owed a huge debt to the Army. This discontent led to civil war. The King dismissed the Parliament claiming the privilege of his divine right.

On this issue—of the king and the army—the House of Commons was intensely divided. The Presbyterian faction was keen to draw an agreement with the king and dismiss the army but the Independents, comprising of the senior offices of the New Model Army such as Oliver Cromwell and Henry Ireton, wanted a full compensation for the army and to restrict the power of the king. It was at this point of dispute that religion played a divisive role.

'Vital theological differences pitted the Anglican Church, which believed in the importance of ritual, the divine authority of its bishops and the special status of the monarch, against the Reformed Christians who held a firm belief in the primacy of the individual conscience and the importance of a Christian life.'[7]

The Reformed Protestants showed disinterest in the doctrine of the divine rights of the kings, whereas the Anglicans steadfastly held on to it. The Anglican Church which was a establishment under the Crown was catholic in nature with King as its supreme governor. Naturally it was advantageous for them to support the doctrine of the divine right of the king.

It was in this setting that the army ranks devised election as a method to choose their representatives for the highest council of their Army. Interestingly the Levellers who popularized Protestantism in the army came up with some very secular doctrines albeit founded on religion. These were firstly, that political rights should be enjoyed by all whether saint or sinner; secondly, that the State should be separated from the church; and thirdly, that people should have personal freedom to choose their own religion whether Catholic or Protestant.

With the arrest of the King, Charles-I, and his execution in 1649, the restoration of Monarchy in 1660 by the Parliament that invited Charles II to take the throne and subsequently deposing his successor James II and inviting William of Orange to occupy the throne it was clear that the Parliament was in ultimate control. It also demonstrated that the course of the world affairs could be changed by very ordinary people rather than kings, nobles, popes and bishops. Yet democracy was repudiated in favour of a Parliament that was attended and run by the affluent.

Finally with industrial revolution, economic boom, printing press and spread of education brought politics into public discourse. As a result the practice of election would vent out the democratic impulses of earlier centuries. This was evident in the Levellers working through the New Model Army. With the workers gaining membership to the Parliament through elections full democracy came to the British Isles.

India

Although from 1919 democratic institutions and practices were partially instituted under the British rule, it was in its post-colonial era that democracy was finally established in India.

While Mahatma Gandhi consolidated his political movement against the British in three stages since 1920, namely, Non-cooperation, Civil Disobedience and Quit India, Dr Ambedkar led movements for social reform and equal rights for the Untouchables. Towards this he led 5000 Dalits in March 1927 to taste water from the public *chawdar* pool in Mahad as per the municipal ruling that 'Mahad tank was open to all irrespective of their caste'; he publicly burned *Manusmriti* on the Christmas Day of 1927; and led *satyagraha* on 2nd March 1930 with B.K. Gaikwad for entry of Untouchables into the prestigious *Kalaram* Temple in Nasik.

These movements were not so much to motivate Dalits to go to the temples as it was to gain their right to enter them. It was not for piety but to procure social equality for them. It cannot be disputed that liberty is best enjoyed in democratic societies. He believed that social equality had to precede political liberty. Concerning democracy Dr Ambedkar held that

> A democratic form of Government presupposes a democratic form of society. The formal framework of democracy is of no value and would indeed be a misfit if there was no social democracy. The politicians never realized that democracy was not a form of Government. It was essentially a form of society. It may not be necessary for a democratic society to be marked by unity, by community of purpose, by loyalty to public ends and by mutuality of sympathy. But it does unmistakably involve two things. The first is an attitude of mind, an attitude of respect and equality towards their fellows. The second is a social organization free from rigid social barriers. Democracy is incompatible and inconsistent with isolation and exclusiveness, resulting in the distinction between the privileged and the unprivileged.[8]

Despite being firmly opposed to Mahatma Gandhi, he was appointed by Jawaharlal Nehru, the first Prime Minister of India, as the Chairperson for the committee to draft a Constitution for India. The Committee was set up by the Constituent Assembly immediately after the Independence from the British.

Dr Ambedkar drew up a clear Constitution to govern India as a democratic republic of federated States but with a strong Centre. It was adopted in January 1950. It also empowered people to elect their government and to remove it by voting and electing their own representatives for the Parliament. It distributed the powers of the government between the legislature, the executive and the judiciary so that the possibility of someone taking over as a dictator was minimised.

What did we learn in this study?

The above query must be fixed in the frame of a larger inquiry i.e. to what extent has India shaped its society in line with Dr Ambedkar's vision of egalitarianism? We know that in the exercise of voting democracy regards all citizens as equals. As there was to be no monarchy in post-colonial India, it was clear that democracy would be a suitable choice for this new republic.

Accordingly its Constitution was drawn up and the influence of Dr Ambedkar, who drew it up, is detectible in the legal provision for people to be free and equal citizens. This political and legal equality was reinforced by the principle of one person one vote and one vote one value, but democracy has failed to achieve social justice in India. Citizens are still not free and equal.[9] This is due to prevalence of caste system in the society.

In this failure religion has also been a culprit. Unfortunately, it turned the system of caste or *varna vyavastha* into a sacred system. The fact is that the Caste System had provided a structure of a social hierarchy which became religiously institutionalised and psychologically ingrained. Consequently it needs no bloody action to maintain the oppressive social condition. Yet in Dr Ambedkar's view the potential of religion to construct a just society was promising only if it was of the right kind.

A religion would exhibit its best feature if it would sacralise justice particularly its egalitarian aspect. Conversely, the fact was that in India it had sacralised caste system. Part of the problem arising as a result of it was that the populace had internalized its mechanism of graded inequality, fixity of occupation and fixation of people. In daily run of life it was visible in the practices of untouchability ans segregation.

Furthermore this mechanism was crystallized by the Laws of Manu *Manusmriti* which was written in the antiquity. It did this by peculiarly increasing the degree of penalties down the line of caste so that the offender of the lowest caste received the highest degree of penalty for a same offence that an offender of the highest caste would commit. This is why Dr Ambedkar held that,

> A just society is that society in which ascending sense of reverence and descending sense of contempt is dissolved into the creation of a compassionate society.

Seeing no remedy of reform in the Brahmanic tradition Dr Ambedkar advocated the annihilation of caste. The way to do this was to convert to an egalitarian religion. To make this possible he created the provision in the Indian Constitution to profess, practice and propagate a religion of one's choice as a fundamental right so that the adherents of egalitarian religions particularly neo-Buddhists would take advantage of this.

With this in view we learnt that leadership should follow a transformative instead of magisterial, ministerial or managerial models. This model aims at social transformation. In this line of vision the leadership should aim to transform a casteist society into a casteless society so that people are liberated from social degradation and economic disadvantage.

Other essays on Identity, Education and Development are written with similar view. The underlying queries in these essays are about social condition e.g. in a society gripped with casteism what is expected of a leader? How is identity construed? And what should education and development aim at?

Justice requires the knowledge of social context

In all these essays the concern for social harmony, representational democracy and justice is highlighted. This means that along with the vision to create a pluralistic and casteless society, endeavours should also be made to ensure that people are free, equal, secure and happy. It is clear that as long as people suffer with social degradation and economic disadvantage these social ideals will never be achieved. At the same time it has been demonstrated that the root of these problems is the Caste System.

Caste System not only creates an unjust society but also enforces a mentality which does not protect human dignity as an obligation under natural and rational or moral principles. But we cannot leave it like that. The presuppositions which rationalize the Caste have to be rationally refuted and justice has to be reinforced. Here we should take John Rawls' Theory of Justice into account. He advocated justice as fairness on rational, not religious or moral, grounds.

So what is fairness? The objective of this foundational idea for John Rawls was meant to avoid bias in our decisions. He developed the idea of the *veil of ignorance* to promote justice as fairness. In his view fairness involved taking note of the interests and concerns of others as well and in particular the need to avoid being influenced by our respective vested interests, or by our personal priorities or eccentricities or prejudices. It is a demand for impartiality. The *veil of ignorance* is an imagined situation of 'Original Position'. Here primordial equality exists i.e., when the parties involved have no knowledge of their personal identities or have vested interests. What is just has to be decided under this *veil of ignorance* i.e., ignorance about personal interests or even actual views of good life—what Rawls calls 'comprehensive preferences'.

However rationality of the *veil of ignorance* as propounded by John Rawls in his idea of 'Original Position'[10] would fail here because *karma* has lifted the veil of future as well as the past. An individual can estimate how he/she might have acted in the previous life and what may become of him/her in the next life based on what actions he/she performs here and now in life. This explains why and what of the personal condition of life i.e. the reason of sufferings or joys in his/her present life.

The idea of *karma* may be metaphysical but its style of explanation sounds rational like the cause and its effect. This explanation has no need of gods or morality, benevolence or generosity but pure rational thinking. However, the benefit of this way of thinking, albeit rational, is reaped by the dominant castes.

If this is the case then the question that begs an answer is this: what should be done to counter the *karmic* way thinking? Here public education with insight is essential. By 'insight' I mean the presupposition behind an idea or a theory. Accordingly, the presupposition of *karma* must be grasped and critiqued.

In other words how does *karma* answer the question of identity e.g. who am I? Or answer the question of prospects e.g. what is my future? Or the question of choice e.g. what should I do? Or the question of morality e.g. what is right and what is wrong? Similarly what is the presupposition of the idea of *karma*? If its presupposition is the idea of transmigration of soul *atman* or the idea of appropriate consequences of one's work then who, it should be asked, benefits from these ideas right now?

The answers to the questions of life, therefore, have to be contextual not metaphysical or religious or rational. It must be accepted that the right to act lies in what the social context exposes and what the condition of the people reveal not by the *karmic* idea of transmigration of *atman* or adherence to the Casteist laws of *Manusmriti*. The context is our society where the culture and practice of caste system is intense. It is here that justice has to be established. If this is the case then the idea of the *veil of ignorance* where the choices are made impartially is irrelevant. It is impossible for the decision makers to be behind the *veil of ignorance* and then decide in a way that will work to their advantage whether they fall in the privileged or the deprived section. The reason for this is that in a casteist society justice cannot be fair unless it is preferentially biased for the victims of caste system.

In a society which will be shaped on the vision of Dr Ambedkar the commitment to recognize individual virtue and natural liberty have to be a part of thinking. The society must be conserved in order to protect individual's freedom of choice. The right to be educated, to form associations, to dissent and the freedom to theologize has to be granted as a natural or civic right. Here it is the role of theologians to demonstrate that all these values which reinforce human dignity also emerge from the being of God.

THESE RIGHTS AND PRIVILEGES THIS WILL BE POSSIBLE IN A DEMOCRATIC SOCIETY. Democracy is not only where diverse and contradictory voices are publically heard for making decisions but also where people elect their government and remove it when they wish. This makes democracy representational and friendly for the masses but ruthless for the rulers. At the end we look for a homeland where along with every human being we Dalits will be free, equal, secure and happy. It is a vision of free and fair society. This will be the heavenly Jerusalem of the Bible which will be our *Begampura*, i.e., a city without sorrows.

Endnotes

[1] Despite its primitiveness, it is the first fully recorded democracy chiefly in Aristotle's book *Constitution of Athens*.

[2] It must also be noted here that although this form of democracy through consultation and consensus was at its height in Athens for two hundred years i.e. C 507—323, it never quiet died out from the civilized world. Though democracy had a torturous history in Athens it came to a definite end by the conquests of Alexander of Macedonia. His vast empire which stretched till India was eventually brought under the political control of Rome. But at the cultural plane the intermingling of the two gave rise to Graeco-Roman culture. Now let us turn to another aspect of democracy, namely, the idea of a republic. *Cf.* Roger Osborne. *Of the People by the People: A new history of Democracy.* (2011) The Bodley Head. London. p. 9.

[3] Roger Osborne, *Ibid.*, p. 69.

[4] The wars was between King Ferdinand, a fierce catholic who was enthroned in 1619 with the support of Spain, and Christian IV, King of Denmark, who led a league of Protestant states.

[5] Roger Osborne, *Ibid.*, p. 72.

[6] Roger Osborne, *Ibid.*, p. 74.

[7] Roger Osborne, *Ibid.*, p. 78.

[8] B. R. Ambedkar, 'Ranade, Gandhi and Jinnah' in *Writings and Speeches* Vol-I.

[9] The words free and equal were used in the "French Declaration of the Rights of Man and Citizens".

[10] Amartya Sen, *The Idea of Justice* (2009) Penguin Books. London. p. 54.

Bibliography

Ambedkar, B.R. 'Annihilation of Caste.' (1936) *Writings and Speeches* Vol-1. Govt. of Maharashtra. Mumbai: 1989.

—————, 'Bhikkhus Should Serve the Buddha by Becoming Preachers of His Dhamma' (1956) *Writings and Speeches* Vol-17. Part-1. 2003.

—————, 'Buddha or Karl Marx' (1956) *Writings and Speeches* Vol-3. 1987.

—————, 'The Buddha and His Dhamma' (1956) *Writings and Speeches* Vol.11. 1992.

—————, 'Buddha and the Future of His Religion' (1950) *Writings and Speeches* Vol.17. Part-2. 2003.

—————, 'Buddhism Disappeared from India Due to Wavering Attitude of the Laity' (1955) *Writings and Speeches* Vol-17. Part-1. 2003.

—————, 'Buddhist Movement in India: A Blue Print' (1954) *Writings and Speeches* Vol-17. Part-3. 2003.

—————, 'Buddhist Seminary to be Started in Bangalore' (1955) *Writings and Speeches* Vol-17. Part-1. 2003.

—————, 'Closing Speech in the First Constituent Assembly of India' in *Great Speeches of Modern India* (Editor: Rudrangshu Mukherjee) New Delhi: Random House, 2007.

—————, 'The Condition of the Convert' (1937) *Writings and Speeches* Vol-5. 1989.

—————, 'Hindus should not be Indifferent to Conversion of Depressed Classes' (1936) *Writings and Speeches* Vol-17. Part-1. 2003.

—————, 'Krishna And His Gita' (1956), *Writings and Speeches* Vol-3. 1987.

—————, 'Pakistan or the Partition of India' (1940). Thackers Publishers. Mumbai. 1946 *Writings and Speeches* Vol-8. 1990.

—————, 'Philosophy of Hinduism'. (1941) *Writings and Speeches* Vol.3. 1987.

—————, 'Reformers and their Fate' (1956), *Writings and Speeches* Vol-3. 1987.

—————, 'What way Emancipation?' (1936) *Writings and Speeches* Vol-17. Part-III. 2003.

_____, 'What Congress and Gandhi have done to the Untouchables.' (1945). *Writings and Speeches* Vol-9. 1990.

Ariarajah. S. Wesley, "A World Council of Churches Perspective on the Future of Hindu-Christian Dialogue" in Harold Coward (Ed.), *Hindu-Christian Dialogue - Perspectives and Encounters*. Motilal Banarsidass Publishers, Lucknow, 1993.

Bayly. Susan, "Caste, Society and Politics in India from Eighteenth Century to the Modern Age" in *The new Cambridge History of India* Vol. IV. 3. (1999) Cambridge University Press. Cambridge.

Becher. Glora, 'Dr Ambedkar And The Jewish People' (1941) *Writings and Speeches*. Vol-17 Part-1. 2003.

Classical Dictionary of Hindu Mythology and Religion 1928.

Constitution of the Church of North India and Bye Laws. ISPCK. New Delhi.

Dalit Bible Commentary. James Massey et. al. (edt) New Delhi. Centre for Dalit Studies. 2015.

Daniel. Monodeep, '*Faith on the Anvil of Justice*.' Amsterdam: Vrije Universiteit. 2013.

Daniel. Monodeep, *Models of Leadership in the Indian Church: An Evaluation in Studies in World Christianity* Volume-13 Part-1. Alister Kee (Editor:) Edinburgh University Press. 2007.

Daniel. Monodeep, *Religions in India: The Vision of Dr Ambedkar* (2016) ISPCK. New Delhi.

Ginwalla, Persis and Ramanathan, Sugune. "Dalit Women as Receivers and Modifiers of Discourse" in *The Emerging Dalit Identity* (1996). Edt. Walter Fernandes. Indian Social Institute, New Delhi.

Habir Angar Ee. *Pali is the Mother of Sanskrit*. Nagpur: Tarachand Chavhan. 1994.

Larbeer. Mohan P., '*Ambedkar on Religion: a Liberative Perspective*.' New Delhi: ISPCK. 2003.

Mani. Braj Ranjan, *Debrahmanising History: Dominance and Resistance in Indian Society*. New Delhi: Monohar Publishers. 2011.

Massey. James, *Dr. B.R. Ambedakar: A Study in Just Society*. New Delhi: Centre for Dalit/Subaltern Studies. Manohar. 2003.

McPhee. Arthur G., *Road to Delhi: Bishop J Waskom Pickett Remembered 1890-1981*. Bangalore: SAIACS Press. 2005.

Moon. Vasant, *Dr Babasaheb Ambedkar* (Translated by Asha Damle) New Delhi: National Book Trust of India. 2007.

Muir. J., Original Sanskrit Texts on the Origin and History of the People of India their Religion and Institutions – II Edition. Trubner and Co. Paternoster Row. London. 1872.

Mukherjee, Rudrangshu. (edt.) *Great Speeches of Modern India*. New Delhi: Random House. 2007.

Nehru. Jawaharlal, *The Discovery of India.* (1961). Asia Publishing House. New Delhi. 1974.

Neill. Stephen, *Men of Unity.* London: SCM Press. 1960.

Omvedt. Gail, *Seeking Begampura: The Social Vision of Anticaste Intellectuals.* New Delhi: Navayana. 2008.

Osborne. Roger, *Of the People by the People: A new history of Democracy.* (2011) The Bodley Head. London.

Outlook. 9th Nov, 2009.

People's Reporter. Vol-21, Issue-17, Mumbai Sept 10-25, 2008.

Rattu. Nanak Chand, *Little Known Facets of Dr Ambedkar.* New Delhi: Focus Impressions. 2001.

Sen. Amartya, *The Idea of Justice.* London: Penguin Books. 2009

Smith. Robertson W. *Lectures on the Religion of Semites.* First Series. London: Adam & Charles Black. 1907.

The Manusmriti.

The Rig Veda.

World Christian Encyclopaedia Vol-1. (2nd edition) David B Barrett et. al. (editors) Oxford: Oxford University Press. 2001.

Index

www.ingramcontent.com/pod-product-compliance
Lightning Source LLC
Chambersburg PA
CBHW030858050726
47500CB00008B/113